D1522771

The Dreams That Bind Us

Echoes of Etherium, Volume 1

Maximilian Lopez

Published by Maximilian Lopez, 2022.

THE DREAMS THAT BIND US

First edition. February 18, 2022.

Copyright © 2022 Maximilian Lopez.

ISBN: 9798799976712

Written by Maximilian Lopez.

To my mother, Margarita Yolanda Gonzalez. We live on through each other's memories. Until this universe takes me, your name will be forever locked inside this book. I only hope that another reality kept us together for longer. I'll always love you and miss you dearly. Special Thanks to my loving and supportive wife, Shirley. The most amazing boys I could ever have, David and Jordan. All those who helped me groom and polish my manuscript along the way, especially Red Lagoe, for the pointed guidance I needed.

PROLOGUE
Thirteen Years ago.

A stranger placed a handful of flowers atop my father's casket. Several unknown faces trampled across the stained carpet in front of the cloth-lined altar. *Why? Everyone knows father's casket is empty.* They had small conversations as they waited their turn; some of them wore military uniforms. As my mother sat in the wooden pew beside me, she pulled my head to her chest. A tear dripped from her trembling chin onto my thin wool-suited shoulder. *Is she trying to console me?*

I glared at the empty handshakes and pandered greetings. "Mother, who are all these people?"

She looked down with tearful eyes. "They *work* with..." Using a red, satin handkerchief, she wiped away her smudged mascara. "They *worked* with your father, dear."

Different servicemen and women approached the podium. Scientists and politicians spoke about how my father's work impacted their careers. No one talked about him on a personal level. *Do they know what his important work did to us? Especially in the last few months.* I sat there in solitude, as the funeral concluded. *He missed my Mathlete competition and now he's going to miss my early graduation from high school.* Faceless masses of strangers emptied from the venue until only my mother and I remained.

I held her warm comforting hand. "Come on, let's talk to him before we leave. I'm sure he heard all those nice people, maybe he'd like to hear our voices, too."

In the backroom of the red brick funeral home, we came upon a long, steel cylinder laid on top of a metal table. Glimpses of my father's naked body through small, glass windows scarred my memory. Hunching over the mechanical coffin constructed to keep my father alive, she sobbed. *Why are we making such a big deal out of this? He designed this device to house his body. It's as if he* knew *that something like this would happen.* A digital read-out displayed his heartbeat and the statistics related to his breathable oxygen inside. *There are other numbers about brain waves that I don't quite understand.*

I tugged at the black dress of my grieving mother. "Don't cry. The doctors said that he's in a coma and that he could wake up at any time." *Although, they told us that weeks ago.*

My mother turned to me, shook her head, and caressed my cheek. "He loved you very much. That's why he worked so hard." *Loved me? It was always theories and science. I rarely heard the word* love *come from his mouth.* I looked back at my mother and grasped her hand. *Maybe he said it to you... before I was born.* My other hand stroked the cold steel of the apparatus. *What we call* love *is a chemical imbalance in our brains.* Soft, docile tones of the medical device delivered a quiet lullaby. *Isn't that right, father?* A vapid expression remained on my father's face from beyond the thick glass portal of his self-constructed coffin.

We lingered around the simple, country funeral home for an hour before we left. Four uniformed men in an armored vehicle brought my father's metallic living apparatus to our home in the mountains. It had a self-sustaining power module but needed to recharge. I looked on through the second-story window as they carried him into our basement. Once they left, I tip-toed down the stairs carefully to not make a sound. *Mother needs all the rest she can muster. We owe her that much.* Father was placed beside a stack of chemistry books and some broken machinery we toyed with over the years. *Look at you now, old man. Confined to our basement.* I shook my head. *You talked about greatness at any cost.* Blood heated inside my veins as I clenched my adolescent fists. *It's up to me now, to show you what greatness* truly *is.*

Dinner that night was quiet. Mother warmed up some minestrone that she made earlier that week. *What should I say?* She sat on the opposite end of the hand-crafted, wooden table and stared down at her silverware. *She'll be alright. She's stronger than she lets on.* Rising steam from the broth-filled bowl warmed my face and fogged the lenses of my glasses, as I ate in silence. *At least she doesn't have to worry about when father will be home. He's right where we left him.* I grinned. *It shouldn't be funny, but he could wake up tomorrow, for all we know.*

As the evening drew on, my mind wandered through various calculus equations and new universal theories. I drifted off underneath the thick, cotton bedspread of my queen-sized bed. As my thoughts danced with their unfounded solutions, it brought me... peace. *They warm my soul... if there is such a thing.* Out through the window on the far side of my bedroom, ethereal moonlight pierced through the scattered clouds. A steady autumn wind pushed against our aged, wooden rafters. My eyes grew heavy. They fluttered and flickered between the dream world and this reality.

It was then that I saw *it.*

At the edges of my bed frame.

A looming, dark figure.

What is that? Did it... stare down at me? Although, it had no eyes. My whole body seemed paralyzed as I fought to regain my foothold in the realm of the waking mind. *Move!* My toes moved. My eyes refocused. While my heart raced, I lifted my head. *Where did it go?* I surveyed the room.

Nothing.

No one.

Gray clouds drifted across the moonlit sky. My breathing slowed as my head sunk into my down-filled pillow. *What was that thing?* Fixated on the stained oak beams that lined our ceiling, my eyes grew heavy as time went on. *It must have been a figment of my imagination.* The creaking of the wooden floors, made throughout the house, faded into silence. Each echo of my heartbeat pulsated an eternity apart. The foot of my bed was vacant. *Good.* As my consciousness succumbed to my slumber, I glanced to my rightmost bedside.

There *it* was again.

A towering, ominous, pitch-black mass.

Is it death? Attempting to swallow, I couldn't. *Are you here for me, or perhaps... my father?* My limbs ached to move, but it was too late. Immobilized, again. *I'm at the mercy of this thing. This... being.* Words wouldn't escape my mouth. *Someone... help me.*

As my eyes shut, *it* reached down to me.

Oozing, bubbling, darkness seeped into my mind.

Unbeknownst to me at the time, that was the last night of rest... I'd ever get to myself... again.

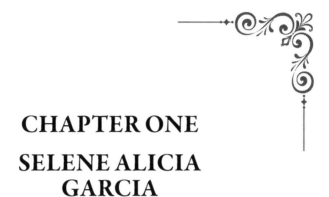

CHAPTER ONE

SELENE ALICIA GARCIA

Present Day.

S elene walked up the gray granite stairs of an old Spanish mission-turned church. *This place is great, albeit a little loud when the choir hits their high notes.* Warm, southern Texas sun beamed through a stained glass celestial saint above the solid oak doors. Squeezing Selene's soft light-brown arm, her mother turned to cough.

She's been coughing more lately. "Are you okay, Ama *(Spanish slang for mother)*?" Selene lifted her sunflower print, button-up, sundress above her worn tennis shoes as she approached the top of the church steps.

Selene's mother turned and smiled. "I'm fine, Mija *(Spanish slang for daughter)*. I've told you before. God has a plan for all of us. Now, focus, it's your big day. Let's go."

Mom's smile is always warm. Two well-dressed male ushers stood on either side of the gapped wooden entrance. They greeted Selene and her mother as they walked in. *The darker one on the right has bloodshot eyes. His sweat is starting to show underneath his armpits. I'm pretty sure he drank too much last night.* Selene stared at the man as she walked past him. *Was he here to ask for forgiveness?* Her mother jolted her hand forward like the tug of a dog leash.

"Come on, Mija, the Lord waits for no one," her mother said.

5

I must have stared too long again. Selene dashed toward her mother. "Yes, Ama."

As Selene and her mother entered the main area of worship they both bowed their heads in front of a massive carved statue. *It's a woman holding a cross. It looks painful every time I see it.* Selene lifted her head and followed her mother to a vacant pew. Pulling unscented lip balm from the front pocket of her yellow sundress, she applied it to her weathered, pink lips. *My favorite thing about wearing this dress.* She shoved the lip balm back down. *Pockets!* One of the apostles walked over to Selene's mother and shook her hand. Bright green and white ceremonial garbs hung off him like window drapes. *Please don't shake my hand.* He extended his hand out to Selene. *Oh, no.* She grimaced and then placed her dainty hand against his rough, meaty palm.

With a smile, he nodded at Selene's mother. "She's making progress. A few years ago she wouldn't even look at me when I walked up."

Selene contorted her thin unblemished face to resemble a smile. *That's because he would follow up with questions I couldn't answer like... how's it going? Or what do you want to be when you grow up?*

As he turned to greet other patrons her mother nudged Selene's ribcage with her elbow.

Ow. "What was that for?" Selene asked. *Was my smile that unconvincing? I've been practicing in the mirror.*

Tilting her head, her mother leaned in. "Fitting in is not that hard. I'm glad that you're making progress."

Why do I have to fit in? "You've always told me that God made me this way for a reason," Selene said.

Her mother's lotion-scented fingers ran through Selene's flowing hair. "Mija, several reasons, but it's on *you* to put in the work. She can't do everything for you."

Selene sat on the hard wooden pew and waited, while she greeted the surrounding churchgoers. When her mother finally sat down, Selene reached across her slim waist for her mother's hand. Fluffy tufts of cotton from her mother's white sweater caressed Selene's nineteen-year-old skin. *God has a plan for all of us. Who are we to interfere with it? Still...* She raised her right-hand fingertips to her moist lip-balm-covered mouth and stared down at them. *How do I know if I'm doing the right thing? I'm trying to control myself, but what if God wants me to focus on other things.* Her short clear-coated fingernails methodically caressed her full rose-tinted lips. *Mom's been working so hard ever since my dad passed away. What if I say something wrong and embarrass —*

Ow. Selene's mother clamped her hand so tight that the pain snapped Selene out of the trance she was in. She retracted her fingers and sunk in the church pew. *I must have zoned out again.*

"Sorry, Ama," Selene said.

A slight morning breeze threw Selene's hair around to her mouth. She blew the loose strands outward off her shoulder. Lightly-dusted blush on her cheeks contrasted her dark brown hair. *Mom must love to torture me every Sunday before church. Does God hate ponytails?*

Her mother smiled. "It makes my heart happy that you've signed up to do this. You're so brave, Mija."

I've got to prove to you that I can do things like this or you wouldn't let me move to the college campus and live on my own. Selene gritted her teeth and assembled a make-shift grin. "I'll do my best, Ama."

Gentle angelic voices of the choir echoed throughout the church. Selene winced and then slammed her hands against her ears. *Too loud.* All those in attendance gathered in their respective seats. The pastor walked down the aisle with a large leather book. It contained the scriptures that were regurgitated every week. *It must be heavy, his small arms are shaking.* He held it open over his head then placed it on the large wooden podium. The elderly pastor quoted passages from the sacred texts as the sermon went on. *His voice sounds shaky.* Their words permeated Selene's mind. *I've been going to the same church since I was little.* She nodded. *I've got this.* The pastor stood in front of the congregation and introduced Selene up to the podium. With his hand extended to guide her, she stared at it. *His hand is clammy. Wait. Focus.* She smiled and walked behind the microphone and adjusted it to her short stature.

"Ahem, I was asked —" Selene's voice squealed like a prepubescent teen. *Focus.* She cleared her throat. "Excuse me. I was asked to speak to you all on my favorite verse from the blessed teachings."

She looked around the church. Two kids fought over the affection of their father as he stood attentive to Selene's next words. She smiled. *I wish my father was here. I barely remember what he was like. It's been so long.*

"Mija," her mother whispered.

Regaining focus, Selene glanced at her mother. *Right.* "Please open your books to page three hundred and ninety-two verse twelve." Her lips trembled. Mild rumblings from the congregation amplified by the vaulted church ceilings made her cringe. *I wish I had my headphones.*

A young woman cradled a baby who wore a pink polka-dotted dress. *Focus. Just like the time I rehearsed in front of my bedroom mirror.* She fiddled with her fingers beneath the podium and took a deep breath. "The Lord came upon them... the humbled masses of sinners and anarchists and offered salvation. His kindness was met with laughter and ridicule."

Selene glared at the seated patrons. "God had told them that they embodied lust, which later transforms into anger, and is the all-devouring enemy of the world. Greed is also a transformation of lust. Together, lust, anger, and greed are the foundations from which the demoniac vices develop. They fester in the mind and make it a suitable ground for all other vices to take root."

Selene pointed her small index finger outward and shook it as she continued. "Consequently, our Lord labels them as gateways to hell, and strongly advised to shun them to avoid self-destruction. So the Lord rebuked unto them. Tell your troubles to the One who is the source of all comfort. How can you forget the One who created your soul, the breath of life? Without it all that we wear and eat is impure. Everything else is false. Burn emotional attachment, and grind it into ink. Transform your intelligence into the purest of paper. Make the love of the Lord your pen, and let your consciousness be the scribe. Let your soul be not destroyed in the fiery inferno of damned eternal darkness that lies between this realm and the next."

Selene glanced around the congregation. *No one is clapping.* Several parishioners mumbled amongst themselves. *I said all the words.* She ground her fingernails against each other inside the cover of the podium. *Wait.* She stopped. *What was I supposed to say at the end? Oh yeah.* "This is the word of the Lord above."

"Praise be to God, Amen," the congregation responded in resonance.

Selene contorted her face to present a smile and then stepped down from the podium. *Thank the lord, that's over.*

The elderly Hispanic pastor bowed to her as he walked past. "Uh... thank you, Selene."

Selene glanced at the pastor's head. *His brow has a few beads of sweat.* "You're welcome, pastor." She walked toward her mother.

Her mother smiled and hugged Selene as she approached the wooden pew. "You do know there's a baptism today, right?"

It feels so safe in her arms. The noise around Selene faded away as her heartbeat steadied. *That wasn't as bad as I thought.*

"Never mind. Good job, Mija," her mother whispered.

Selene genuinely smiled.

As the aged holy leader instructed the choir to perform the next hymn, the entire church fell silent.

Her mother gasped. "Mija, turn around."

Selene turned just as the pastor fell to the floor grasping his chest. Everyone else in the congregation stood still. *Something's wrong.* She rushed over to the pastor's body and then knelt beside him. She lifted his left wrist with her middle two fingers and bent her ear down by his mouth to listen for a breath. *He's not breathing.* One of the apostles reached out to touch Selene's shoulder. Her mother intercepted the man's arm.

He turned to Selene's mother. "What do you think you're doing, Mrs. Garcia? We need to help him."

She released his arm away from Selene's vicinity. "Trust me, no one here is more qualified to help him than my daughter."

Selene raised her head and surveyed the evergrowing crowd of people. She reached into her pocket, pulled out a worn black scrunchy, and then gathered her long hair into a ponytail.

Not him.

Her heart was steady.

Not her.

Her breaths were calm.

Selene zeroed in on someone. *She was a home inspector.* "Mrs. Rangel will you please look for the church's AED."

Mrs. Rangel stepped back and looked about.

"Please hurry, we need to resuscitate him. He's had a heart attack." Selene furrowed her small brow.

Mrs. Rangel nodded and scurried off through the huddled mass toward the rear of the church.

Selene waved at the apostle that tried to touch her earlier. *He looks strong.* "You. Please come here." She yanked his arm down until his knees buckled so that he sat on the opposite side of the pastor's body. "Kneel here and press down on his heart like this." She locked her hands together and showed him where to apply pressure.

"Are you sure? How fast do I do this?" he asked.

Selene raised her finger and wagged it in the air, closed her eyes, and smiled. "Ah, ha, ha, ha, stayin' alive, stayin' alive. Ah, ha, ha, ha, stayin' alive..." She opened her eyes. "Just. Like. That."

He stared at Selene in disbelief.

Why is he not doing it? "Please hurry," Selene said.

Shaking his head, he compressed the pastor's chest as Selene instructed. Mrs. Rangel barreled through the lumbered crowd and presented a small encased device that displayed large red letters that read: AED.

"Here you go." She handed the device to Selene.

Selene looked to her mother. "Ama, please call 911 and tell them exactly what happened and that we're going to use an AED to resuscitate him."

Her mother pulled out her cellular phone, without hesitation, and called 911.

Selene opened the AED and dumped its contents on the floor. *Just follow the instructions. Easy.* A few birds chirped as they hovered around the large mesquite tree beside the entrance of the bright-colored stucco church. *I wish it was always this silent.*

"Ah, ha, ha, ha, stayin' alive, stayin' alive," the hulking apostle mumbled as he continued compressions on the pastor's chest.

Selene tapped him on the shoulder once she prepped the AED. "Please remove the pastors' garbs from his chest area. I'll need to apply these pads around his heart."

She looked down at the AED and turned it on as he removed the clothing from the pastor's chest area. His light brown skin lost its natural pigment and turned a bluish hue. *Follow instructions.* She removed the plastic film from the electrode panels and stuck them to either side of his lifeless body. *It recommends a shock.*

Selene sat up. "No one touches his body." She looked around the immediate area. *No one is touching him.* "All clear." She pushed the button on the AED. The pastor's back arched up as the electricity coursed through his body and then slammed against the cold stone church floor beneath. She looked down at the AED as it recalculated the state of his health. *God has a plan for all of us. I hope it involves you living for a little longer.* The AED finished. *It recommends another shock.*

Her mother leaned down to Selene. "An ambulance is on its way, Mija. They said to keep doing what you're doing."

The apostle scoffed under his breath.

Selene waved her hands above his body. "No one touches his body." No one approached. "All clear." She pushed the button again. The AED shocked the pastor. His body rose, as if it was summoned to the heavens above, then returned to the earth below.

His chest expanded and recessed.

Selene reached for the pastor's wrist but stopped short. *Wait... Instructions.* Retracting her hand back to her lap, she looked down at the AED. *It recommends that his body be turned to its side, monitor his breathing, and await emergency personnel.* The pastor's natural skin tone returned to his face. She smiled. *I was able to follow instructions.*

"Is he going to be okay?" the apostle asked.

Everyone waited with bated breath.

"Mija," her mother said.

Selene raised her head. "Please roll him on his side just in case he throws up." She reached for his wrist and felt a faint pulse. "He's going to make it." *If God wills it.*

As some of the stronger followers turned the weakened pastor to his side, ambulance sirens screeched in the distance and grew louder as the seconds ticked away.

Selene stood up and walked toward her mother's side. *I wish I had my headphones, but... this is an emergency.*

Her mother leaned in. "Good thing I made you focus on your schooling. You'll be a great biologist someday, Mija."

Biochemist. Selene smirked. "Good thing I forced myself outside of my comfort zone and took those free CPR classes."

Her mother turned her head and coughed into a red handkerchief.

Should I ask the paramedics to take a look at mom when they get here? She escorted her mom to the bathroom as the medical personnel burst through the historic church entryway. Her mother's cough echoed from inside of the Ladies' restroom. *Is mom going to be okay without me around to help?*

Members of the congregation parted making way for the medical personnel who rushed to the pastor's side. They checked his vitals, placed him on a gurney, and then secured an oxygen mask on his mouth. *Mom is tough. I can do this.* Once the suspense and commotion died down, several high notes reverberated off of the vaulted church ceiling from the choir as they sang their hymns. Selene covered her ears. *Too loud.* Inspired prayers were reaffirmed as they knelt in front of the large female statue. *If God has a plan for* him *to live then surely there's a plan for all of us.*

SHORTLY THEREAFTER, Selene and her mother retreated outside toward a 2001 white Honda Civic. Selene drove half an hour past the city limits, down dusty country roads before she parked in the gravel driveway of their small, rural South Texas home. Her mother headed to the kitchen to finish cleaning their dishes from breakfast. Selene wandered down the narrow hallway toward one of the two bedrooms. She opened the thin wooden door and waltzed in. Small toys and trinkets had their exact placement along her shelves. On a twin bed, two worn soft pillows remained in the same spot from when her father taught her how to make her bed, a decade ago. Library books filled the make-shift bookshelf on the top of her light-blue, hand-painted dresser.

Selene glanced back at the long, thinly-framed mirror that hung on her door. *I'll remember to pack this dress for our trip.* She smiled. *It's got pockets.* She changed out of her sundress, slipped into baggy, gray sweatpants and a white tee, and then placed a set of large black headphones around her ears. The clacking of washed dishes in the kitchen and the rustling leaves outside her cracked window faded away. *That's better.* Leaned against the pillows lay three stitch-worked plush animals from her childhood. *Hello, my animal friends. You won't believe the day I had.*

Selene hummed as she meandered toward the white flea market nightstand that sat between the headboard of her bed and the paint-chipped wall. Above the light-blue, Texas sky, the sun perched and beamed through her dusty cracked window pane. She reached into the drawer of her nightstand and pulled out a green and white notebook. The lines on the pages inside resembled small squares instead of the horizontal lines found in an average ruled journal. On the cover, the words ~~for official use by engineers and architects~~ were scratched out.

As Selene opened the engineering notebook, a whiff of clean, blank paper crept into her shallow nostrils. *Stable and sturdy.* She inhaled. *Did Dad smell like this?* She exhaled. *Maybe that's why Mom married him.* In the other room, her mother's cough came through above the silence. Selene looked back toward her door. *Should I pick up some cough medicine on my way back from work tonight?* She reached the open drawer, pulled out a purple mechanical pencil, and laid across her bed.

Selene clicked the end of her pencil and then wrote:

I focused on speaking in front of real *people! No one clapped.... Boo! I think I did a good job. Mom said I did well, so who cares. Also, our pastor had a heart attack. I managed to check my impulses without any prompting and I followed instructions to the letter. I wish Dad were alive. Mom needs the help, even though she'll never admit it. And Alex, you're missing out...* Selene glanced at the top of her dresser at a picture of two small Hispanic kids perched on a rusted, dent-filled, metal slide. *How can you be out there in the big city by yourself? If I was more independent like you, mom wouldn't worry as much.* She smiled. *I got a scholarship. Mom said you were a straight-A student before...* Her smile faded. *We're going up north to Freshman orientation.*

"Mija, please help me with the laundry and bring your work uniform," her mother shouted from the living room.

Selene turned her head. "I'll be right there, Ama."

I'll show mom that I can go on an adventure by myself. As long as it's not noisy... and I don't have to shake hands with anyone. She closed her notebook and placed it back inside her uneven nightstand.

My next adventure begins soon.

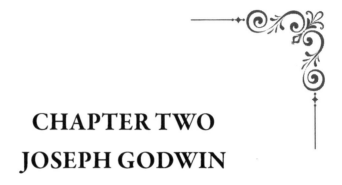

CHAPTER TWO
JOSEPH GODWIN

Joseph looked down at the audience from the brown wooden podium on the stage. "My father trained me to be successful at an early age." *Although no one ever distinguished him from the rest of the custodians he worked with.*

Overhead, a bright stage bulb radiated on Joseph's professionally-cut tufts of greying golden-brown hair. An angelic-type glow emanated from his head, similar to a halo. "When I was five years old, I won my school talent show. When I was sixteen, the Committee of Performing Arts awarded me the highest individual award due to my role as Mr. Otto Frank in my high-school one-act play of The Diary of Anne Frank." He lifted his chin. *That's when I fell in love with the cheers and accolades.*

Distilled drinking water kissed his thin, light-pink lips as he sipped from a glass hidden inside the ingress of the podium. "However, it wasn't all rose petals and runways." He pointed his long, tanned finger at no one in particular. *Dramatic pause...* The seated crowd remained silent. "I honed my craft through hard work and perseverance. I sacrificed countless nights and days to get where I am today." *I sacrificed... almost everything.* The thin microphone wobbled as his left hand jittered. *I could use a cigarette or, at least, a cigar right about now.*

"It's an honor to stand here before you. I am humbled to accept this award. Most of all..." *I wish you were here to watch me.* Joseph looked up at the massive center rafters. *Who am I kidding? You'd be too busy working your knuckles to the bone.* "I'd like to thank my mother, she's the reason I was able to get here. Even though she passed away shortly before mother's day, I know she's looking down on me from heaven." He kissed the top of his manicured hand and raised it high above his head. *The critics love all this personal sensitive shit and the religious zealots swoon when I mention heaven.* "This is for you, mom!"

A single loud clap echoed from the back row of the well-dressed audience. Waves of applauds joined in as the cheers and whistles grew. The audience stood and praised Joseph as he raised the golden award with his left hand. The male and female hosts walked over to Joseph, who stood five to six inches over their heads. He bowed to the clapping of several hundred of the most influential people in the performing arts world. *Just keep smiling.* He blew a kiss to the adoring crowd as he exited the stage per the direction of the stage manager. *Another award to add to the shelf.*

"Great speech, Mr. Godwin," a stagehand said.

Joseph caressed his freshly shaved jawline. *My beard.* "Thank you." *Another sacrifice I had to make.*

A female producer approached him. "Mr. Godwin, this way to the backstage access area. Several media outlets would like to get a photograph with you and your award."

Joseph looked down at his custom-tailored suit and followed. *Just like last time, I suppose.*

Flashes from the cameras and cell phones reflected off Joseph's straight, polished, white teeth. He posed for each media representative. *Every photo will cement my image in the history books.* From the most well-known media corporation to the smallest, independent, underground video blogger. *I'll be remembered, once all the lights dim and all the cameras have faded away to time.*

as Joseph took the last of his pictures, a shorter, disheveled, brown-haired woman with a bright yellow sweater, black suspenders, and khaki slacks snuck up from behind. "Joseph, did you have to lay it on that thick? I'm pretty sure the critics got a sweet tooth from that sappy little number."

Joseph turned around. *She's starting to know me a little too well.* "Well, if it isn't my favorite manager slash agent. So glad you could make it, Julia, my dear."

Julia smirked and switched the assortment of folders, planners, and calendars cobbled together on her hip, from her left side to her right. "I'm the *only* manager slash agent slash friend willing to help you land the gigs that can snag you the best actor award."

Slash friend may be pushing it. "Speaking of which, what's on the docket for my next project." The back of his suit jacket stretched taught as Joseph crossed his bulging arms. "Come on. Out with it."

Looking up at Joseph, Julia grimaced. "Wow. Just enjoy this moment will you?"

How can I? Joseph narrowed his light-brown eyes at Julia. *I'm not getting any younger.* He tapped his wing-tipped leather dress shoes on the convention center floor.

Julia shrugged her small framed shoulders. "I'm working on it. With the state of the world as it is, and more prominent actors coming up, the gigs keep getting harder and harder to find."

Joseph's light-skinned face turned somber. "If there's more competition then that's more of a reason to push me harder, my dear." *That's what makes* me *special. Unique.*

Julia switched the jumbled mess of papers to her right side from her left side, raised her right hand to Joseph's face, and squeezed his thin cheeks. "Oh no, don't look so gloomy. I'll find something by the time the hype from this dies down. You'll be out there researching a role in no time."

Ow. "Alright, fine, will you let go now?" Joseph mumbled.

Julia retracted her hand. "Good. Now go enjoy yourself, for once."

"Wait." Joseph leaned in. "Do you have a *you-know-what* on you, perhaps?"

Julia looked around, then reached down her sweater and pulled out a cigarette. "Look, don't let the cameras see you with one of these, you know how the health nuts will get if you get caught." She, discreetly, handed Joseph the cigarette, like a drug dealer exchanging a stash of narcotics.

Yes! Joseph slid the cigarette down the front jetted pocket of his cream-colored suit. "Julia, my dear, you're a lifesaver." *Does she have a husband or boyfriend? I've never asked.*

Joseph shook his head as Julia walked away. *Who am I kidding? I don't have time for things like that. I need to focus on my career.* A nervous sensation enveloped his being. *I need to focus on where to smoke this cigarette so I don't get caught.* A young well-dressed man holding a serving tray of scattered finger foods walked past.

I bet he *knows.* Joseph reached out and pulled the young man aside. "Excuse me. Do you know where I can smoke a cigarette in peace around here?"

The young man perked up. "Yes sir, there is a cigar lounge for guests on the other side of the green room, just beyond backstage."

Joseph turned where the young man pointed and then pulled him in close. "No, no, no." His gaze pierced the young man's eyes. "Where do *you* go to smoke." He reached in his pocket, pulled out a twenty-dollar bill, and slid it into the server's red vest.

He nodded and motioned for Joseph to follow.

I knew it. He led Joseph to the loading dock through the other side of the kitchen. A large paint-stained metal door opened to the back alley behind the convention center. Joseph smiled. *This is more like it. None of those camera jockeys would be caught dead back here.*

"Thanks, kid." Joseph pulled the cigarette from his front pocket. "You don't happen to have a lighter on you, do you?"

He handed Joseph a book of matches with a nude girl on the outside cover. *Classy, kid.* He lit the cigarette with one of the matches, Joseph handed the book back to the server before returning to his station.

A calming wave of endorphins washed away the jitter that grew within Joseph throughout the evening. *Finally.* He leaned against the brick wall beside a large, blue dumpster. Smoked escaped from his mouth, like the enslaved remnants of harmful energy; accumulated from a lifetime of stress. *How will I be remembered? I need that* one *role.* He smiled. *I believe in you, my dear, Julia.* Several voices from the other side of the dumpster penetrated the decaying stench. *Shit.* He took one final drag of his cigarette and threw it on the ground beside his expertly stitched dress shoes. Bright red embers turned to black soot blending with the juices running between the cracks of the poorly laid asphalt. *Must be some random paparazzi.* Joseph inched his way toward the green door. *Hopefully, they won't notice me.*

"There's no fucking way someone will read your shitty screenplay," a male voice echoed from the other side of the dumpster.

"You don't know that. Do you know how many big names are out there? If I could just hand out some copies," a female voice said.

They don't sound like paparazzi. They must be the staff. Either way, I need to get out of here. He reached for the door handle.

"It's such a pipe dream, you'll never make it, no one knows who you are and they never will," the male voice said.

Joseph hesitated. *Dad said those exact words when I said that I wanted to act.* He scoffed. *Look at me now.*

"Maybe your right..." the female voice said.

Joseph's light-brown eyes widened as he retracted his hand from the door handle. *No. Never. You can't give up.* He dashed around the garbage-filled dumpster.

Two people in their mid-twenties stood around an old coffee can filled with wrappers and butts of different cigarette brands. They looked at Joseph's tall figure and leaped back.

Shit, I must have scared them. "Sorry, I didn't mean to eavesdrop, but I overheard your conversation," Joseph said.

Dumbfounded, they stood there in silence.

"You." Joseph pointed to the average-sized, female staff member. "Give me your elevator pitch..." He crossed his arms and bowed his head to listen. "...and go!"

"Uh... a *what* pitch?" She asked.

Oh boy. Maybe this was a bad idea. Joseph unfolded his arms and placed his hands on his hips. "Elevator pitch. It's a brief few sentences that you use to hook some high-end executive on an elevator. That's what they call it, in the industry." He eyed the pack of cigarettes in the young man's pocket. *They're smoking my favorite brand.*

Joseph extended his light-skinned palm out. "Tell you what, hand me one of those and, if you can pitch me your screenplay by the time I finish, I'll let you know if it's a good one or not."

Bewildered, they looked at each other.

"And you are...?" the boy asked.

Joseph's eyes widened. *They work here and don't know who all the important guests are? Kids...* He held his chest high and raised his chin. "My name is Mr. Joseph Godwin. Best actor, award-winning, Joseph Godwin."

"Oh, shit. Sorry, Mr. Godwin, we didn't know," the girl said.

"We aren't into the theater, so we weren't familiar. What are you doing back here?" the boy asked.

I can't tell them the truth. "Never mind *why*." Joseph pointed at the female staff member. "You have a chance to sell me on your screenplay, my dear. Now, it's your choice to waste this opportunity but I'd advise against it." *More importantly, I can smoke another cigarette while you do so.*

"Uh..." She hesitated. "Alright, I'll give it a shot."

"First, hand me one of those, will you, kid?" Joseph held his hand out toward the male staff member.

Endorphines from the nicotine filled Joseph's aged, fit body as she fumbled through the main plot of her screenplay. He nodded and smiled just as he did for the cameras and bloggers before. A final puff of smoke left his mouth, as he extinguished the cigarette on the alleyway below. "Listen... you're close. It's got promise —"

"Really?" Her eyes lit up.

"Work on that elevator pitch. Three or four sentences max. I'll give you the number to my agent, Julia, and we'll go from there."

"No fucking way." She looked around and then covered her mouth as her hands trembled.

Maybe I am *putting it on too thick. Julia was spot on. I need to dial back the ham.* "But you've got to work on it and make sure the story is airtight, alright?" Joseph extended one of Julia's cards out to her.

Shaking, her hand reached for the card. "Of course, thank you. Thank you. Thank you!"

Joseph pulled the card back millimeters before she touched it, "Last thing, kid."

Her eyes fixated on Joseph's lips.

"Don't let someone talk you out of success, *no one* remembers a person who quit halfway, but..." *Dramatic pause.* Joseph closed his eyes and clenched the business card in his left fist. "...*everyone* remembers the person who succeeded."

Opening his palm, Joseph handed the scrunched business card to the young woman. "Thank you so much, Mr. Godwin. I'll never forget this and I'll work on that elevator pitch," she said blushing as her coworker rolled his eyes.

"Of course, and please..." Joseph winked. "I was never back here." And then retreated into the convention center.

Some people will believe anything. He sighed. Everyone *has an agenda.*

AS THE CELEBRATION wound down, Joseph stood out in front of the convention center leering at the rest of the theater talent who formed around their various social cliques. *They scurried away, like cockroaches, from the bright lights and cameras. Some of the naive ones get caught up in the rush... the need to feed their insatiable desires.* He hopped into a long black limousine, alone, and headed back to his hotel, which sat upon the white-sanded Florida coastline. *It's a hard and lonely life, but I don't care. I can't slow down now.* Out of the tinted back window, a young couple held hands while walking down the sidewalk. A black leash snapped taut around their wrists as their small white dog stopped to pee on a leaning sapling. Joseph smiled. *I miss Velma and Roxie.* The street lamps illuminated fewer people as the limousine skirted further from the city along the northern Florida coast.

Joseph glanced into the rearview mirror at the chauffeur's eyes. *What does* he *think of all this, outside looking in? Jealousy? Spite?* He reached to lower the middle window of the limousine that separated the back seat passengers from the driver. *Maybe he's oblivious to which of us had to put in the work and which of us were gifted a seat at the table because of family ties.* As the window slid down, his phone vibrated in his pocket.

He placed his index finger up, then reached for his phone and looked down at the screen. *It's Julia.* "Hold on my man, I want to ask you something, but I need to take this."

The window extended upward as he accepted Julia's phone call. "Hello, my dear, how is my —"

"What the shit, Joseph? A girl who can barely pitch her screenplay. Are you shitting me?" Julia asked.

What is she... oh crap. Joseph chuckled. *I didn't think she'd call Julia until tomorrow at the earliest.*

"I swear to god, you'd better not be laughing. This shit is serious, Joseph," Julia said.

With the phone to his ear, Joseph laid back against the patchwork of black leather stitching. *I should talk her down.* "Julia, for real, I wouldn't have given her your number if I didn't believe she had talent." *And my favorite cigarette.* He nodded. "Come on. It's me, your favorite client." *At least... your highest grossing client.*

Julia was silent.

Maybe, this time, I need to lay it on as thick as I can. "Listen, I get a warm feeling inside when I'm able to inspire people. It's like... the more people who remember how I impacted their life, the longer I'll be remembered. You're young and beautiful so —"

"Don't try to bullshit your way around this one," she said.

"I'm being honest, my dear. No cameras. No microphones. You're still young and beautiful. I'm old and faded. This girl could be my replacement. And I'm..." *Dramatic pause.* "...I'm okay with that. As long as you both remember me."

Thick like peanut butter. Joseph looked down at his phone. "Julia. Hello?" *Did she hang up?*

"Don't be such a drama queen, you're not even forty yet... Fine. I'll give her a chance," she said.

Oh, thank god. Joseph placed the phone back against his ear. *She bought it.*

"Speaking of chances. I got you another gig," Julia said.

That's fast. "Julia, my dear. Are you sure? I thought you wanted for me to enjoy this win for a little while longer."

"It's in San Francisco, in three days. You'll have to fly commercial the whole way. I booked you a seat in first class, 'cause I couldn't schedule a private jet in time," Julia said.

That's too *soon*. Joseph shook his head. "Nope. I hate flying proletariat."

"Excuse me? I wasn't asking. I told them that you'd be there straight away. Not only do you owe me from *this* fiasco of a mess you call talent, but we don't say *no* just because of some inconvenience. Don't you want to be great? Don't you want to be remembered? People who say *no* to opportunities will never be remembered. Isn't that what you told me?" she asked.

With his phone at arm's length, Joseph gritted his teeth. *I bet she made those reservations because I gave that girl her phone number... well played, my dear. Even so, she's got a point. Any sacrifice. Any opportunity to be great...* "I'll take it."

"That's more like it. I'll send you the itinerary and contact numbers in the morning. Enjoy the night while you can," she said.

As if I can, now that I have to lament my fate. "Good night, my dear, and if you skimp on the alcohol budget, I'd advise against it. I'm going to need several stiff drinks to deal with the dregs of humanity and, especially, the airline servers."

"Just watch the limit, and you better show up on time. This gig might be your greatest yet," Julia hung up.

Joseph looked ahead after he placed his phone in the front pocket of his suit. The driver blew smoke out of the window from a lit cigarette. *I need one of those... immediately.* He reached toward the middle of the limousine and lowered the window again.

"Yes, sir. Can I help you with something?" The driver glared at Joseph through the rearview mirror.

"May I have one of your cigarettes? I'd be forever in your debt, my man." Joseph stared into the driver's eyes.

"Of course, sir." He pulled a pack of cigarettes from his pocket.

Joseph's dry mouth salivated.

As the driver pulled up, the luxurious hotel teemed with crowds of people. *Cell phone cameras. Damn it.* He waved off the cigarette as it dangled in front of him. "Sorry, I'll have to decline for now." *He's going to think I'm a jerk.*

Joseph's door opened and stepped out onto the hotel entrance toward the flock of awaiting fans.

No matter.

It'll be worth all of the sacrifices.

To be remembered... forever.

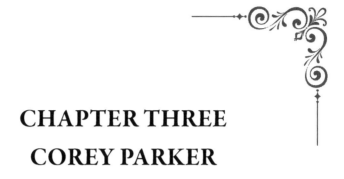

CHAPTER THREE
COREY PARKER

Corey marched across the aluminum brow toward the bridge of the newest ship in the United States Navy. With his bike in tow, sweat from his wavy black hair cascaded down onto his bronzed cheeks. He wiped his round clean-shaven face and cast the excess into the cold pacific water below. As he removed his helmet the mid-morning air ran across his ashy, cracked, dark-skinned knuckles. *Damn, I should've put more lotion on my hands before I left.* He rummaged through the pockets of his blue camouflage pants and pulled out his identification to show to the sentry ahead. A stocky, ornery, older Irish fellow greeted him at the Quarterdeck.

Crow's feet entrenched themselves in the naval chief's pale worn face from years of grimacing at young inept sailors. His gaze bore a hole into Corey's soul. "Petty Officer Parker, follow me to the mess, we need to talk."

Corey glanced at the black waterproof watch on his left wrist. *I'm not late. What's this about?*

Marching into the depths of the ship's hull his Chief turned. "Let's go."

"Yes, Chief." Corey handed his bike and helmet to the sailor who stood watch and then raced to catch up.

Did I do something to get on his bad side? Failed an inspection? Did I have a low score on my last physical? He shook his head. *No, that's not it.*

As the dried sweat crept back onto the surface of his forehead, his heart rate rose. Down the narrow brightly-lit passageways, through the loud well-oiled machine rooms, Corey followed him to the Chiefs Mess (*A special area where sailors who have earned the rank of Chief are allowed to enter*).

"Please close the door behind you Petty Officer Parker," the Chief grumbled as he sat behind an affixed table that adorned the ships' insignia.

"Yes, Chief." Corey walked in and closed the door.

A tall, dark-skinned sailor in his mid-twenties with dull black boots and an unkempt uniform stood at attention in the corner of the Chiefs Mess. *Crap. Now I know what this is about.* The other sailor mouthed the words *my bad* to Corey as he walked in. He stood on the opposite side of the table, put his arms behind his back, spread his legs shoulder-width apart, and held his chest high.

Turning to the other service member, the Chief leaned in. "Do you understand that this is not the first time you've been late to the ship while under my command, Petty Officer Carter?"

Dried sweat settled across the skin grooves on Corey's forehead. "Petty Officer Carter is a hard worker, Chief. I'm mentoring him on the gear, and —"

"I'm gonna stop you right there Petty Officer Parker." Chief lifted his arm and extended his hand out. "Don't make excuses for your fellow shipmate. I asked if he understood that this wasn't his first instance of tardiness. All I want is a yes or no answer... so?"

Corey closed his mouth. *Just answer the man and, for god's sake, please don't mouth off to him.*

Petty Officer Carter inhaled and exhaled slowly. "Yes, Chief."

Chief leaned back against the bulkhead of the Chiefs Mess. "Listen, you're not a bad sailor. You just seem to be a little... unfocused. What is it that you want out of your time in the Navy?"

Corey tightened his lip. *Unfocused? Naw. He's prolly focused on girls and a steady paycheck.*

"To be a Chief like you. How many years until you're on out and on easy street, Chief?" Petty Officer Carter asked.

It's no use trying to suck up to him. Corey shook his head.

"I don't think about my career that way. I still have work to do before I get out. Sure, you can keep your head down and get to my rank before you retire, but you'll miss the important parts along the way. The people you meet will bring out the best in you and sometimes... the worst." The Chief's eyes gazed down at the table.

Where do I fit in on his scale of best to worst? Corey raised his thick bushy eyebrow.

Several shipmates shuffled by the passageway behind the door at Corey's back. Muddled immature conversations woke the Chief out of his thoughts. His gaze narrowed in on Petty Officer Carter once again. "Fortunately for you, I have the remedy for that. It'll help keep your attention on one thing. Have you seen all the dirty brass we have on this ship?"

Corey grimaced. *I know where this is going.*

"Yes, Chief," Petty Officer Carter said.

"It's a shame that such a new ship has dirty brass already, don't you think?" the Chief asked.

"Yes, Chief," Petty Officer Carter said.

Good. Corey nodded. *Just keep it up. It's the only thing he wants to hear at this point.*

"You'll be cleaning the brass throughout this ship, every handle, and rail," the Chief said.

Petty Officer Carter gritted his teeth and shook his head.

"Do you have something to tell me, Petty Officer Carter?" the Chief asked.

Corey flung his head over toward Petty Officer Carter and pursed his full brown lips. *Don't do it, Charles. He's baiting you.*

"Chief, this is bullsh—"

A bell rang throughout the ship.

Corey zeroed in on the beige speaker mounted in the corner of the room.

"Fire. Fire. Fire. Class Charlie Fire reported in the Forward Port Antenna Equipment Room. Away the at sea flying squad, provide from repair locker two," came over the 1 M.C. *(The central intercommunication network on every naval ship)*

"Head to your assigned duty stations and then get started on the brass, Petty Officer Carter. Dismissed!" The Chief stood.

"Yes, Chief. I'll make sure he gets it done," Corey said.

I never thought that I would be happy to hear a fire alarm. He turned, gathered Charles, and ran to his assigned area of responsibility.

Corey's heart raced as he changed into his flame-retardant gear. *What's with me?* His rubber boot slipped out of his moist, clammy hands. *Shit. I forgot to take my anti-anxiety pill this morning.* He bent down to pick up his boot.

Charles sat beside Corey on the steel bench next to repair locker two. He leaned over toward Corey. "Man, that's so dumb the chief would make me clean brass just for being a few minutes late to duty, right?"

"He *was* going to write your ass up if it wasn't for this emergency." Corey jimmied the rubberized fire suit over his stocky midsection.

"Aye, yo, fuck that! He's just angry 'cause I get laid every night and his ex-wife takes half his paycheck," Charles said.

Wow, are you kidding me? With his shoulder halfway inside the gear, Corey scrunched his face. "Do you even hear yourself talk? I don't think anyone cares if you get laid every night, especially the Chief. We're part of a system, a system of rules and regulations. We follow them for the greater good. People are counting on us. Otherwise, the whole thing comes tumbling down and we're left... lost."

Charles smirked as he effortlessly pulled his safety gear over his slender, fully dressed frame. "Yeah, bro, I'm sure the Navy will just fall apart if I show up late a couple of times. You're the same rate as me and we went to boot camp together. Why did he put you in charge?"

That's a good question. Corey squeezed his remaining upper half into the reflective, brown suit. "Maybe 'cause I do what I'm told, good at my job, *and* show up to work on time."

"Fuck that. I'm older so I should be in charge." Charles dawned his mask.

"Fire. Fire. Fire. Class Charlie Fire reported in the Forward Port Antenna Equipment Room. Away the at sea flying squad, provide from repair locker two," resounded over the 1 M.C., again.

As he stood up, Corey pegged Charles in the chest with the back of his meaty hand. "You know who else is old? Our Chief, and he'll bust our asses if we're late getting this fire resolved. Let's go!"

Corey dawned his Self-Contained Breathing Apparatus and rushed up the ladder well toward the bow of the ship. Poised to breach the electrical compartment, he stood behind four fellow shipmates. *What's taking them so long?* Heat emanated from the latched door. *They need to secure power in the room.* He put his hand on Charles' shoulder. His heart rate increased as the bindings of the hatch creaked from the pressure caused by the fire behind it. *We've been through this drill, what feels like, a hundred times. We got this... I hope.*

A bell rang throughout the ship. "Fire. Fire. Fire. Class Charlie Fire. Power secured at zero eight twenty-two Zulu," resounded over the 1 M.C. above Corey's head.

Gray smoke billowed out as the Fire Team Leader opened the hatch and the team breached the space. "Go! Go! Go!"

Corey peered through the small, rectangular window of his breathing apparatus. He let go of Charles' shoulder and headed toward the bright flames shrouded by thick, caustic, grey smoke. Fluctuating electrical hums played an ominous background. He used a nearby fire extinguisher on a large electrical transformer engulfed in small flames. He surveyed the spaces behind rows of mountainous cabinets filled with multi-million dollar radar equipment. A large, thick cable lay bare on the deck, severed and mangled. Blue sparks flared through the amassing gray smoke. *Did someone take a chainsaw to the poor thing?*

Corey tapped his Fire Team Leader on the shoulder. "Fire. Fire. Fire." He pointed to the starboard bulkhead. "Between the Transmitter and Signal Processing cabinets."

I can squeeze in between two of the biggest pieces of gear to get close to the power cabinet. Corey turned to Charles. "Hey Charles, I need to get on the other side of those cabinets before this thing sparks another flame in here."

"Alright man, I got you." Charles moved tools, parts, and debris from the front of the larger metal cabinet.

Corey wiped the rectangular plastic viewing window of his hood. *The sparks are growing in frequency... it's going to get worse.*

"We need them to secure power, stand down," the Fire Team Leader said.

By the time they do that, it'll cause another fire and we'll be trapped. Corey's hands trembled.

Charles raised his lanky arms. "Can't *we* cut the power to this thing?"

Corey knelt on the rubber safety mat on the floor by the power unit adjacent to the mangled cables. "You'll have to turn off the power switch from the front of this panel and I'll have to open it up from the back to get to the power input side."

A dance of smaller sparks intensified.

Corey motioned to get the team leader's attention. "We've got to secure power ourselves before —"

Snap!

Pop!

An arc of electricity crackled through the moat of smoke and danced across to nearby uncovered ducting. Sagged ducting material fed the flames insatiable hunger.

Another fire. Shit! Corey stood up and turned away from the expanding heat. The darkness from the smoke supplanted the remaining light from the space.

"Corey! Are you okay?" Charles grabbed the fire extinguisher and offloaded the extinguishing materials between the spaces toward the starboard wall.

A white cloud exterminated the flames and splashed Corey's only means of vision. He wiped away the foam and soot from the plastic window of his headpiece. "Yeah! I'm alright. I need to open the panel and shut down all the breakers."

The Fire Team Leader pressed a black, short-range radio against his mask. "Secure power to the whole space, goddamn it!"

We can't wait for them. Corey knelt and pulled out his screwdriver to remove the panel. *I'm sorry.* Beyond the exterior panel, each circuit breaker was connected to exposed wires. Four hundred volts of alternating current ran throughout the conglomeration of crimped connectors and label-faded contacts. *I picked the wrong day to forget my pill.* He chuckled as his hands grew clammy. Several sparks grew and crackled around him. *I've got this.* He reached in and secured all the breakers in front of him.

Bright flashes of electrical sparks ventured further from its source. A sudden foul stench of burnt electronics funneled into Corey's cavernous nostrils. He winced. *It's like it knows that we're here to destroy it.* He narrowed his eyes. *It won't go down without a fight.*

"That didn't do it." Corey clenched the screwdriver in his right hand. *What will kill the power?*

"Corey, what's up?" Charles asked.

"Hold up, asshole. I'm thinking," Corey said.

Charles laughed, "Well, think faster or we're fucked."

I prolly can't get far enough inside from back here, but... "Voltage is running through the line, somehow, and we need to dissipate it," Corey said.

As he peered through the circuit breakers, sweat dangled from Corey's long curled eyelashes and dripped into his mouth. He spat out the salt droplets and then shook his head to expel the remaining moisture like a long-haired dog after a bath. The power input wires were fused. Brittle plastic coating melted off to expose the shiny copper and silver wires. *We need to disconnect them from each other somehow, but if we don't know where the source of electricity is coming from, we'll get fried.* He shivered. *The source of the electricity will go through me before it finds ground.* His deep brown eyes widened. *Ground!* He jumped up and flailed his arms at the Fire Team Leader. "Rivas, I need to ground the system with a grounding rod, or else it'll keep starting fires."

The Fire Team Leader pulled a radio up to his breathing apparatus. "Central, this is Fire Team Leader Rivas. I need a status, now. Over."

"We're still trying to find the correct switchboard to isolate the power source. Over," resounded from the radio.

Fire Team Leader Rivas nodded. "Petty Officer Parker and Petty Officer Carter proceed with extreme caution."

Corey searched around the back wall of equipment. *There's one.* He yanked it from its secure place on the side of another cabinet. He shied away from the sparks as he mated the grounding rod to the amalgam of exposed wires and cables. *Here goes nothing.*

A large blue electrical arc flew out of an assembled wiring harness and penetrated the thick, smoke-filled space to get to the grounding rod in Corey's hand. The vibration of millions of colliding electrons coursed through his rubberized grip. *Oh no, you're not going anywhere.* He cinched his fist harder.

Ominous electrical hums faded.

The popping and crackling settled.

Corey moved in to inspect the exposed wires. *Did we... do it?*

Charles turned to Corey and the other fire team members. "We. Fucking. Did it!"

Fire Team Leader Rivas raised his fist in the air signaling for them to stand by while he talked on the radio. His mumbled words were hard to hear above the ambient noise and rubber headpiece that surrounded Corey's small, thin ears.

A bell rang throughout the ship. "Class Charlie Fire secured. Power secured at zero eight thirty-nine Zulu," resounded over the 1 M.C. located somewhere in the space.

"Shit. Thanks to us," Charles said.

More like, thanks to our naval training. Corey returned the ground rod to its home and squeezed his stout midsection through the metal cabinets. Once the fire was secured, they ventilated the space. His hazed vision cleared and his heart calmed. *Thank goodness.*

Corey regrouped with the other members in the space. *I'm glad no one got hurt... or worse.*

Fire Team Leader Rivas placed his hand on Corey's shoulder. "Good job, Petty Officer Parker. Alright. Move out and report to repair locker two."

Corey looked back at the charred equipment as his shipmates ran out of the space. *That was close.*

Fire Team Leader Rivas stopped at the entrance of the space and turned to Corey. "Return to repair locker two, remove your gear, and get cleaned up. I'll report this to the Chief."

Good. Corey removed his headpiece and turned to Charles as they walked down the passageway. "Hey, maybe I can get you off the hook if I tell the Chief it was *you* who saved this space from being a total disaster."

Charles removed his breathing apparatus. "Yeah right, the Chief will still be jealous of me."

"That's *if* you can keep your big mouth in check." Corey chuckled. *I guess that's asking a lot from my shipmate... my friend.*

LATER THAT EVENING, a knock came from Corey's beige barracks door. Corey placed a black wax container down on the table where he sat. He removed his hand from a faded black boot and set it on the floor next to his chair. *Goddamn it, Charles.* "I told you that I'd help you with your boots after I was done with mine."

"Petty Officer Parker. It's your Chief. Open up, please," the Chief said.

"Come in, Chief." Corey opened the door then stood at attention. *I hope he's here to confirm the good deeds he heard about Charles.*

He walked in wearing black and white basketball shorts and a sleeveless gray moisture-wicking shirt. *He must have just finished PT'ing.*

"At ease," the Chief said.

He looked around the room. Stainless steel faucets shined. Books on basic electronics and digital logic lined the shelf above Corey's desk.

Corey relaxed his stance, sat back in his seat, and reached down for his boot. "What can I do for you, Chief?"

The Chief sat in a chair that faced the television in the corner of Corey's barracks room. "Petty Officer Rivas told me how well you reacted while putting out the fire in the antenna equipment room."

"Thank you, Chief." Corey smiled as he brushed the black wax in a circular motion on the heel of his boot.

"However, he didn't tell me how Petty Officer Carter saved you all from burning up. Just as you eloquently put it," the Chief said.

Corey froze. *Shit.* He looked into the Chief's blue eyes. "Rivas's, I mean, Petty Officer Rivas's vision must have been blocked. Prolly 'cause of all the smoke."

Crossing his arms, the Chief narrowed his eyes. "Mmhmm. Must have been."

Corey continued to brush the wax along the toes of his boot. *I hope he bought it.* Sweat accumulated on the curled hairs of his chest.

"Just as well, I've submitted temporary active duty orders for you and Petty Officer Carter. It's to a reserve unit in Waco, Texas. A Senior Chief friend of mine said he needed some reliable and trustworthy help. I told him that I knew the right men for the job," the Chief grunted as he rose from the mass-produced barracks chair.

Corey's eyes widened as he dropped the wax-filled brush on his lap. "For real, Chief?"

"Normally, we don't send second-class's TAD, but I've got high expectations for you. Against my better judgment, I'm letting Petty Officer Carter go along as well. I hope you'll use this opportunity to mentor him." The Chief pushed the chair underneath the table across from Corey.

Charles, you owe me big time, bro. "Yes, Chief. I'll do my best." Corey swept the flaked black debris off of his lap, stood, and then escorted the Chief out of his room. *You can count on me.*

From the doorway, the Chief looked back. "You'll be leaving in a few days. Make sure your room stays inspection-ready while you're gone. That goes for Petty Officer Carter, too."

"Yes, Chief. Have a good evening." Corey held the door open. *Yes!*

As he walked across the cracked concrete catwalk, the Chief grumbled until he was out of view.

Corey closed the barracks door behind him. *If I was alone, in a new duty station, I don't know if I could handle it. Now, I've got my chance.* He smiled. *I can't let the Chief down.* Corey looked down at the muddled wax on the tattered black boots. *We all have rules to follow, or the whole system crumbles away, just like this wax.* He reached for the black cell phone that lay on his rack, connected to a white wall charger.

Can I convince Charles to stay out of trouble long enough? Corey texted Charles the good news. *He better not mess it up for his sake... and mine.* After pressing send, he hesitated. *Should I tell* them *that I'm doing well?* He shook his head and then folded his phone into the pocket of his government-issued sweatpants. He stared at the rope-draped anchor insignia on the blue camouflaged uniform that hung in his closet. *It's been a long time since I talked to them, but it doesn't matter 'cause...* His smooth brown cheeks swelled as he grinned.

I think I've finally found the place where I belong.

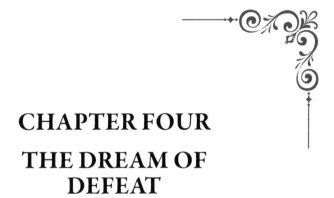

CHAPTER FOUR

THE DREAM OF DEFEAT

Shrieking sirens blur by as two police cars speed past the dirty, scummy alleyway I call home. I glance down at the sheen of oil and liquid on the asphalt beside my torn white tennis shoes. Black hair dangles beside the fresh bruises of my arms contrasting what used to be light brown and supple skin. A damning, thin-cheeked reflection stares back at me. *Damn, Selene, you let them have their way with you last night, didn't you?* I pull down my rolled-up sleeves wiping away the day-old mascara from my misty eyes. *Whatever. Fuck them. I got what I want.* The backpack strap feels heavy on my boney shoulder. *It hurts. I bet one of them bit down on my shoulder.* As I reach for my tender shoulder a phone vibrates in my pocket. Pulling it out, I see who it is. *Just my brother again. Why does he try to stay in touch with me? I haven't been a part of that family since my sixteenth birthday.* The squawking of several crows fighting over a decaying mouse carcass breaks my train of thought. *That was three years ago.* I stuff my phone inside my baggy hoodie pocket. *Damn, just leave me alone.* Walking out on the nearby downtown sidewalk, the full magnitude of the sun's rays hit me right in my face as it peeks over the tall brick buildings and shops.

I turn away to protect my eyes. "Fuck."

A couple passes me on the sidewalk and collectively gasps. Once I regain my focus, I sneer at them and their perfect relationship. *Hold-*

ing hands like some sappy chick-flick on TV. Get a fucking room. Walking down the street different people jaunt around doing their best to avoid me. *Do I look that fucked up?* Walking by a bookstore, I remove the hood from my head and reach out to the glass. *There's dirt underneath your fingernails.* I smile. *Your teeth need a good cleaning. Damn girl your whole fucking soul looks faded.* While laughing, I look up at the mannequin in the window displaying the latest book fad and the sun pegs me right in the eyes again. *I don't need a makeover, I need a pair of sunglasses.*

Darting through two parked cars toward the other side of the street, I get halfway across and then stop. *Didn't that asshole have glasses on last night?* I unhitch the backpack from my shoulder and whip it down in front of my feet. *Ow, fuck. I forgot.* My shoulder throbs as I look into the dark crevices of the frayed backpack; none of the little pockets in the front have glasses. The main holding area has bags of drugs, pipes, syringes, and... *There they are!* "Bing—

Screeching tires echo off the nearby buildings.

Burning rubber stings my nostrils.

A fog of white smoke shrouds the street.

An obnoxiously loud car horn decimates my concentration.

I dig the sunglasses out of the main compartment and put them on my small thin ears. A frat boy asshole driving a blue sedan hangs his head out of the car window and curses at me. *Fuck you for interrupting my train of thought, shit-head. I was going to say* bingo. I zip the bag back up, flip off the douche bag, and continue to walk across the street. My phone vibrates again. *I swear to God if it's my brother Alex, I'm deleting his ass.* I take my phone out and look through my notifications. *It's Tommy. It looks like he needs some green, fast. Luckily, I recently refilled my supply.* I shake the backpack on my shoulder. *Ow. And I need the cash.* I text him back. *Does he still go to school down the street from that gas station?* I text Tommy again, letting him know that we'll meet behind that. *It'll take me forever to walk there.* From my front right pocket,

I pull out a plastic white card. *Hopefully, that lady didn't report her bus pass stolen.*

Loud, heated, vent exhaust blows my hair about as bus forty-two passes by me on the street. *Shit. I think that's the one.* Racing half a block to the stop I look ahead. There's a line of people waiting to get on the bus. My running turns into a fast-paced walk. *Holy shit, I am out of shape.* With that *holier-than-thou* look in her eyes, the overweight bus driver looks at me like everyone else in this fucked up world. I walk up the bus steps. *She's got blotches on her skin. Her hands are jittery. She smells like an ashtray and — stop doing that, Selene!* I hit myself on the side of the head. *I don't give a flying shit about her.* Through the slot of the scanner, I slide the bus pass. *Come on...*

The light turns green.

Fuck yes, it worked. Navigating to the blue cushioned back seat of the bus, far away from everyone else, I pull the top of my hoodie over my head like a shroud.

As the bus meanders along its route, I stare at the houses and businesses as we get closer to the suburbs. *People and their perfect lives.* I tighten my grip on the black backpack on my lap. *What do they know of pain? What do they know of sleeping under a trash bag as the rain pelts you throughout the night? Each droplet slams down like the symbols on a drum solo at a live concert. You can't even hear yourself think, much less sleep. Surviving day-to-day.* I smugly smile. *But they don't understand life as I do.*

A tall dark-haired man in blue jeans and a brown suede sports coat walks up. "Mind if I sit here, miss?"

Get fucking bent. I look him up and down. Before I open my mouth, I hesitate. *He's got a bulge on his side and something shiny on the opposite side of his waist.* My eyes narrow. *He's clean-shaven, smells of old man cologne, and uses manners.* He stands there waiting for me to answer. *He's a cop.* I grip my backpack tighter. *Shit. I can't tell him to go fuck him-*

self or it'll arouse suspicion. I can't get sent to juvie anymore. This time it's big girls prison for me or worse... rehab.

With gritty fuzzy teeth, I force myself to smile. "I don't mind at all, please."

Scooting over, I create as much distance between me and him as possible. My palms are sweating. *Shit.* My heartbeat speeds up. *He's going to try to have small talk with me and find out that I'm jonesing.* I avoid making eye contact by staring out of the smudged back window.

He leans over and glances out of the window toward whatever I'm staring at. "How are you doing today, ma'am? Where are you heading on this lovely Saturday afternoon?"

The overbearing stench of his bargain-bin cologne causes me to gag. *He's definitely a pig. His inquisitive nature is fucking annoying. Although... to him, I'm just some young high school girl.* Glaring into his eyes, I shake my head. "I'm sorry, mister, my parents taught me not to talk to strangers. Especially if they're on a bus with a bunch of empty seats and decide to sit next to me." *That ought to shut him up.*

He sits upright, crosses his arms, and smiles. "I'm glad that your parents were so thoughtful and specific. It's Saturday, you have a backpack, but there's no school. Your hands... have cuts and bruises. Are you in some sort of trouble? You can trust me." He pulls a badge out and flashes it in front of my face. "I'm a detective."

Yeah, I know, dick-for-brains. My smile turns into a grimace as I fold my arms and stick my hands into my armpits. *As if he can help me. I don't need him... or anyone for that matter.* "Do you think I should trust you just because you've got a badge and a cushy job? I'm on my way to visit my sick grandmother and I've got her medicine in my bag... happy?"

As the bus continues along its route more passengers get off but no one else gets on. *There's an old woman and a Hispanic dude in headphones to the left.* I survey the remaining spaces. *She's old as dirt and he's*

THE DREAMS THAT BIND US

oblivious to the world around him. Maybe I'll just leave early. I poke my head up. *It's six or seven blocks away now.*

His textbook smile turns somber as he reaches inside his sports coat toward the bulge I noticed before.

Is he posing as an officer to stick me up? Or is he a real detective and about to arrest me at gunpoint? I pull my backpack around to the front of me and hug it against my chest to protect me from whatever this guy has in store. *Was he waiting for fewer witnesses?* The glass pipes and syringes dig into the bruises on my arms as I squeeze my bag tighter. *Why did this have to happen, of all days, Selene?*

He stands in front of me. Resolute.

He's blocking my only way out.

As his arm comes around from behind his sportscoat, I catch a glimpse of what he grabbed.

Is this... it? *Fuck. My. Life.*

CHAPTER FIVE

THE DREAM OF SELF

A tall tan girl with blond hair and an athletic physique nestles her head in my tone, muscular, left arm. "Joseph, you said that you'd take me to your parents' cabin this weekend. We're still going, right?"

Step-dad's, but still. I flash my perfect white teeth at her. "Oh yeah, of course, beautiful and you can call me Joey."

She looks up at the ceiling. "It's gonna be awesome, I'll bet that you're gonna have some of the best weed." She turns and smiles. "Right?"

"I *am* the king of partying babe, you know that." *Shit. I'll have to ask TJ to hook me up before he leaves for winter break.* Looking around my dorm room, I grimace. *The six hundred dollar bong. The top of the line gaming console. The curved flat-screen TV. How much will it set you back, Joseph?* I shake my head. *It doesn't matter. Everyone already thinks that I run this place. I can just return it all before the credit card companies come for it.*

Reaching over, she pulls my chin millimeters from her budding pink lips. "What are you looking at?" She grabs my hand and presses it against her voluptuous right breast. "You *should* be putting all your attention on me."

My mouth waters as my heart races. *She's everything I want.* Her scent brushes over my cheeks like an enchanting fog, capturing my every thought. My thin, bottom lip quivers at her touch.

Her hazel blue eyes pierce my mind. "You know, I only date winners, right?" She pulls my hand from her breast behind her back along with her flowing blond hair down to the lace panties covering her taut tone ass. *I can't believe I convinced her to spend the night with me.*

Turning right before our lips meet, I smirk. *I can't look too desperate.* "Of course, and I only date ten out of ten girls." I gaze back at her. "But you, my dear, are an eleven."

She smiles, leans in, and presses her soft moist lips against mine. Pulling away, she waves her finger in my face. "Tsk, tsk, we have to save some guilty pleasures for later, Joey."

I grin. *She's such a tease.*

She glances up at the ceiling of my dorm room, again. "Do you know what gets me in the mood? Like, saddle you up all night, American cowgirl style?"

Anything, I'll do it. I stretch my arm out and create some distance between us. "What's that, Lisea, my dear?"

"That top-of-the-line weed you told me about last night. Do you still have some laying around?" She asks.

Shit. "Naw, beautiful, we smoked it all..."

She pouts and lifts the blanket to her neck covering her slender, yet curvy figure.

"But... you know me. The king's got his connections. I'm the man, remember? Let me make one phone call and I'll have some in no time."

"Really?" She tosses the blanket off of her body, turns, and rubs her knee up my thigh across my bulging manhood. She creates figure eights with her finger on my chest. "Go ahead and make that call, I'll be here... waiting."

The only thing between me and that smoking hot body is a bra, panties, ...and TJ. I leap out of bed, grab my cell phone, and then duck into my bathroom. I turn back at the door frame. "Sorry, beautiful, I need to make this call in private. I don't want you to get involved with my connections. I know some dangerous people." I wink at her. *Hell yeah, I'm a badass.*

I close the door behind me, flip open my cell phone, and call my best friend. "Yo, I need you to do me a favor, like emergency bro." *He answered. Thank god.*

"Another favor? After you ditched me the other day for a ride in that new Camero. No chance," Tommy says.

Fuck. I did *do that.* "Screw those guys, I just wanted to see if it was worth it to buy one or not. You know that you're my best friend, TJ. Look, I've got that exchange student from Prague in my dorm room *right* now, no lie."

"Oh shit, dude, she's smoking hot. How did you manage that?" Tommy asks.

Looking in the mirror, I flex my chiseled twenty-two-year-old chest. "Cause I'm the man, you know this."

"Sure. Did you call just to brag?" Tommy asks.

I don't brag, do I? "No, I need an important favor from you right now. I need for you to call up your connection for some top-shelf, pri-mo, weed. Like, right now. Do you think you can do that for me? The most awesome friend in all of bum-fuck Texas." My slim, clean-shaven cheeks turn red. *Come on man, If I can score this broad then I'll be fa-mous around here.* Beads of sweat form in the tan-lined creases on my forehead.

"Just call me TJ, you sound like my mother. Fine." Tommy sighs. "This is the *last* favor, Joseph. You still owe me from last time."

As I clench my fist and curl my arm inward, my blue-veined bicep swells. *Fuck yes!* "Oh my god, dude, you're the man, I won't forget this, bro. Anything you need, I've got you." *Within reason, of course.*

"You should worry about how to pay for all the expensive shit in your dorm room before promising me that. I'll see what I can do and text you if I have something." He hangs up.

He needs to hurry. I wash my face and then run my wet fingers through my short dark-brown hair. Looking at myself in the mirror I pinch a small fold of skin on my mid-section as I tighten my abs as hard as I can. *Damn, still a little flabby. I can't skip the gym today.* I dry my hands on the white towel hanging by the mirror. *Unless* she *gives me a good workout.* My cell phone vibrates against the countertop. *Come on TJ, don't let me down.* I grab my phone.

The text reads:

Mr. Lameski

OK, you lucked out. My connection will meet you behind the gas station up the road in 30 mins. Don't be late and don't forget the money. It's going to be 120 bucks. Be nice. She's not the friendliest.

Monday 12:55 PM

Yes! I text him back.

Joey

I wish it was sooner... but I'll take it. Thanks.

Monday 12:56 PM

I poke my head out of the bathroom. *Please, still be almost naked.* My pillow rests between her legs. *Damn. I wanna be that pillow.*

She bats her dark brown eyelashes. "So, Joey, are you the party king, or am I going back to *my* dorm room... alone?"

Damn right, I am. I grin. "Of course, my dear, my hook up is coming in a little bit so I have to step out but I'll be right back."

"Hurry, I don't know how long I can wait. I *need* you here." She squeezes my beige overpriced pillow between her smooth thickset thighs.

Say no more. I step out of the bathroom.

"After, you bring me what I need," she says.

I change direction toward my dresser in the corner of my dorm room and put on shorts and a shirt. *It's cold outside.* I pull a black hoodie from my closet. *My favorite metal band, The Dread Snakes.* I drape it around me. *Damn, it still smells like weed from the other night.*

Walking up behind me, she wraps her arms around my chest. "Mm-mm, you smell so good." She twists me around and kisses me. She corrals her tongue around mine in a circular motion, pulls away, and then slides toward the bathroom. "I'll freshen up while you're gone. Hurry back, my king."

The door closes behind her.

Damn... she knows how to use her tongue. I dash toward the door, down the stairs, and then head to the gas station a few blocks away from campus. Walking along the sidewalk, my breath fogs the way ahead. *I should have worn pants.* The poorly maintained concrete turns into broken asphalt beneath my feet. *No one is around.* I look down at my watch, then toward the gas station. *They're late.* Kicking scattered rocks toward the street, I stuff my shaking hands in the front pockets of my hoodie. Dulling, gray blankets of clouds above my head move through the sky like an avalanche of snow cascading through a mountain. As I exhale, the fog from my breath bellows around my mouth. *I spent a ton of credit to impress those seniors. Maybe, I should take that shit back to the store.* After, *I score with this foreign exchange girl, of course.*

A short Hispanic girl with mangled, matted, black hair walks up to my side. "Hey, are you Tommy's friend?"

This is TJ's connect? Is she still in high school? "Yeah, my name is Joey and —"

"I'm not looking for a friend, bro. Do you have the money or not?" she asks.

TJ was right, she's not friendly. Whatever. "Yeah, you're late," I reach for the wallet in my pocket.

"If you're gonna be an asshole about it, I can leave." She stands, frayed backpack at her feet, and stares up at me.

Shit, be nice. "I'm sorry, I'm cool. Promise. Just in a rush, that's all. One hundred and twenty right?" I thumb through the money in my wallet. *My parents gave me two hundred for the whole month. Fuck it. I'll tell them I got robbed or something.*

Glaringly, she looks me up and down.

What's she doing?

She smirks and unzips her backpack, reaches in, and pulls out a small clear bag of green, leafy goodness. "I had to get off the bus a few blocks short, some asshole cop harassed me." She hands it out toward me.

I furrow my brow. "Is that all?"

She retracts the bag before I touch it.

Shit, be nice. "I meant if I want to get some more from you, would I be able to?" I smile.

She grabs the money from my grip and hands me the drugs. Her hoodie sleeve pulls up as she reaches out.

There's a detailed tattoo of a weird lion-eagle-snake monster drawn on the inside of her wrist along with some healed cut marks. "Strange tattoo, you've got there. I like it, though, it's cool. Did you have a local guy do it?"

She pulls her arm back into her sweater, zips up her backpack, and slings it over her right shoulder. "TJ knows how to get a hold of me. We're done here, pretty boy. If you let anyone know who you got that from, we won't be cool anymore, got it? And... it's called a Chimera."

"Good to know, Mrs. Dealer. And it's Joseph, not *pretty boy*." I nod and look down at my watch. *One-thirty. Shit. I hope she's still in bed.* I put the bag of weed in my front pocket and walk away.

She scoffs. "Hey, pretty boy. Do you have food at your place?"

I turn back around. "In my dorm room, not really. Why?" *Does she think that I was flirting with her? She's cute... but pretty fuckin' wrecked.*

"After you smoke that, you'll be crazy-hungry. Most people get too wasted to move. If you're going to smoke it now, you should grab some food." She points to the gas station on the corner of the street. "Maybe from there."

Damn, I need to hurry, but she's got a point. That is... nice of her. I smile. *I've got to make sure I don't fuck this up with that beautiful goddess laying in my bed.* I jog past her toward the gas station. "Thanks, maybe I'll see ya around."

Police sirens ring out in the distance. *It's coming from downtown.* They get louder as the seconds tick down.

She pulls a hood over her frizzy black hair, looks down, and then heads to the gas pumps as a topless, red car pulls in. "Maybe not, pretty boy."

Whatever. As I round the corner of the gas station, I look down at my watch and bump into a slender dark-skinned man. "Sorry man, I'm in a rush."

I open the door and dart inside.

As I dash head-first into the snack aisle, the same man waltzes in and says, "It looks like everyone's in a rush... to die today..."

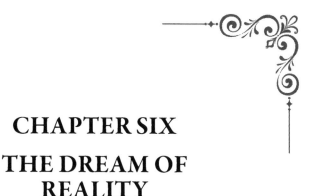

CHAPTER SIX
THE DREAM OF REALITY

A shadowy figure lurches forward. "I'm a powerful supernatural creature, capable of circling the globe in forty minutes or of enshrouding unsuspecting mortals in a deep fog. One who enjoys playing practical jokes on mortals. I'm more mischievous than malevolent. The fairy world is not all goodness and generosity," I bellow from the darkness behind the stage. *Remember, your doing this for the kids Corey. Just like we practiced.*

Emerging from the foliage, a Norse demon, sometimes associated with the devil. "I can invoke the spirits of the dammed that wander home to graveyards after a night of evil-doing. Even though I accidentally caused Lysander *my son Elliot* and Demetrius *Elliot's classmate* to fall in love with Helena *my daughter Eliza,* I enjoy the pleasure of their folly." *My role in this play is to make them aware of the darker side of life, the underworld realm of shadows and magic, and, ultimately, death.* I return backstage.

Maybe I need to rethink our involvement with a play containing concepts of this nature. I smile as the children perform an over-dramatic death scene. *They just like dressing up in robes and holding swords, what kid doesn't?* My lower back aches from all the crouching and menacing poses. *I'm just too old for these dark undertones of death and mortality. Caroline spent an hour getting Eliza's hair curly and I went to countless*

*stores looking for a replica sword that a twelve-year-old could swing...
legally speaking.* Elliot, playing Lysander, raises his sword toward the
ceiling as he fumbles through his lines. Sweat beads on top of my green
and black face paint. *Come on, buddy, you got this.* I clap with the audience at the end of his monologue. The crowd grows silent. All the char-
acters empty the stage.

Oh crap, Corey, it's your turn. I hobble out from the makeshift foliage toward the center of the stage where two strips of gray masking
tape form an X. "If we actors have offended you, just think of it this
way— you were asleep when you saw these visions, and this silly and
pathetic story was no more real than a dream. Ladies and gentlemen,
don't get upset with me. If you forgive us, we'll make everything all
right. I'm an honest faerie, and I swear that if we're lucky enough not
to get hissed at, we'll make it up to you soon. If not, then I'm a liar.
Good day to everyone. Give me some applause and, if we're friends, I
will make everything up to you." I bow.

Every student of Mrs. Ganther's fifth and sixth-grade theater production of A Midsummer Night's Dream return to center stage. The
audience cheers and applauds as the deep wrinkles on my face break the
paint and form a grin. *Retirement is not so bad. I'm able to work on stuff
like this with the kids.* Salty sweat drips from my painted face, down my
full lips, to the wooden stage below.

"Good job, Puck!" my wife, Caroline, shouts from the front row.

I blow a kiss to her and shuffle off stage with the rest of the class. *I
was hesitant when they asked me to do this, but...* My slim bronze shoulder twinges with micro-muscle spasms. *I had fun. It gives me an excuse
to dress up like a monster outside of my favorite holiday.* I wipe my sagging brown eyes. *Now I need to wash this off my face before I break out
like a teenager.*

Once we freshen up and change back in our clothes we gather outside by our car. As I walk up to Caroline, I hung my sweater off my
arm. Her skin has the slightest wrinkle, and her sexy, slim figure hasn't

changed since high school. *She still warms my heart, after all these years. Does she have any plans after this? We need to schedule a date night.*

"You were super scary, daddy." Eliza runs up behind me and jumps into the backseat of the car.

I look on and grin. *My sweet little girl. Her future is as bright as her personality. She'll always have me in the palm of her delicate little hand.*

"He wasn't *that* scary, Eliza. Did you see my fight scene with that big sword? Wasn't that cool?" Elliot walks to the right side of the 1983 cherry red convertible.

My heart swells. *My big boy. I can't wait to teach you so many things. How to be a man in a world that wants you to fail.* I shake my head and smile. *You're going to be a better man than me someday.*

I grab Caroline by her waist and kiss her.

"What was that for?" She asks.

I look into her reflective brown eyes. "No reason, my love. Today... was a good day."

"Eww," echoes collectively from the backseat of the car.

My eyes roll as I open Caroline's door so she can sit down in the newly upholstered, passenger seat. I kiss Eliza on her small, soft forehead and Elliot on his chubby, brown cheek as I round the back of the car on the way to the driver's side door. *I can get used to days like this.* We discuss doing more plays as a family on the way back home through the suburbs. *The kids may be future theater performers.* We arrive at our two-story house away from the downtown noise. Caroline unlocks the door as Eliza and Elliot rush into their rooms to leave me all the costumes and props from the trunk. *Of course...* Walking up with my arms full of belts, straps, and swords, Caroline approaches.

She looks back to ensure that the kids are out of hearing range. "You said that if they did great with their lines that they could have ice cream cones. Remember?"

Oh crap, nope. "Yes, of course, my love. I'm going to the store as soon I drop these off inside."

She stood smirking. "Mmhmm."

I know what that means... I better hurry. I throw the costumes and accessories on the brown, suede, living room couch, grab cash from the counter, and then ditch my coat on the passenger seat of my convertible. I drive to the nearest gas station and rush inside. A young man, my height, darts in front of me. *If I was still Puck I would have turned him into a river toad.*

I'd announce to the faerie world. "I guess we're all in a rush to die this eve. Now the hungry lion roars and the wolf behowls the moon."

As the store clerk glances in my direction, I stop and wave at him. *Did I say that aloud?* I creep toward the ice cream inside their frozen section and select the most expensive and extravagant ones. I stroll to the line behind that same young man that bumped into me earlier, as he grabs several assorted snacks. *Is he going on a trip?* He runs his left-hand fingers through his brown, feathery hair and taps his shoe against the white, convenient store floor. He fiddles with his sweater. *Cool shirt, it's got two giant snakes fighting each other. What's got him in a rush?* I shake my head. *He's just young and impatient.* I grimace. *Is this what retirement is going to be like, from now on? Judging young people like some old fogey.* I laugh.

He hands the clerk a hundred-dollar bill.

Woah, big spender. I check my back pocket for my wallet. *Shit, it's in my coat.* Reaching into my front pocket, I feel the cash I grabbed from the house earlier. *It's fine, I'm almost done here.*

"And if you try to short me one dime, I'd advise against it," the marijuana-smelling kid tells the clerk before dashing out of the store.

That's a strange thing to say. I walk up to the counter and place two ice cream cones on the counter. I pull out the cash from my pocket, pay, and then walk out to my convertible. When I reach for the door handle, I hesitate. *My coat is on the floorboard and not on the seat where I put it.* I survey the area, but no one is around. I get in my car and reach my hand inside both pockets of my coat. *Shit.* My heart palpitates. *Oh, no.* I frantically search underneath the passenger seat. *My wallet. Crap.*

I slam my thick, withering fists against the woodgrain steering wheel. "Damn it!"

Caroline, my love, is going to kill me.

I take a deep breath... *But first* ...and then start the car.

Eliza and Elliot deserve some ice cream.

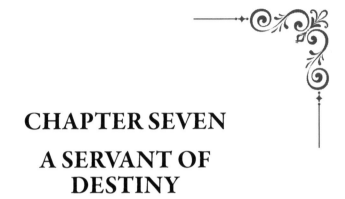

CHAPTER SEVEN

A SERVANT OF
DESTINY

During the next warm, humid, southern Texas afternoon, Selene walked into the Mexican restaurant where she worked. Burnt orange paint, with hues of red, outlined trim along the walls. A local artist interweaved cultures of native North Americans and early Mexican history into several vibrant murals displayed throughout. Lacquered wooden tables lined the sides next to the windows. Hand-woven blue, red, and white ponchos hung from the wooden rafters. Freshly kneaded tortilla dough filled the staff area where she hung her thin, purple coat. Newly waxed floors reflected the light from the indoor lampposts that stood throughout the restaurant. As the rest of her coworkers meandered in, Selene tied her long brown hair into a ponytail and then waltzed into the bathroom to wash her hands before beginning her shift; like clockwork.

Selene walked out of the restroom toward her manager. "Carlos, I'm going to college in a month, isn't that great?"

Carlos nodded. "Wow, already Selene? Yes, congr—"

"So I need to quit." Selene stepped outside of his personal space.

His expression went blank.

I must have made him upset. Maybe he needs some reassurance. "My mom said that it was standard practice that I give you a notice before

I quit. I'll have to keep working for two weeks up until that point though," Selene said.

"Oh, okay." Carlos tilted his head. "I'm sorry to hear that, you're a great waitress."

"You're awesome too, thanks, Carlos." Selene genuinely smiled. *Yay, he's fine with it.*

As the customers filed into the restaurant during the evening rush, the clashing of pots and pans from the kitchen increased. Locally farmed spices ground with red, yellow, and green peppers filled the air. Conversations in Spanish and English from a diverse swell of customers carried throughout the venue.

Toward the end of the night, the crowd noise dissipated. The sloshing of dish rags against dirty plates replaced the clashing of pans. The perfume of homemade Tex-Mex food morphed into a pine-scented cleaning liquid that one of Selene's coworkers lapped on the floor with an old ragged mop.

Selene brought the check to the remaining guests. She conjured the same smile she used throughout the day. *I'm pretty sure, I've nailed the smile thing.* She looked at the massive tin clock shaped like a sun and moon. *Thirty minutes left then I can head home and pack.* She nodded. *I'll prove to mom that I can handle college on my own.*

A dark-tinted luxury vehicle pulled into the desolate restaurant parking lot. A tall light-skinned man walked through the double doors. His black dress pants hung perfectly down to his leather stitched shoes. A grey and teal cardigan stretched across his chest underneath his tan sportscoat.

"Bienvenidos, Señor. Please have a seat anywhere you'd like." Carlos smiled as he extended his hand back toward the empty venue.

Carlos, you're too nice. Selene leaned against the painted wall that lead to the bathroom in the back. *I'm gonna miss this place. I was so stressed at first.* Trumpets, tubas, and accordions blared from a small radio in the back corner of the kitchen. *All the noises made me wish I had my headphones on. Over time, I got used to Tejano music and the hollering.* Her coworkers gossiped around the kitchen window. *Then... it became comforting. I hope... every adventure is like this.*

Selene grabbed a bowl of chips and the last cups of homemade salsa and then walked over to the table where the fancy-dressed, taller gentleman sat. She set the free chips and salsa in front of the man. "Hello, welcome to Roberto's Taqueria, I'll be your waitress Selene. Please enjoy these free chips and salsa while you decide what you want."

The older man stared at Selene. "I realize it's late, my dear, but my plane had some turbulence so it had to land in your..." He glanced around with eyes narrowed. "...beautiful city."

Strange. I thought he was going to call this area trashy. Selene mustered the best smile she could. "I always thought it was trashy outside, especially around here, but it's good that you think it's beautiful."

He chuckled, "Thank you for your honesty. Do you have any specials?"

"Yes sir, our specials of the day are..." Selene raised her fingers to her lips. *If he orders any of the specials now, then the cooks will need to remake some of the ingredients that take a long time. Then* we'll *be here for a long time. Then he'll yell because he looks hungry.*

He tilted his head. "What's a matter, my dear, did you forget the one job you're supposed to do?"

Oh, I must have zoned out for too long. "No. I'm sorry sir, we only have what's on the menu," Selene said.

Selene stood and held her smile as the tall, fair-skinned gentleman perused through the large laminated menu.

He tapped his fingers melodically on the wooden tabletop.

Does he think that I'm rushing him because we're gonna close soon? "Sir, please feel free to take your time. I can come back with some water. That'll give you time to make a decision. In the meantime please feel free to enjoy all of the hand-painted murals along the walls."

"Very good, my dear." He motioned his hand as if Selene was a dog to be shooed away.

She walked to the window to retrieve a glass of ice water.

One of Selene's female coworkers walked up. "I hate people like that. Pinche culero."

Selene leaned over. "Why do you hate him already?" *He just walked in here.*

Her coworker put her hands on her hips. "Baby girl, I don't know how you didn't cuss him out. Some guys think the world revolves around them."

Selene turned to her coworker as she filled the plastic cup with water and ice. "He's hungry and tired." *He's got dark bags under his eyes and the color faded from his cheeks.* "Irritation and impatience are a bad combination for empathy." *At least, that's what I've read.*

"Sabes que, I don't think you see what everyone else here sees sometimes, baby girl. He's super conceited," her coworker said.

Is he? Selene walked back to the table where the dark-brown-haired man sat and set the water down on the table in front of him. He held his sports coat in his lap. "Are you ready to order, sir?"

"I think it was less of a decision and more of a gamble on which of these dishes wouldn't upset my stomach on tomorrow's flight." He looked up at Selene.

"I rarely get stomach aches, so I can't imagine how hard it is for someone to gamble on delicious Tex-Mex food," Selene said.

He scoffed. "Aren't you going to write my order down, my dear?"

Selene shook her head. "No sir, it's only you so it'll be easy to remember."

He narrowed his eyes again. "Is that so? Well then, I'll have a taco of Carne gui... guisa..."

"Carne guisada, sir. It's stewed beef marinated in bold rich Texas flavors," she said.

"I'm sure it is... I'll take a flour tortilla with that. One cheese and shrimp enchilada. Two rolled chicken flou-things," he said.

"Those are called Flautas, sir," she said.

He raised his left index finger in the air. "I'm not done yet."

Selene stood there with a cobbled faint smile as the man berated her with specificities on each order. "Will that be all, sir?"

"Are you sure you don't want to write it all down?" He sneered. "I would hate for you to forget as you did so earlier."

Selene closed her eyes. *Think.* "No sir. I've got it." *How did he say it?* "Shrimp enchiladas. No onion in the enchilada sauce, extra shrimp, but not too many. Two chicken flautas and they better be crispy, not hard. One carne guisada taco with cheese in a flour tortilla. Instead of cheddar cheese, you'd like Munster cheese on top. To drink, a Mexican cola with the top still on so you could see it opened yourself. And... less chunky salsa than what I set out for you earlier."

His eyes widened. "Impressive, my dear. Where did a young girl like you hone your memory?"

"School, mostly. I'll be starting college soon to become a bio-chemist... hopefully." Selene stood by. *If I convince mom well enough.*

"I see, yes, well I'm glad you didn't say *acting*. Stick to biochemistry, my dear." He handed her the laminated menu.

Wasn't that a compliment? Selene held the menu behind her back. "Oh, thank you. I'll put your order in right now. Please enjoy our de-lightful Mexican culture and atmosphere, sir."

"One last thing, my dear." He held his tan, sports coat at arm's length. "Hang this up somewhere, I don't want it to get dirty, thanks."

Selene took the man's coat and hung it close to the entrance where an empty coat rack stood. *He must have missed it.* She walked over to the kitchen window and then let the chefs know what he ordered.

Blaring Tejano music in the kitchen muffled the chef's Spanish. The two cooks looked at each other, then at Selene, and shook their heads. "Pinche culero."

I'll need to ask mom what that means when I get home. Selene retrieved the cold bottle of Cola and the bottle opener from the kitchen. She walked to the table where the toned, fit-looking man sat. He caressed the stubbled, brown hair along his groomed jawline and leered at the murals painted throughout the restaurant walls. She opened the bottle in front of him as he requested. "You're right, my dear. The scenery on these paintings is exquisite."

Selene set the bottle down in front of the man. "Here you go, sir."

"You remind me of my manager," he said.

Is that another *compliment?* "Alright." The bell by the kitchen window rang. "Excuse me, that means your food is ready." Selene brought the plates and set them in front of the man. *Hot. Hot. Hot.*

He leaned in. "It smells... decent."

They sound like compliments. I thought conceited people were mean. "Alright." Selene retreated to the back of the restaurant.

As she approached, the cooks complained about the complexity of the man's requests. She pulled out her phone from underneath the cashier's stand and checked her messages.

<u>Mom</u>

Mija, when are going to be home? You'll need to get sleep if we're heading up to the college tomorrow. I can't wait. If it's not too late, grab some cough medicine and I'll pay you back. Cuidate. I love you.

<u>Wednesday 10:08 PM</u>

Selene raised her fingertips to her lips. *I wish we could afford to be home or pay for her to visit a doctor. It's bad enough that we're barely making it off of her janitor salary and this job. This is the third bottle in a month. My dad is gone forever but my brother doesn't have an excuse.* Clacking dishes and high pressured bursts of water broke Selene out of her head. She held her phone up to her chest.

<u>Selene</u>

Alex, it's your little sister. You should come home. I don't know why you can't just keep an eye on mom from time to time, just...

check-in so I know you're alive. I love you and... I miss having you around. I don't know if I told you but mom is gonna let me live up north when I go to college. Crazy right?

Wednesday 10:44 PM

Selene set her phone on mute and slid it back into the crevice underneath the cashier's station. *He never responds except to ask for money or to borrow my car.* She sighed.

The tall man waved. "My dear... Uh... miss..."

I hope he liked the food. Selene rushed over to the table. "Selene, sir."

His plates were empty. *He must have been starving.* He pointed at the wall. "These hand-painted murals are intricate in their details to capture the history of your people."

My people? She looked around at the murals. "I think these paintings are of early indigenous Native Americans. I don't know any of those people. I think they're made up. Honestly, the one I like is the Chimera in the corner by the restroom."

He canted his head. "The what?"

Selene pointed at a large, colorful creature displayed in the back corner of the building. "A Chimera."

He turned his head.

Selene clasped her hands and smiled. "It's an ancient mythological creature with the body and head of a lion, tail of a scorpion, wings of an eagle, and the venom of a snake." *It's so cool. The best of everything.*

His brown eye's widened. "That's..."

Selene grabbed her arm. "I wanted to get a —"

"A tattoo... on your wrist," he mumbled.

Selene revealed the unblemished, light brown skin of her wrist. "That's right, but mom would have killed me. So I asked Andrea, the artist, to add it with the murals. She said that it had nothing to do with Aztec culture." *I think that's why she put it next to the restroom.*

He furrowed his brow then stared at Selene. "I just had the weirdest case of déjà vu, my dear. You look like a cute yet disheveled girl in my..." He shook his head. "Never mind."

"Alright," she said. *For someone conceited, he sure likes to hand out compliments.*

He grinned. "What's your name, my dear?"

He must be happy because he's full of food. "Selene, sir." *It's all part of God's plan.*

He held out his hand.

No. Selene grimaced. *Why do people shake hands?* Selene clasped his hand with her fragile fingers.

"You won't believe this, Selene, but..." He elevated his chin. "...I'm the star of stage and theater, Joseph Godwin."

Selene manufactured the best smile she could and leaned over. "Joseph... Who?"

CHAPTER EIGHT
ON THE ORDER OF CHANCE

The next afternoon, Joseph's plane landed in Salt Lake City, Arizona. He grabbed his carry-on, zipped past the airline agents, and then darted into the Tequila Sunrise bar across from the gate of his final destination, San Francisco. *This place had better serve alcohol.* He looked down at his intricate, gold, Swiss-made watch. *It's noon... They'll make an exception for me.*

A short female server approached Joseph. "Sir, welcome to the Tequila Sunrise. Where would you like to sit?"

What's with all the small female servers? Joseph walked past the few employees who meandered around the newly opened venue. "Preferably in the back corner somewhere. I'd like to be left alone, however, I want your bartender to make me an old-fashioned with your most expensive bourbon."

The server tilted her head. "Sir, I'm sorry but we don't serve alcohol until —"

Of course, they don't. I hate flying proletariat. Joseph smiled. "Not even for someone like me, my dear?"

The confused look on her face means that she doesn't know who I am. Uncultured... Joseph pulled a one hundred dollar bill out of his wallet. "Please split this between you and the bartender. Hopefully, you can make an exception on the matter."

The server's eyes lit up as she reached for the money. "I think we can bend the rules a little." She looked around. "After all, we're not too busy, Mr. umm."

Joseph loosened the collar of his dress shirt. "Mr. Godwin. Star of stage and theater, Joseph Godwin. Don't let the word out or you'll end up with a huge crowd."

She grinned. "Yes, sir, Mr. Godwin. It'll be *our* secret."

After a few minutes, the server came back with his drink and placed it on the table in front of Joseph. He nodded to her, and then she smiled and walked away.

Joseph unbuttoned his sports coat as he sipped on his Old Fashioned in the corner of the bar. His phone vibrated in his front coat pocket. He took it out and read the message. It was his manager confirming the exact time and place for him to meet the producer to review the lines with the crew and accommodate any concerns that Joseph had with the play. *It's a dual leading role. Damn it, Julia, she knows that I hate dual leads.* He smirked. *This must be payback for the phone number I gave out to that aspiring screenwriter.* Glancing into the bottom of his glass of bourbon and bitters, he chuckled. *Well played, my dear.* A couple walked past Joseph as he put the glass down. *It's getting busier.* He sat and waited. The server was preoccupied with the influx of people. *My tip doesn't go as far as it used to.* He swallowed the last drops of bourbon and headed to the bar.

The biggest gap in the crowded airport bar was between two African-American men. One had black curly hair, was clean-shaven with a high faded haircut, and broad thick shoulders. The other had lighter skin, was skinny, and was generally unkempt. The one on Joseph's right was shorter than the gentleman on his left. *I hope they don't mind if I squeeze in between them.*

He interrupted their conversation, "Excuse me, gentlemen, can I squeeze in between you two to get the bartender's attention?"

"No problem, sir." The one on the right nodded. *Glad to see that some people have manners still.*

After Joseph ordered another drink, he scanned the area. Kids shouted at their parents while a group of Europeans with fabric face-masks walked by. *I hate flying proletariat.* He fiddled with his hands.

"You alright, sir?" The man on the right asked.

"I'm fine," Joseph said. *Other than the fact that I hate having all these distractions.*

"My name is Corey." He pointed to the other side of Joseph. "The jumbled mess over there is my friend Charles."

"Nice to meet you both. My name is Joseph." He held out his hand. Corey shook Joseph's hand.

"That'll be twelve dollars, sir." The bartender placed Joseph's drink on the bar top.

"Put it on my tab." Joseph pointed to the back corner where he sat.

"We're in the military, but we don't make much," Corey chuckled. "So we decided to just sit here and slowly sip on a drink to pass the time until our flight." He glared at his watered-down drink.

"You should buy us a few drinks to show you're appreciation for the military," Charles said.

"Hey, bro. That's not cool." Corey reached around Joseph and smacked Charles on the back of the head.

Corey shook his head. "I'm sorry about that. Ignore my friend over there, his mouth doesn't have a filter."

Joseph took a sip of his drink. *Of course, everyone has an agenda.* "Look, I love what you guys do for our country, but there is no such thing as a free lunch. I worked hard to become this successful. I can't just hand out drinks to every stranger that I meet." Joseph turned to Charles. "And if you're thinking about asking someone else I'd advise against it."

Joseph turned away. *Kids these days.*

Corey put his drink down, stood up, and tapped Joseph on the shoulder before he could move out of reach. "I'm sorry, sir. Can you please say that one more time? I didn't hear that last part."

Sighing, Joseph turned around. "I said that I respect you boys but if you want something for nothing —"

"I'd advise against it," Corey and Joseph said in unison.

Joseph raised his eyebrow. *Hey, that's my line.*

Corey shook his head. "Sorry, sir. I just had the strangest case of déjà vu. Except, I think it was from... a dream I had. Weird, right?"

Joseph looked into Corey's eyes and smirked. *That's also my line... This might be interesting to hear.* "You know what?" He grinned. "I was too harsh on you boys earlier. I'll get the next round of drinks for you fine gentlemen if you'll tell me about this déjà vu of yours, kid, deal?"

Charles chimed in before Corey could answer. "Deal. Corey, tell him about your lame dream. I'm gonna go to the head, then I'm going to try one of those, old what-cha-ma-call-it, he ordered."

Charles walked to the bathroom.

Corey told Joseph everything he could remember. The details about the play, his wife and kids, and his stolen wallet. Joseph just stood there and listened intently. *Maybe I was wrong.* Corey told him about standing in line in the convenience store and how he heard a young man repeat those words... *I'd advise against it.*

Joseph's light-skinned face turned ghostly *No fucking way.* Time came to a crawl as he released the drink from his hand.

It shattered on the bar floor.

Shards of glass exploded over Corey's black shoes. He stumbled back as the busboy came around the corner to clean up the mess at their feet.

Corey placed his hand on the front of Joseph's light-blue dress shirt. "Are you ok, sir? Did I say something wrong?"

Joseph kicked through the fallen glass and around the busboy's wet rags. *This can't be a coincidence.* He gripped Corey's shoulders. "Describe the guy you waited in line with. Was he tall? Was he fat? Did he act strange?" *I don't remember someone that looked like this guy in my dream, so what gives?*

Corey's eyes lit up as he inched back. "Uh, he was my height, young, and skinny. He had board shorts and a hipster band hoodie on. The front of his hoodie had some band that I've never heard of."

Joseph's eyes widened. *Don't say The Dread Snakes.*

Corey scratched the side of his head. "It was black, green, and had some serpents on it, I think."

His heart thumped.

Warm sweat beaded on his chest.

Joseph leaned in, inches from Corey's face. "Is that it?"

"Um... Oh! He also smelled like smoke. Like marijuana smoke, I think. I prolly just smelled someone vaping outside of my barracks room and imagined the smell inside my dream. No big deal, right?" Corey pulled back from Joseph's grip.

I'm freaking this kid out as much as he's freaking me out. Joseph retracted his hands from Corey's shoulders. *Play it cool.* "I'm sorry, please, continue."

Corey told Joseph the rest of his dream to the extent that he could remember. Just as Corey concluded his tale, Charles arrived.

Joseph looked into Corey's eyes. *First the painting and the Hispanic girl, now it's a thing with this soldier.* "Thank you for telling me about your weird dream, Corey. For a second there I thought you and I were in the same dream along with..." Joseph chuckled. "Never mind, it's no more than a mere coincidence." *It can't be as simple as that.*

Charles nodded his head. "Oh, cool, so can we still get those drinks?"

My hunch was right. "Of course." Joseph smiled. "Bartender!"

"Yes sir?" The bartender asked.

"Please get these boys one drink each and put them on my tab in the back," Joseph said.

The bartender nodded and asked Charles what he wanted first.

Joseph shook Corey's hand. "Thank you. You boys have a safe trip."

Corey put down his drink and looked toward Charles. "Yo, that guy was cool, but kind of weird. He didn't have to buy us drinks. Next time don't be so rude about it, alright?"

Joseph walked back to the corner of the bar. *I've got to find out more, but it's not like I'm flying back to Texas to talk to that waitress, what's her name.*

"Yeah, whatever. I heard something break while I was in the head. What was that about?" Charles asked.

Joseph sulked in his seat. *I've got to be crazy. Or maybe... I'm special.* He pulled out his phone and did a quick internet search on dreams and sharing them with strangers. *Nothing obvious. Some books about dreams and what they mean. Conspiracies about government testing in the early nineteen seventies but nothing recent on having shared dream experiences.* He sighed. *What am I doing? I need to focus on the production notes.*

The female server walked up to Joseph. "Can I get you a fourth drink, Mr. Godwin?"

Maybe I've had too many? Joseph shook his head. He reached in his wallet and pulled out a credit card for the younger woman. A folded slip of white paper fell out on the table in front of him. *What was that?*

She smiled, took the credit card from him, and then walked away.

Joseph opened up the piece of paper. *It's a receipt.* It read:

Roberto's Taqueria

12909 San Pedro Drive

San Antonio, Tx. 78122

Telephone #210-781-4598

Server: Selene Garcia

His eyes widened. *Selene. That was her name.* Joseph reached for his phone and stared at the screen. *What am I going to do, call the restaurant and ask if she shared a dream about me? I would immediately block myself if I were in her shoes.*

She slid back into Joseph's view and handed him a black enclosed booklet that contained his credit card and the receipt.

I've got it. Joseph grinned as he stared into the server's deep brown eyes. "Excuse me, can I ask you a personal question?"

She blushed and nodded.

"If I needed to get a hold of you, my dear, after I've left this venue, what excuse could I use to get your attention?" Joseph asked.

She smiled and wrote on a blank piece of paper then handed it to Joseph. "You don't have to be shy," She winked. "Just ask for my number," She handed the paper with her phone number on it to Joseph.

Ugh. Maybe I do lay it on too thick. He accepted the slip of paper and placed it in his pocket. "Thank you, my dear, but what if someone already left and wanted to get a hold of you for say... a missing coat or if I left my credit card inside of this envelope." He tapped the black envelope against the top of the table.

She contorted her lips. "Well, you could just call and ask the manager for lost goods. Or..." She placed her hands on her hips. "If you wanted to add more to my tip, my manager better let me know, for sure."

Of course. Joseph smiled. "Thank you, my dear, you've been quite helpful."

"Anytime." She winked then walked away.

"Flight 1554 departing for San Francisco, California will begin boarding shortly through gate A24," rang throughout the terminal speakers above.

Joseph slid his wallet into his back pocket and then dialed the number to the restaurant where he met Selene.

"Hello, this is Roberto's Taqueria, is this order for takeout or delivery," a man's voice answered.

"This is not a food order, my name is Joseph Godwin. I dined in your fine establishment last night. I was hoping to speak to one of your servers, a young woman named Selene. Is she working today?" Joseph wedged the phone between his shoulder and ear as he wiped his hands with a napkin and walked out of the bar.

"I'm sorry, she's off for the next few days. May I take a message?" he asked.

Shit, I need to speak with her now, before she forgets about the dream. "I forgot to leave her a larger tip. I noticed after I reconciled my books. I must speak with her. Does she have a number that I could reach her on?" Joseph asked.

"My apologies sir, I can't hand out the phone numbers of our staff," he said.

Joseph held the phone at arm's length, sighed, and then pressed it against his ear. "She mentioned that she was heading off to college and I want to do the right thing. I'm sure she would let me send her off with a sizable tip. What kind of manager would deny money to a sweet girl like that?" *That should do it.*

"I'll give you her number sir, but... don't tell her that you got it from me or I'll be in big trouble. Deal?" he asked.

Joseph grinned. "Of course, my good friend. I'll make sure that all my inner circle gets wind of your remarkable establishment the next time they're in good 'ole south Texas." *However unlikely that scenario will be.*

"Flight 1554 departing for San Francisco, California boarding First Class through gate A24," rang throughout the terminal speakers, again.

He rattled off Selene's phone number as Joseph stood in line to board the plane. He wrote it down on the back of the receipt with a pen then fumbled the phone wedged between his ear and his shoulder. He hung up with the restaurant and touched the airline's application on his cell phone to retrieve his boarding pass. *Just in time.* He scanned the pass and boarded the plane. Joseph couldn't concentrate on the task that Julia had laid at his feet. His thoughts solely focused on his conversations with Selene and his recent encounter with Corey. *What does it all mean? Are we connected... somehow? I need to find out.* Joseph sat in his seat and peered outside of the window.

A flash of light enveloped the whole of his vision. He blinked and looked away for a brief moment. *What was that? It was brighter than the main stage light.* He turned back toward the open window of his first-class seat and saw nothing out of place. *It must have been a glare off the metallic airline equipment scattered throughout the gate entrance.* Joseph reclined his adequate first-class seat. Buckling his seat, he pulled out his cell phone from the front of his sports coat pocket. He entered Selene's number and text her the prospect of a large generous tip awaiting her response.

The flight attendant leaned in. "Please turn off your phone, sir. We're taking off."

And... sent. Joseph looked up and smiled. "Of course, my dear, right away."

Joseph turned off his cell phone. *By the time I land, she'll be clamoring to find out when and where to collect the money.* He sat back and closed his eyes. *Maybe I'll dream again, this time as a less insufferable juvenile.*

CHAPTER NINE
SEE THROUGH THE HOLLOW DARKNESS

Corey arrived at the Naval Warfare Training Facility in Waco Texas. *I've got a good thing going here. Even though it's only for a few weeks.* He let the Senior Chief in charge know that he was not going to cause any issues and that he would do what he was told without question. Once he checked into his room at the barracks he made his rack. While Corey folded creases in his bedsheets, he shook his head. *Sharing a dream is impossible. How could someone who looked successful and smart possibly believe in such a thing?* He rolled down underneath his rack. *I don't remember dreaming about* him, *but I remember that* someone *stole my wallet.*

He pulled a boot band out of his pocket and joined one side of his bed sheets with the other side underneath. *This will make sure that the bed sheets stayed tight and look uniform.* A knock echoed from his door. He rolled out from under his rack. *If it's a surprise inspection by the Senior Chief. I'll pass with flying colors.*

"Open up, fucker. I know you're not asleep yet. It's only twenty-one thirty," a voice cried out on the other side of the barracks door.

Corey turned the knob to let Charles in. *Or should I leave him outside until he grows tired of shouting?*

"What's up? I'm already headed to bed." Corey walked back toward his closet and pulled out a sleeping bag.

"Bro, are you nine years old? Who goes to bed at twenty-one thirty? Besides, I just hooked us up." Charles followed him into the mostly vacant barracks room.

Corey stopped and turned around. "*You* hooked *us* up? I'm interested."

"Listen, homie. Senior Chief needed two more volunteers for a working party out in town. It's to provide security at some high-class event. I told him that we could do it, no sweat. Cool, right?" Charles asked.

Nice work, Charles. Corey smiled. *It's a good chance to prove to Senior Chief that we're here to help.* He sat down in his desk chair. *There's a catch.* "That's great man, but I know you, brother. Spit it out. You never volunteer for shit."

"I was getting to the sweetest part. It's a high-class event for the university in Waco. A welcoming party for all the freshmen." Charles' face lit up like how I pictured a kid, from a wholesome family, on Christmas morning.

Corey crossed his arms. *Yup. I knew it.* "That sounds like trouble."

"Come on man. Think about all the pretty females. Maybe you'll find someone who loves your pudgy ass," Charles chuckled.

Corey looked down at his waist. *Hey, I'm not that chunky. Will I end up with a wife and kids like my dream or crusty and divorced like Chief?*

"Besides, if you wanna back out now, Senior Chief might be disappointed," Charles said.

He knows the exact buttons to press. Senior Chief is counting on us. Corey sighed. "Alright man, we can't let Senior Chief down, but if you try to bring some chick back here, you're on your own. When do we gotta be there and for how long?"

Charles clapped his hands together. "Tomorrow evening the duty van will pick us up in front of the barracks at seventeen hundred. Then, drop us off at the theater out in town and pick us back up at twenty-three hundred to take us back to base."

"Twenty-three hundred?" Corey sighed. "Alright, now can you let me finish getting ready for bed?"

Charles meandered out of the room. "Hey, I'm just trying to get you laid for once? With your lame ass twenty-one thirty bedtimes."

Corey chuckled then looked at his mirror as he escorted Charles out. *Hey, I've been laid before.* "Yeah, yeah. Good night. I'll see you tomorrow, man."

SELENE WALKED WITH her mother through the R.E.B University campus. Green well-kept grass fields surrounded tall marble-pillared buildings. A growing warm front broke through the expectedly chilly autumn North Texas day. Young adults scuttled about the grounds with smiles and laughs. A budding relationship had a picnic beneath the canopy of an aging oak tree at the edge of a walkway. *There's no way we could afford this without my scholarship in biochemistry.*

Selene's mother stopped, retracted her arm from Selene's grip, covered her mouth, and coughed.

"Ama, I don't have to stay here. I can always drive back and forth," Selene said. *She's going to tell me that she's fine.*

Selene's mother closed her eyes and inhaled, then slowly exhaled. Opening her eyes, she shook her head. "Don't be silly, Mija. Look at this place. Don't worry about me, I'm fine. As long as you remember to be safe, I want you to enjoy your time away from home." She reached into her purse, retrieved a cough drop, and popped it in her mouth.

She's getting thinner. The rose color from her cheeks has faded. Is this part of God's plan? Selene walked up to her mother and laid her head against her bosom. *Her steady heartbeat is comforting.* "I love you Ama. I'll do my best. I'll make sure to visit when I'm not studying. Promise."

Selene smiled as her mother's gentle fingers ran through her long brown hair.

Selene held orientation papers and fliers underneath her right arm, as they headed to the parking lot toward the far end of the campus. She pulled a flier for a ceremony held by the professors and alumni at a local theater. "Maybe we shouldn't go to this tonight. It was a long ride up here and you shouldn't push yourself." *Besides, the dress mom picked out doesn't have pockets.*

Selene's mother walked toward the passenger side door. "If it makes you feel better, I'll stay in the hotel while you go. I'll be fine, but you need to show up. You've got to make a great first impression. This is your future." She opened the door, sat down, and buckled her seatbelt. "I can't believe you're going to college, Mija." She sighed. "If only your father was still with us. He'd be so proud." She sniffled.

Selene started her car and smiled. *I like it here during the daytime.* As she exited the university parking lot, she drove her mother back to the hotel. The quiet humming of the radio provided a backdrop for their car ride. As they came to a red light, Selene turned to her mother. "Ama, if God has a plan for everything and is all-knowing, then was the plan for Dad and Alex to be out of our lives? Wouldn't you be better off with them around to help you around the house?"

Her mother's demeanor went from cheerful to sour. "No one knows God's plan. Not you, not me, no one. She's the only one that knows everything. We just have to keep the faith."

Grasping the steering wheel with both hands, Selene ensured that every signal was pressed as the driver's manual instructed. Each yellow light caused her to slow down and she looked into the rearview mirror to give the vehicles behind her the appropriate amount of space to stop. Several colorful papers sat between both women that contained printed directions to the hotel from the university and from the hotel to the freshman introduction ceremony tonight. Selene's cell phone rattled as it rested on top of the papers so that they wouldn't fly away. *Who is try-ing to get a hold of me while I'm trying to drive? Do they want me to crash?*

Her mother reached for the cell phone. "Do you want me to see who it is Mija?"

"Not right now. Can you put it on silent please, Ama?" Selene asked.

Her mother turned her cell phone to silent as they drove.

Arriving at the hotel, the two ladies unpacked the car, then made their way up to their room. Once in the hotel room, her mother took cough medicine with a bottle of water then laid down on one of the white-sheeted twin beds in the room. Selene turned on the television but reduced the volume so that her mother could rest undisturbed. *I don't like wearing formal dresses, but I don't want to keep mom up.*

Selene leaned at the edge of her mother's bed. "Ama, I'm going to take a shower and get ready for the event tonight. Try to rest. I'll bring you something to eat before I go."

Her mother nodded then closed her eyes. Selene unpacked her dress, sweater, shoes, and accessories then headed to the bathroom to shower. She glanced down at her cell phone. *Oh, right, someone was trying to get us killed earlier.* She took her phone to the bathroom and reviewed the text messages. *Who is...? That older guy from the restau-rant thinks the world revolves around him.* She removed the notification from her messages. *I have more important things to worry about... like which biology and anatomy subjects will help me understand what mom's sickness stems from.* She turned the water to the hottest setting. Steam emanated from the bottom of the bathtub. *Maybe I'll get a nice job and help mom with bills.* She smiled as she entered the shower stream. Scald-ing hot water pummeled her body like a professional massage therapist. *Or at least make more than a waitress does.*

Selene got dressed, walked out of their room, and softly closed the door behind her. She took the elevator down to the lobby then ordered Tex-Mex from a local restaurant for her mother. She received the food and journeyed back to their room. She snuck in the room and placed the plate of tacos down on the nightstand next to her mother. Selene glanced at her sleeping mother. *Don't worry Ama, I'm sure God's plan is for you and me to face the world together.* Vibrating in her pocket, she took the phone out and opened her notifications. *Another text from that man.* She glanced at the time. *Shoot.* As her mother snored, Selene bent over and kissed her on the forehead. *I'll be right back.*

A large full moon illuminated Selene's small figure as she walked outside during the autumn North Texas night. Her warm breath created a fog of mist she opened the driver's side door. She set her handbag down on the cloth-torn, passenger side seat of her car. *My A/C might be busted but the heat still works.*

As she leaned toward the center console and turned the heat knob, a surge of blinding light enveloped her sight. *Is someone going to hit me?*

Selene's heart rate increased.

She peeked over her peeled blue vinyl dashboard. The light caused her to shield her eyes with her arm and look away. The flash receded as fast as it appeared. She blinked and removed her arm from her field of vision. She looked around. *What was that?* She sat in her car as her heart calmed. She put her hands on the steering wheel and headed to the ceremony. *I hope I don't get blinded like that on the way.* Clutching the steering wheel harder, Selene proceeded down the darkly paved Waco city streets.

AS THE COLD SEATTLE rain pelted the window of his high-rise condominium, Joseph pulled his phone out of the front pocket of his sports coat. *Nothing from Selene yet.* Walking into the bedroom he turned into an office space, he placed his coat on the back of his brown leather computer chair and sat down. Roxie, his small, professionally-groomed dog, rubbed her fluffy white fur against his ankles.

Joseph bent down and scratched behind Roxie's right ear. "Don't worry, my baby girl, she'll get back to me soon."

Roxie wagged her tail and curled up on the floor between his feet. Joseph searched online for any information on dream sharing. Among his search tabs were conspiracy theories on government experimentation, alien influences, and multi-dimensional time-traveling beings. *Damn. There has to be more to this.* The tabs compounded until he couldn't click on them individually. He looked down at the diamond-embedded watch on his wrist. *It's already five. Shit.* His ab muscles tightened as the grumbling of his stomach caused Roxie to awake from her nap and bark.

Joseph patted Roxie on her side. "Shh, girl. It's alright, daddy just needs to get something to eat."

He scratched her head, then stood and stretched his arms. *Oh shit, Selene.* He pulled his cell phone out of his coat pocket and looked down at the screen. *Nothing... strange. I'll text her again so she doesn't think I'm just some shmuck.* Joseph grinned as he typed.

Joseph

Selene, it's Joseph Godwin, the star of stage and theater. I wanted to let you know that it causes me immense guilt that I shorted such a sweet girl out of money, right before she left for college. Please return my message so I can make things right for you. Hope to hear from you soon. :)

Wednesday 5:08 PM

If she doesn't reply to that then I need to rethink my acting career. Joseph's stomach grumbled, again. Roxie growled. Velma, his golden retriever, barked from the first floor.

Joseph looked down at Roxie. "Great, see what you started? Now you've got your sister riled up."

Roxie trotted at the edge of his heels as he darted out of the computer room and down his aluminum-railed stairs. Her pedicured paws tapped on the hardwood floors of Joseph's condominium. Velma intercepted Joseph as he reached the bottom of the stairs. He bent down and scratched the golden tufts of hair by her tail. Her tail ceased to wag as Velma raised her chin and closed her eyes. She was intoxicated by Joseph's preference for heavy-handed butt scratches.

"All you wanted was some attention, huh?" Joseph pet Velma on her side and her tail resumed wagging. *They only demand the slightest attention and they'll love you eternally. Genuine love. Unlike people and their façades.*

"I know daddy just got home, but you both need to wait here. I'll be back in a minute." Joseph grabbed the keys to the luxury sedan that hung by his door and exited the condominium.

Joseph started his car and connected his phone to the car's Bluetooth. *No answer yet from Selene.* He scoffed then sped off into the city arriving at his favorite take-out place, K.D.'s Noodle House. *They have the best ramen.* He walked past the huddled patrons straight up to the counter and ordered.

An older Asian woman smiled and greeted him at the counter, "Oh, Mister Godwin, it's good to see you, again. Welcome back."

The scent of soybean and miso paste permeated his nostrils. His belly gurgled and croaked at the prospect of their homemade noodles and choice cut pork belly. Joseph couldn't order fast enough. He handed the woman cash. She gave him the change, turned her head, and yelled the order to the chef in the window of the kitchen in the back. Joseph moved out of the way of the next patron but hovered around close enough to snatch the order immediately as it came out. He surveyed the area for a temporary place to sit. *Damn. This place is busier than usual.* He paced back and forth like a hyena on the prowl of its next scavenge.

Joseph stopped.

A lone man stood against the sidewall of the restaurant.

He was shorter than Joseph and wore a black trench coat and a black fedora. *Does he think this is, a speakeasy?* The lone man stared at

Joseph, as he paced back and forth. The man's eyes never averted. *Talk about a stalker, jeez. It's best to ignore people like him.* His phone vibrated in his back pocket. *Selene?* Joseph pulled his phone out and read the notification. *Damn, it's just the executives from San Francisco.* He read the long-winded text. *Yada, yada, yada, you did great. I'd love to have you on our team. Whatever.* Joseph closed his phone. *This should make Julia happy... and me... I guess. I hoped it was Selene.* A patron walked by with their bowl of ramen in hand. A miasma of deep rich pork and chicken broth encapsulated Joseph's head. *What am I thinking? Of course, this makes me happy. It's the chance to etch my name in the history books.* He shook his head as he tucked his phone away. *I need to forget about this dream nonsense.* He glanced to see if his stalker left.

The man was gone.

Joseph examined the walls of the restaurant as nonchalant as possible. *Thank goodness, I can eat in peace.*

A flash of ethereal light engulfed the whole room. It caused Joseph to shield and squint his eyes for a brief second, then the light receded into the darkness. He lowered his arm and opened his eyes. *What was that... again?* All the other patrons went about their conversations. *How did they not see that bright-ass light?*

A sharp point tapped his tall shoulder.

Joseph leaped back.

"Here you go Mister Godwin, sir." The aged woman handed Joseph a bag of soups and sides.

Oh thank god, I thought she was my stalker. "Did you just see that light?" Joseph pointed behind him at no one in particular.

She shook her head. "Sorry, no light, but my eyesight has been getting worse over the years so I probably missed it."

Joseph received the food from the woman. *No, you definitely would have seen that.* "Okay, thank you."

"That reminds me, someone called for you before you arrived... asked if you've been here recently," she said.

The only person I've taken to this place is Julia, although she should have just called my cell phone. "It must have been my manager Julia, she's a strange one," Joseph chuckled.

"Hmm, I don't know, it was a man's voice. Sounded serious. Didn't give a name though," she said.

A man!? Joseph scanned the area again. *Mr. wanna be noir detective, I'll bet.* He cradled the bag of food. "Thank you for the heads up, my dear. If he calls again, tell him you never saw me." *I shouldn't eat here.*

Nodding her head, she shuffled away behind the counter. "Alright, Mister Godwin, until next time."

Joseph walked out to the sidewalk and headed to his car. His eyes focused on every person that passed him along the way. *The last thing I need is a stalker.* His heart pounded faster as he looked back and to his side. His pace quickened. The heat from the mouthwatering containers of broth and his uneasiness compounded to make his palms sweat. *I usually order my food online and come pick it up anyway. He must have seen me eat here and I never noticed him.* He reached his car, stood, and swiveled his head. *The coast is clear.* He put his food in the passenger seat, locked the doors, and headed home. His heart calmed. He wiped his palms on his khaki pants before he gripped the gray, leather-bound steering wheel.

Velma and Roxie pranced around at the entrance of the door as he entered and locked the door behind him. They sniffed at Joseph's feet, wagged their tails, and followed him to the dining room area. He placed the bowl of ramen and side dishes on the thick glass dining room table, removing all the containers and ramen ingredients. A deep, rich aroma from the chicken katsu caused Roxie to tap on Joseph's shoes with her small white paws. She sat on her hind legs and limply joined her front paws as if saying, "Please may I have some too, daddy?"

Joseph looked down at Roxie's eyes. One was green and one was blue. Her curly white fur was trimmed around her eyes but engulfed the rest of her facial features. "Of course, daddy wouldn't forget my girls."

He pulled some chicken katsu and pork belly out and laid them in their respective bowls in the kitchen. *That should keep them occupied for a bit.* He poured the broth into the bowl of noodles, mixed in the meat, and then added the fermented egg. Joseph slurped every last noodle and drank every drop of broth. *That hit the spot.* He burped. *Good thing no one's around to hear that.* He chuckled then looked down at his watch. *It's getting late.* The dogs ate their fill as Joseph lurched up the stairs. He walked into his office space and looked at the hundred tabs open on the screen. He scoffed. *What am I doing?* Joseph pressed the power button on the computer until its light was extinguished.

Velma and Roxie barked and snarled. *What the hell?* Joseph walked out of his office room and looked down at his door where the dogs scratched and howled. A shadowed figure stood silhouetted against the hazy glass of his door.

Joseph's eyes widened. *Shit! Who the fuck is that?*

Joseph froze. His eyes fixated on the figure. *Is it my stalker? How does he know where I live? Maybe he'll go away if he thinks I'm not here. Even if I call the cops, they'll take forever to get here. I need to remain still.* The silhouette of the man remained resolute like he was playing chicken with Joseph. *The first one that flinches... loses.*

Joseph's back pocket vibrated which jolted him back a step. The hardwood floor creaked. *Shit!* He looked down to regain his foothold then looked back at the hazed glass window of his door. As the shadowed figure remained, he reached into his pocket, pulled out his cell phone, and glared at the notification. *It's from Selene!*

Selene

Thanks for the offer, but no thanks.

Wednesday 8:22 PM

He looked back up at his door, but the figure disappeared. Joseph took a deep breath and exhaled. *Whatever, little girl, I'm over it. Fuck off and have a good life.* Joseph descended the stairs and the dogs ceased their commotion. *Thank God. I should call the police.* He turned the corner at the bottom of the staircase. A small white folded piece of paper jutted out from underneath the door. *What is that?* He reached down and picked it up. *Did that psycho stalker leave this?* He unfolded it and it read:

IF YOU KEEP PURSUING THE DREAMWORLD THEN YOU AND THE OTHERS WILL EVENTUALLY HAVE TO DEAL WITH THE NIGHTMARES THAT ARE CAUSED IN ITS WAKE.

STOP NOW!

YOU HAVE BEEN WARNED.

CHAPTER TEN

WARDEN OF THE KEY

The next evening, Corey jumped out of the white duty van that arrived at the front of the Hippodrome Theatre. They were dressed in their formal white uniform. The fluorescent light from the marquee sign above his head spelled out WACO in giant neon letters. The paint on the outer brick layer was fresh. The businesses that surrounded it teamed with patrons. Down the street hipster bars and exotic eateries teemed with young patrons. He put his military ID in his pants pocket then approached the plaza area where his Senior Chief stood.

"Are you the last group to get here?" the Senior Chief asked.

Corey stood at attention. "Yes, Senior."

"Listen up!" The other eight junior sailors gathered around the Senior Chief. "Our job is to provide security, check invitations at the entrance, help the staff hand out hors d'oeurves, and clean up afterward. We are to be on our best behavior. Then, meet back here to get picked up at twenty-three hundred to go back to base. Got that?"

"Yes, Senior Chief," they all replied.

Senior Chief pointed at Charles. "You will be with me at the front greeting everyone and collecting invitations. The rest of you go to the back and get with the staff to help set up and get ready because we'll have a full house in thirty minutes."

"Yes, Senior Chief," they all replied.

Corey walked toward the back of the venue. *Senior Chief picked you for a reason, Charles. Don't blow this.* He helped move tables and chairs around the newly renovated theater. Corey looked up at the beautifully lathed woodwork on the vaulted cathedral-like ceiling. The lacquer that emanated off of the dark mahogany hardwood ballroom floor smelled of hickory. He had never been to an event at such an elegant meeting place. Corey's eyes wandered throughout the room as he set up the tablecloths and chairs. He looked upon a painting that depicted epic scenes that highlighted the rich history of the local theater. He ran his hands against the mural's deep colors.

A surge of light covered the inside of the Hippodrome Theatre from the deep brown wood-stained flooring to each hairline fracture of the dome overhead. Corey shut his eyes and covered them with his right hand. *What in the world?*

Charles strolled by Corey on his way to the restroom. "Hey, homie, I will let you know if any fine girls walk through these doors."

Corey winced, removed his hand, and peered through his narrow eyelids. "What in the hell was that?"

Charles looked behind him toward the entrance. "What was what?"

Corey looked up at the light emanating from the chandelier hung far above his head. *Maybe they turned the bright ones on just now?* "Don't worry about me, man. You can take them all. Just let me be."

Charles shrugged then walked into the restroom.

Where did that come from? Heading into the backroom, the staff prepped several plates of hors d'oeurves. As Corey conversed with his fellow shipmates, the sound of idle conversations in the ballroom area grew to a rumble.

A staff member walked up to Corey with a giant silver serving dish. "Take this and visit all the tables to ask if they'd like one. When you're done with all the tables or when you run out, come back here and we'll give you another one. Got it?"

"Yes sir. Easy-peasy orange squeezy," Corey said.

Grabbing the large plate of what looked like fancy Shish Kabobs, Corey headed out to the ballroom floor. Several elaborately decorated tables lined either side of the venue leaving a clear pathway in the middle for the sailors and guests to maneuver. He asked each table if they wanted the various plates of food while keynote speakers were up on the lit stage. The speakers welcomed the new freshman class and gave guidance on the future they would mold. *I could have gone to college. I would have ended up like Charles if I did. Not that he's a bad dude, he just can't see the benefits that the military provides.* Corey looked up at the lights again as he walked forward. *Those weren't as bright as—*

Slam!

His plate of skewered meats and cheeses fell over onto a young woman's dress and then crashed to the ground.

"Oh, my god! I am so sorry." Corey knelt to pick up the scattered pieces of food. He looked at the dress and sweater of the woman he stumbled into. *Shit.* "Please, let me get something to clean your clothes. Miss... um..."

"Selene, and it's okay. I was looking down at my phone and didn't see you either." Selene sat on her knees and leaned down to help pick up the scattered toothpicks, exotic cheeses, and sliced meat.

He took the random scraps of food items from her and put them back on the tray. "Please, wait here for a minute while I go to the back room and get you a wet towelette. I'll be right back."

Selene wiped off small meat and cheese crumbs from her dress and sweater. "Thanks."

Darting off into the backroom, Corey handed off the tray of discarded partially skewered food items and explained the situation. *I hope Senior Chief didn't hear that.* He turned to the staff member that handed him the meat tray. "Can I get something to clean up a small mess outside? I accidentally spilled my tray." *I gotta clean up this mess and apologize. I hope she isn't too pissed.*

Another staff member walked up and handed Corey a moist tow-elette. "Thank you, ma'am, you're a lifesaver."

He headed to the spot where the meats and cheeses were sprawled across the floor and looked around. *She's gone.* He searched the ball-room but did not see her. *Well, shit.* Corey performed his duties as the ceremony progressed. He kept a watchful eye out for Selene but nev-er saw her throughout the evening. Charles infrequently swung by to tease him only to disappear into the crowd of nicely dressed people. To-ward the end of the evening, the guests vacated the ballroom and, once the last of the guests trickled out, the staff told the sailors to commence cleaning efforts.

Corey went into the restroom, wiped his eyes, and splashed water on his face as twenty-three hundred slowly approached. After the staff thanked the sailors for their efforts, the Senior Chief called for the duty van. While the group waited out front to be picked up, amplified con-versations at the bars across the street and the constant traffic noise filled the stiff night air.

Charles turned to Corey. "Yo, I got a number from this girl. Sorry, bro, I couldn't find one that was interested in chubby guys who go to bed at twenty-one thirty," Charles chuckled.

Good one. Corey shivered and smiled. "As long as you didn't give Senior Chief a hard time, I don't care."

"I was on my game man, we got this." Charles high-fived Corey. "Oh, there was this *one* girl that rushed out before I could talk to her. She left during the middle of the whole thing like she forgot something important."

Corey raised his eyebrows as he leaned in toward Charles. "Was she a light-skinned Hispanic-looking girl with dark brown hair, thin lips, and big brown eyes? Was she about five foot five and wore a white and blue skirt?"

"Oh snap. Did you find a pretty little senorita?" Charles laughed.

"It's not like that man... Well?" Corey asked.

Charles scratched his head. "Actually. Yeah. How the fuck did you know?"

"Shit, which way did she run off to?" Corey moved beyond the group of sailors.

Charles pointed beyond the noisy bars and crowded sidewalks.

Corey surveyed the busy streets. *Did I ruin her night? Poor girl. Damn.*

Senior Chief motioned toward Corey. "Hey, knuckleheads. The duty van is here, get in."

Corey and a few other shipmates got in the duty van and buckled up. Looking out the window, he sank into the black vinyl seat. *It's so late.* The city's vibrant lights blurred through the van's back window. His eyes grew heavy as the collective chatter of the other sailors turned into indistinguishable murmurs. Blaring late-night traffic transformed into a melodic lullaby.

The duty van stopped.

Corey's head jolted forward.

"Everyone, get your IDs out for the sentry to check," the duty driver commanded.

Corey rummaged through his pockets and every opening in his pure, white, dress uniform. *I can't find my military ID!*

Shit. He looked up.

Everyone in the van looked back at him. *I am so screwed.*

SELENE PULLED INTO the parking lot of the Hippodrome Theatre, per the directions printed on her paper. Reaching for her handbag, her phone vibrated. *What if mom woke up and needed something.* She read the messages on her phone. *It's that man again. What the heck? His name is Joseph Godwin.* She looked up. *I've never heard of him.* She continued to read. *How did he get my number?* She replied to Joseph.

I don't want money, but mom always told me to be polite. Selene tucked her phone back in her beige handbag.

Walking down the busy Waco street, horns shrieked from the backed-up traffic, and the dissonance from the mixed music that blared out from the bars and outdoor food venues made Selene wince. *If I'm going to go to school here I need to get used to this without my headphones on... but for now...* She jogged.

Two sharply dressed men in all white stood at the entrance. Selene walked up to them and stood there; still and unwavering.

One of the men leaned down. "Excuse me, ma'am. Are you here for the R.E.B University freshman welcoming ceremony?"

Selene nodded.

"Do you have your invitation?" the taller man asked.

Oh. Selene reached in her handbag and pulled out a small decorated black paper invitation and handed it to the man.

The slender dark-skinned man accepted the piece of paper. "Thank you, ma'am. Please come in." The younger man winked at Selene. "And if there's anything you need tonight, don't hesitate to come to get me. I'll take good care of you."

Selene canted her eyes toward the taller man placed her hand on his shoulder. "Thank you, but no thank you."

Smirking, the older man held the door open for Selene as she walked in. Several groups of faculty and fellow freshmen filled the main ballroom. While the first keynote speaker stood on stage and announced the commencement of the activities, Selene found a seat farthest away from the loudspeaker. She set her handbag on the red cloth-lined table in front of her. The waitstaff was dressed like the two gentlemen outside. *I like their costumes. So clean and white.* She took a drink from her glass filled with a mix of apple juice and seltzer. *Is this supposed to look like champagne? I suppose its purpose is to make you feel like you are drinking adult drinks even though we're all underage.* Selene snorted and chuckled. *I should bring this back to the hotel and stumble to the bed.*

Ama will freak out. She'll likely kill me... Selene pushed her drink away. *Bad idea.*

Selene nibbled on the small finger foods dropped off on her plate from the wait staff. Her handbag vibrated against the tabletop. *I should ignore that.* The phone vibrated inside the handbag again. *I told Joseph that I wasn't interested. Perhaps... it's mom. Maybe she needs me to pick up the medicine on the way back.* As Selene got up and walked toward the nearest wall, she pulled her phone from her handbag. Walking away from the rest of the nicely dressed people, she accessed her notifications. *Ugh. Joseph. This time I'll have to block him.* It read:

UNKNOWN NUMBER

Selene, we don't have time for games. I believe we shared a dream.
    I know how crazy that sounds, but me, you, and some other guy shared a dream and I think people are on to us for some reason. Please allow me to explain and be careful. I think someone is following —
Crash!

Selene slammed into one of the waitstaff. She fell back and her phone fell beside her. A taller, portly, dark-skinned man apologized and picked up the foodstuff around her from the floor. Selene sat on her knees and gathered her phone after she brushed the pieces of food from her navy blue sweater and white dress. *Joseph's message is beyond creep status.*

She glanced at an ID card on the ground. *I'll block him right —* She picked it up and looked around for the sharply dressed waiter but he was gone. She stared at the name on the ID card. *Corey Parker. Why does that look familiar?* Selene rose her right-hand fingertips up to her mouth. *It's the same name ID I found in the wallet I stole... from the red convertible... in... a dream a few nights ago.*

Chills went down her spine.

She shot up off the ground.

Her fingers caressed her lips. *This can't be. It's just like that shallow man said.* She ran to her table, snatched her handbag off of it, threw the two items in it, and ran out of the venue past the two gentlemen greeters. She dashed to her car, opened the driver's side door, got in, and locked the doors. Selene clenched her hands on the steering wheel to steel herself from the shaking. She closed her eyes and exhaled. *The rest of Joseph's message.* She pulled out her phone, saved Joseph's number, and read the rest of his message.

<u>Joseph</u>

...I think someone is following me. I'll bet it's our shady government. They spy on us at every opportunity. Call me tomorrow, please! Just let me have a few minutes of your time and I won't bother you again.

<u>Wednesday 10:13 PM</u>

Is someone following me too? Selene scanned the parking lot. A loose vagrant piece of trash tumbled by the street around her car. She retrieved Corey's ID from her handbag and took a picture of it with her phone. *I'll ask him if he remembers dreaming of a red convertible. Do guys always dream of cool cars? It may be a moot point, but I'll ask anyway.* Joseph's message haunted her mind. *The person that I am in my dreams is the worst. I can't believe God would have a plan for her.* Selene shook her head. *I don't even know if this is all a coincidence, but I need to ask Corey about his recent dreams.* She jettisoned out of the driver's seat and rushed back to the Hippodrome Theatre.

Only the older gentleman greeter was left. The venue was dark and the doors were closed. *Oh, no.*

"Excuse me, ma'am. I'm sorry however the ceremony is over and they've closed the doors. Can I help you with something?" he asked.

His demeanor is rough but the look in his eyes is sincere. I can trust him with this. Selene pulled out a piece of paper from her handbag and wrote her phone number on it. She handed the man Corey's ID and her phone number. "You guys were all dressed in the same costume so I assume y'all are part of the same group."

The man chuckled, "Yes, ma'am we're sailors in the United States Navy." The man took the ID and paper from Selene's slender light brown hand.

"Great. Please return this to Corey and have him call me. It's super important... and" *What did mom say about the military people? Oh, yeah.* "Thank you for your job."

A white van pulled up to the street where they stood.

The man nodded to Selene as he got in the van. *Great. Now what?* Her phone vibrated. *Maybe it's Joseph again.*

She reached into her handbag as she stood on the sidewalk in front of the empty venue and pulled out her phone. The message read:

<u>Mom</u>

Mija, where are you? Can you bring me a coke on your way home?

<u>Wednesday 11:08 PM</u>

Selene looked around, put her phone back, and dashed back to her car. She texted her mother back and drove back to the hotel. *I hope they didn't see me...* her *in my dreams.* She cringed. *She's the worst.* She headed up to the hotel room and greeted her mom with an ice-cold coke from the vending machine in the hotel lobby.

"How was the event? What did I miss?" her mother asked.

I can't tell mom, she'll think I'm crazy and never let me stay here. Besides, I can't trust Joseph without talking to Corey first. "Loud... but welcoming. I don't know if I like this place at night. I'll stick to exploring during the daytime," Selene said as she got ready for bed.

"Good, Mija. You don't need to mingle with any troublemakers anyway," her mother said.

I hope Corey and Joseph aren't the types to make trouble. "I did manage to make a friend," Selene said from the bathroom.

"Is *he* cute?" Her mother asked.

Selene retracted her face. *Why does she think the only friends I make are guys?* "I know girls too. We just don't stay friends for long." *...for some reason.*

Selene walked out of the bathroom in gray sweatpants and a long-sleeved shirt that had a picture of two kick-boxing pandas on it. *I can't tell her why...* "I'm waiting for him to text me back to see if he wants to... grab coffee tomorrow."

As Selene sat down on the other twin bed, her mother leaned over. "I'm lucky. Any other mom would tell their daughter to be careful when they talk to new people in a new town, but you're special, Mija. You're a better judge of character than anyone I know. I'm more worried that he won't stick around long enough for me to meet him because you've decided that they're not too something-or-other."

Selene tilted her head. "I'm not that picky, Ama, am I?" *In this case, I'll need to find out if these guys are telling the truth or not.* She tightened her lips. *Not whether or not they'll make good boyfriends.*

Her phone vibrated against the black end table by the twin bed where Selene sat.

"Is that him? Can I answer it?" Her mother's complexion brightened as she leaned toward Selene.

Why is she suddenly cheery? Selene smiled. *I can't let you see either of these guys' texts. Not unless this is all a prank.* Selene reached for her phone. "Ama, I don't even know who it is."

Her mother crossed her arms in a fit like a disgruntled teenager. "Only boys text this late, Mija. You must have made an impression on him."

Quite the opposite, I'm afraid. Selene looked at the message. It read:

UNKNOWN NUMBER

Um... Selene, this was a Corey. I thought I'd at least text you a thank you message for returning my ID. It saved my ass for sure. Sorry... if I ruined your dress. Have a good night, it was nice to meet you.

Wednesday 11:55 PM

My dress? Selene ran her thumbs across the phone's tiny digital keyboard.

Her mother waved her hand between Selene and her cell phone. "Don't reply too soon, Mija. If you like him then wait a bit before responding."

Selene sighed. "But I'm not..." *I can't tell her why.* Selene assembled a smile. "Thanks, Ama. I'll respond tomorrow." *I'll have to send it later.*

She turned off the lamp on the black nightstand and placed her phone on the charger plugged in the middle of the twin beds. Selene stared through the drapes into the night sky the dark gray clouds unveiled a large full moon.

Immense, all-encompassing light entered the room and dominated the whole of Selene's vision. "Ahh." She turned away and covered her head with both her arms.

"What's the matter, Mija?" Her mother sat up.

The light retreated, out of Selene's view, back into the unknown.

"A bright light just flashed inside this room. Didn't you see it?" Selene blinked as she wiped her eyes. *Do I have a cataract or some eye protein deficiency?*

Her mother shook her head. "Maybe the cars from the highway flashed their lights through the window."

She's got a point. Selene looked around and then sank beneath the bedsheets. *The last time I saw the light was in the parking lot. Maybe... I'm just not used to this city.* "It's nothing, Ama, please rest."

Selene waited until her mother went to sleep then stealthily disconnected the phone off the charger and hid it under the guise of going to the bathroom. Once she was in the bathroom she sent a flurry of messages to Corey.

Selene

Corey this is Selene. I don't think our meeting was a coincidence. I think I saw you... your ID to be exact, in a dream I had. This sounds crazy but this other person told me the same thing, shortly before I ran into you.

Thursday 1:20 AM

<u>Selene</u>

Did you happen to have a cherry red convertible with a white vinyl top and white striped tires in any dreams recently? I know this sounds impossible, but please just answer the question. If so, we need to talk.

I'd like to have coffee with you tomorrow to discuss. Thank you.

<u>Thursday 1:22 AM</u>

She reached for the door and then sent another message.

<u>Selene</u>

Oh, and thank you for your job.

<u>Thursday 1:23 AM</u>

She placed the phone back on the charger and nestled herself underneath the hotel room bed sheets. *I hope I never dream of her... of me... again.*

An intense ray of sunlight beamed across her eyes as Selene woke the next morning. She turned her face away from the window and pulled the closest pillow over her head. *Am I a magnet for beams of light?* Through one half-opened eye, she glanced at the other twin bed. The bed was neatly made and her mother was gone. She sat up. *Where did mom go?*

Cracking open, the handle of the hotel room door jiggled. Her mother held a plate of scrambled eggs, bacon, and French toast. A cup of coffee rested precariously on the plate as she balanced it before setting it down on the desk next to the television in the room. Under the plate was a folded piece of paper.

Her mother handed the paper to Selene. "Good morning, Mija. I thought I'd grab myself some breakfast since you're going on a breakfast date."

What is she talking about? Selene unfolded the paper. *These are directions to a local coffee shop. Oh.* She reached for her phone to see if Corey replied to her messages late last night. She clasped her phone close to her chest. "Ama, you didn't look at my messages did you?"

As she took a sip of coffee, her mother shook her head.

Selene read the messages from Corey. *I can't believe this. He's interested in discussing this. Perfect.* Selene smiled.

"Oh, I see your new prospect said yes." Her mother bit a piece of bacon. "I told you that you needed to wait a little while. No man likes a needy woman."

"That's an archaic way of thinking, Ama. Besides, we're going to grab a coffee, that's it." Selene text Corey that she would meet him in thirty minutes.

Selene slid out of bed and into loose-fit blue jeans, a long-sleeved tan blouse, and white cushioned sneakers. She threw her hair into a ponytail and kissed her mother on the forehead.

"I'll be right back Ama, then we can explore more of the town," Selene said.

"Alright, Mija. Maybe give him a follow-on date if he gets nervous," her mother said as she cut into her eggs.

It's not a date and... "I'm not that picky, Ama." Selene waved as she grabbed her handbag, phone, car keys, and paper directions.

As she exited the hotel, Selene observed all the hotel staff in the lobby. Several people sat and enjoyed their breakfasts. *They seem happy in this town. Maybe I'll like it more in the daytime than the nighttime.*

SELENE DROVE HER VEHICLE to the location, just outside of the base, where Corey notified her to meet. She aggressively waved her hand out of the driver's side window. He took his time and looked both ways before he crossed to the other side of the street. As he walked up to the vehicle, Selene rolled down the passenger side window.

He bent down and peaked in. "Selene?"

Selene leaned over. "Corey, get in, please. We need to have a conversation."

He opened the door and sat down on the worn, cloth passenger seat. Selene waited for Corey to lock his seat belt before she drove away. Selene sat in silence as she navigated her way to a local coffee shop.

Corey looked around. "So..."

Selene turned the radio volume up to a quiet hum as she approached a stoplight. "This should help. Sorry, but I need to focus."

She picked up and read the instructions. *First here, then on the highway, two miles down here... got it.*

"Oh... alright. You know I could GPS the location if you told me where we're going," Corey said.

Selene shook her head yet kept her eyes on the road ahead. "No thank you. I've read the instructions."

Corey looked out the passenger side window and smiled. He tapped his hands against his knees. *He's fidgety, but his eyes are warm. He reminds me of my brother, but a little pudgier.* Selene cracked a smile.

They turned into an old pancake house turned drive-through coffee shop. They sat in line behind a few cars.

We don't have much money, but I did ask him out to coffee. Selene turned to Corey. "Please feel free to order what you want. I'll pay for it."

Corey shook his head emphatically. "Not a chance. I still owe you for getting your dress dirty. I'm not trying to insert gender roles but I'd feel bad if you drove out here and had to pay." He reached for his wallet.

My dress was the last thing I was worried about, but... Selene raised her thin eyebrows and scrunched her small nose to replicate a smile. *Mom said to be nice, so...* "Sure."

Pulling up to the drive-thru, Selene ordered their drinks. She parked in the parking lot of the coffee shop. No one appeared around the faded outdoor wooden tables. Crisp Waco morning air bit at Selene's smaller frame as she sat on her heels with her knees bent opposite Corey.

Corey tilted his head. "Is that comfortable?"

Selene looked down at her feet and thighs. *It doesn't look comfortable?* "Yes." The current of steam from their drinks wafted between them. She sipped her white chocolate-flavored coffee.

Corey blew the top of his Limblini latte to cool it down. "So..."

Selene leaned forward. "Did you have a dream where you drove a cherry red convertible? Was it at a gas station? 'Cause I... sort of stole your wallet."

"Sort of?" he asked.

Okay. Lay off the interrogation. Selene glanced off to her left. "*She* stole it in a dream. I never saw someone that looked like you... just your name."

Corey bit down on his lip and shook his head. "Yeah, I remember that sweet classic car and that my wallet was gone." He whispered under his breath, "Joseph was right."

Selene brought her fingertips up to her lips. *He knows Joseph. This is too freaky. What does this mean?*

"Are you alright?" Corey reached out to Selene's arm.

What is he doing? Selene retracted her hand before Corey could touch her. "Sorry..." She sat on the bench seat with her feet underneath the tabletop. "Did you say you knew Joseph Godwin, star of stage and theater?"

Corey's eyes widened as drops of latte spilled on his lap. "Don't tell me you know him too?"

Selene took out her phone and showed Corey the cryptic messages that Joseph sent. She held her phone against her chest after they reviewed the messages. "Here, let me start a group chat with us. I remember some young cocky kid that had a similar vibe as Joseph."

Corey sipped his latte. "Yeah, he seemed impatient but looked like the typical college person our age. I was... a bit older in my dream."

"What does this mean?" Selene held herself and shivered.

Corey shrugged his shoulders. "Maybe Joseph is being paranoid. What's the big deal?"

Selene laid her phone between them on the red wooden table. "Let's call him. I'd feel better if you were here. He creeped me out the last time we met, but I can't shake this feeling." *How does this fit in God's plan?*

She called Joseph.

Joseph answered after the first ring. "Selene! Thank god you called back. Don't hang up, what I'm about to tell you is —"

Corey leaned in. "Hello, again, Joseph. We're both here."

The phone fell silent.

"Hello?" Selene gazed into Corey's brown eyes. "Where did he go?"

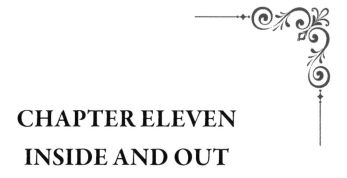

CHAPTER ELEVEN

INSIDE AND OUT

S elene hovered above her phone. *Did his heart explode from the shock? He* is *old.* "Hello, sir, are you in need of medical attention?"

"No... What? I'm fine." Joseph's voice was steady. "So, it's true. We did share some type of dream."

Corey sipped on his latte. "Yeah... now what?"

"Shit, shit, shit." A clattering of several objects disrupted the silence. "Okay... I need you to make sure no one followed you."

Selene and Corey looked up at each other then Selene looked left and Corey looked right. Discarded coffee cups drifted across the sidewalk on the street and a homeless person was huddled in an alleyway in the distance.

Selene leaned in. "I don't think anyone is following us."

Corey smirked. "Yeah, I haven't noticed super-secret spies around the fenced-in, heavily-guarded naval base."

I'm surprised that Corey looked for spies before he knew about this. Selene nodded. *Impressive.*

"Listen, there is something to this. Every thread I've pulled and rabbit hole I've looked down has stopped. Like someone or something doesn't want anyone to find out the significance," Joseph said.

"I agree that it's a strange coincidence, but don't you think you're being a little bit paranoid, sir?" Corey sat back.

Selene received a notification on her phone.

Joseph sighed. "I sent you a picture. Look at it and tell me that I'm being paranoid."

Selene grabbed her phone and opened the attachment. *It's a picture of a note.* She showed Corey. They read the warning together but to themselves.

Selene put her phone back in the middle of the table. She rose her fingertips up to her lips. *He's not paranoid.* Selene swiveled her head back and forth. "Maybe he's right." *I need to go back to the hotel.*

Corey folded his arms. "I doubt some dude is going to rush the main gate, somehow survive, then run into my barracks room to snatch me up. Not without a fight, that's for sure." He cracked his knuckles.

"Alright, Mr. Military. That's not a bad plan. Stay back on base. Selene and I have to be extra vigilant. Also, until I can figure out who is stalking me, I suggest we don't tell a soul about the dream or each other," Joseph said.

Mom wouldn't believe me even if I told her. Selene hovered over the phone. "My mother thinks Corey and I are on a date and knows nothing about you, Joseph."

Corey choked on his Limblini latte. "She what? This is not a date." He covered his mouth as he coughed.

"Good thinking, my dear. I don't know how you both ended up in the same place, but I don't like it. It's like someone planned it. We'll update each other via texts," Joseph said.

Someone like God planned it. I knew it. Selene nodded. "We don't know anything. Just gotta have faith."

"Thanks, Selene. Now if Mr. Military can help out by asking around for any government involvement," Joseph said.

Corey coughed. "Yeah, I'll ask our dream science, civilian interrogation division."

Selene's eyes widened. "You guys have a dream —"

Corey waved his hand and shook his head toward Selene. "I'll keep an eye out for suspicious individuals. Let me know if you find anything. Alright?"

"Great. I'll be in touch." Joseph ended the call.

Corey gulped the last drop of nectar from his latte cup. "Just in case he's right, you could always stay with me." The dark brown color faded from his cheeks. "That wasn't a ploy to get you to stay with me. This is NOT a date. I just wanted to apologize for last night's fiasco."

Selene snorted and laughed. *Is this what a brother is like? He's nice... but...*"I need to get back to my hotel. My mother is alone. If he's right then we'll need to stay in populated areas and not take the same daily routes to school or work." *That's what the freshman orientation said about staying safe.*

Corey exhaled and wiped the sweat from his forehead. "Sounds good."

Selene remained silent and focused until she dropped Corey off at the main gate of the naval base.

Corey turned to Selene. "Text *me*... I meant... text *us* if you feel like you're in trouble. I'm on duty, so I can check my messages this afternoon and into the night. I'll be available if you need to talk."

Selene nodded as Corey closed the door, and then drove to the hotel. Selene got out of her vehicle and scouted the parking lot. *It's mostly empty. A few new cars. There's one black van at the edge of the property, but...* She squinted her eyes. *No one is in it.* She scuttled into the hotel. The staff greeted her as she entered. *Same staff, I saw this morning.* Selene headed toward the elevator. A man in a green polo shirt and khaki pants sat in the hotel lobby. *He was there this morning when I left.* He hid his face behind a newspaper. *I don't think there's that much information in a newspaper.* His hands were rough. No rings. *Besides, who reads a newspaper nowadays?* As Selene approached the elevator he set the newspaper down and walked toward her. Her heart rate increased.

She dashed into the elevator as it opened and then pushed on the close button as fast as she could.

The man's hand reached between the door, but the elevator shut before he could reach inside.

I need to get Ama and head to a public place. The door opened and she looked back as she exited. The floor numbers on the other elevator counted up. Selene's breaths sharpened. She ran to her room and fiddled with the electronic key card before she launched into her room. She slammed the door behind her, cringed at the sound of the collision, and locked it. She rested her head against the white wooden door and exhaled.

Selene's heart rate slowed. "Sorry Ama, I didn't mean to make so much noise."

Selene turned around. "Ama?"

No one else was in the room.

Selene checked the bathroom. *She wasn't in the lobby.* "Mom?"

No one else was in the room.

Where is she? Selene's heart rate fluttered again. *Did she text me while I was out?* Selene reached in the handbag and pulled out her phone. She dropped it on the floor as her hands shook. She sat on her heels then picked it up. *No missed calls or messages.* Selene called her mother. *Come on, pick up, Ama.*

The docile tones of a catchy pop song came from the middle nightstand. Selene stood up and looked over. *Her phone is still on the charger.*

God. What plan do you have in store for mom? Selene paced back and forth between the door and the window at the far end of the room. *Or me?* She held her fingertips against her lips. *Mom could have walked around to get some air. She's been coughing more lately. Did she go to the hospital?* Selene shook her head. *No. I would have seen the ambulance and the staff would have said something. If Joseph's right then whoever is after us may have taken her, too.* She gritted her teeth and slammed her hand down from her lips. *I've got to find her.*

Selene opened the door and walked out. *Maybe I can sneak —*

On the far side of the hallway, silhouetted against a large window, stood the man in the green polo shirt and khaki pants. Turning to Selene, he slowly accelerated.

Oh crap, how did he know what floor I was on? Selene ran away from him, down the hall, past the elevator to the emergency exit, flung open the door, and hurried down the stairs. *I need to head somewhere safe.*

Selene burst through the exit door out into the unimpeded, relentless brightness outside. She looked behind her. No one descended the stairs. *Corey said he'd keep me safe.* Ensuring to remain vigilant, she ran up to her car. *No green polo, khaki panted, body snatcher. Good.* She took out her keys along with her phone and messaged Corey.

Selene

Corey this is Selene. I think someone is following me. Can I meet you on base?

Thursday 11:40 AM

A chilled breeze swept across the soft thin hairs of Selene's neck. She shivered. *I don't like this.* She poked her head up and scanned the edge of the property. *Where did that black van go?* She opened the car door and sent her final group text.

Selene

I've got to find my —

An overwhelming force covered her mouth and pulled her back. *No! I can't...* She struggled helplessly as if fighting against a raging current that would drag her out to sea, destined to drown beneath an ever-consuming maw of darkness. As Selene's phone hit the pitted asphalt below, the screen cracked and shattered.

An unmarked surveillance vehicle door slammed shut.

Squealing tires echoed across the North Texas sky while the dark-tinted van turned out of the hotel property.

A demolished cell phone lay next to an open driver's side door of a white 2001 Honda Civic in a mostly vacant hotel parking lot.

JOSEPH LIFTED HIS HEAD from atop of his folded arms. Opening his eyes, the end of a video from an obscure website played on his computer monitor. Printed papers and pictures were sprawled across his wooden desk. With his left sleeve, he wiped away the speckles of drool that sat on the side of his mouth. His throat was parched as he picked up his phone at the edge of the desk. *How long was I out?*

Thirty-four missed calls. A dozen missed messages. He caressed the stubble gray and brown hairs along his jawline as he stared out of his second-story window through the dusty white shades. Velma's bark echoed from downstairs. *Is it* that guy *again?*

Joseph grasped the baseball bat that he placed at the office doorway and darted toward the top of the stairs. Roxie, rambunctious and unyielding, antagonized Velma's tail by batting at it. The two dogs romped across the lower level as Joseph trotted down the stairs.

"Girls, you *almost* scared daddy." Joseph leaned his bat against the edge of the cream-colored trim of the door entrance.

Velma glanced up toward Joseph then Roxie jumped on Velma's head. Velma, being the larger of the two, shook her head to escape capture and continued to play. *If neither of you are worried then I won't worry.* Joseph trudged up the stairs of his condominium, returned to his office, and then sat in front of his home computer. *There's got to be something out there.* He scanned the still open internet tabs. *Decade-old message boards mentioned experiments and theories about lizard men belonging to untraceable government agencies.* He scoured through anonymously submitted photos of the afterlife, parallel universes, and demonic dimensions. Each photo or video appeared unfocused or blurred beyond the point of recognition. Joseph shook his head as the sky grew dark outside. With his left hand, he wiped his dry red-tinted eyes as he pushed away from the keyboard. Velma and Roxie were silent. *They must be tired from puppying all day.* He pulled his phone out and reviewed his messages.

Julia – Manager/Agent

What the fuck Joseph? Call me back. Where are you?

Thursday 8:30 AM

Julia – Manager/Agent

For real, I'm getting worried. Please call.

Thursday 9:07 AM

Oh, my dear Julia. I don't think you'd understand. Joseph stroked his chin. *Nothing from Corey... as expected. But...*

Selene

Corey this is Selene. I think someone is following me. Can I meet you on base?

Thursday 9:40 AM

Joseph's eyes widened. *I warned those kids to be careful.*

Selene

I've got to find my

Thursday 9:41 AM

Joseph thumbed through his phone to figure out why he didn't receive the remaining message from Selene's text.

Joseph

Selene, can you send me that last text? I didn't get it all. Corey, are you still holed up on base?

Thursday 4:09 PM

The doorbell rang.

Velma and Roxie barked.

Joseph placed his phone in his back pocket and headed downstairs. Two figures were silhouetted through the front door window. *Oh shit.* While they stood outside in the rain, Joseph descended the stairs and reached for the baseball bat he placed by the door earlier. Peeking through the side window slot on the left side of the door, two men in black uniforms and several black cars were parked along the street curb. *I knew it. It's the fucking government.*

The doorbell rang again.

That's it. Joseph opened the door.

Both of the men flashed their identification badges to Joseph. "Mr. Godwin. We're with the FBI. May we have a word with you?"

Joseph leaned against the inside of his door. His left hand held the baseball bat behind his back out of their field of view. "What is this about?"

"May we come inside, please?" One of the men asked.

Joseph shook his head. "No, you may not. I know my rights. I don't have to invite you inside my property and you can't come inside without a warrant."

The two men looked at each other then stood there as the cold Seattle rain pelted their raincoats. "We think you may be in trouble. We can keep you safe."

"Safe from what exactly? Harassment? First, you guys creep me out at the noodle place, then you slide me notes like a fucking sixth-grader, now you're attempting to abduct me without my permission."

They glance at each other again then look at Joseph. "Listen, we don't know what you're referring to. This is our first attempt at contact with you. Mr. Godwin, a former associate that you worked with on your last project is being convicted of funding illegal shipments of sex workers into the United States."

Joseph chuckled. *What the fuck are they talking about?*

One of the men leaned in. "The men behind the trafficking are afraid of being identified. Even if you weren't involved directly we wanted to take the precaution of having a few of our agents positioned around your condo until the culprits are found."

Joseph shook his head. "Talk about a lame excuse guys. So you don't want to take me in with you?"

The shorter man on the left tilted his head. "Not unless you feel unsafe, sir."

Joseph smirked. *So that's what I've been sensing.* "No thanks. You can tell your minions to get as far away from me as possible."

They nodded. "Very well sir, but don't say we didn't warn you."

Joseph stood there until every last agent left the premises. He shook his head. *Fucking faceless drones.* As the door closed, he locked it behind him. From the side window, their taillights disappeared against the misty Seattle rain and fog.

"It's alright girls, they won't be bothering us anymore." He turned around.

Velma and Roxie weren't downstairs. *Where did you both run off to?* Joseph looked around the corner into the living area then walked into the kitchen by their food and water bowls. "Velma baby. Roxie honey. Come here, girls. I know you're tired but you're scaring daddy."

Joseph whistled.

Thunderstruck and the lights went off.

A whistle echoed from behind Joseph. The hairs on the back of Joseph's neck stood on end. He jolted his head around.

Nothing.

Quiet darkness.

From the second story, the dangling aluminum ID tags from Roxie and Velma's collars clanked and clanked. *Is someone up there?* Joseph tip-toed upstairs and held the baseball bat at the ready. Several paws scratched against the wood at the bottom of his closed office door. *How did you girls get stuck up here?* He reached for the doorknob. *I don't re-member closing —*

A dark gloved hand reached from behind Joseph's tall frame covered his mouth with a pungently scented cloth. *Who the fuck?!* He was pulled backward.

The dogs frantically scratched at the wooden door.

Joseph whipped the bat over his shoulder as he tried to regain his balance.

He inhaled. *Shit!*

Velma's whine came through the small gap below his office door. Joseph's eyes grew heavy. His grip loosened. The baseball bat smacked the hardwood floors. *Who is...* As his limbs gave way, Joseph reached out for the doorknob and mumbled, "Don't you... fucking touch... my... girls..."

COREY TOOK AN ANTI-anxiety pill before he dawned the uniform of the day. *I'll have anxiety from boredom before anything else on duty.* He put his phone on silent and slid it in his pocket then marched down the barracks steps en route to his assigned duty station aboard the heavily guarded naval base. *Twenty-four hours on watch is mind-numbingly boring.*

Charles approached him on the sidewalk toward the duty hut. "Hey, I came by your room earlier to see if you wanted to grab chow. Where did you go?"

If I tell him about all this dream stuff he'll laugh and it turns out to be not a big deal like I expect it is. Charles will never let me hear the end of it. Corey hesitated. "I went on a date." *That's more believable.*

"You? No fucking way." Charles slapped Corey on the shoulder. *Ouch, so violent.* "Don't tell me it's that little Hispanic girl? Senior told me that she gave you her number. She returned to the theater just to look for you."

Corey nodded. *Good, he bought it.* "Yeah. Her name is Selene, we just had coffee. I've got duty today so I'll prolly tell you about it later."

"Alright, my man." Charles gave Corey a high-five. *I need to sit him down and explain that having a date isn't that big of a deal.* "I'll be doing laundry most of the day, then maybe go out and check out the mall downtown."

"Sounds good man." Corey nodded as he looked down at his black watch. *Shit.* "Alright brother, I'm gonna be late."

Corey darted to the duty hut at the entrance of the barracks and relived the off-going duty. He made his rounds walking the parameter of the barracks to check for unusual activity. Two Marines held another smaller Marine over the edge of the second story of the barracks as forty-five decibels of thrasher metal music blared out of their open door.

God damned Marines. "Hey, hey. Knock it off!" Corey jogged toward the commotion.

The Marines looked over and pulled their fellow knucklehead up as Corey approached.

"Come on guys, it's going to be a long day if you're out here doing stupid shit like that." Corey sighed.

"We got ya, Petty Officer." They walked inside their barracks room and closed the door.

"And turn the music down!" Corey shook his head as he continued to rove around the building. *I had to get duty at the mixed service barracks. By comparison, mentoring Charles is painless.*

For four more hours, Corey walked around the barracks without another incident, then he relieved the duty inside who stood phone watch. *Finally, air conditioner and a cushioned seat.* He looked up at the large tan government-issued clock mounted above the aluminum and wood duty desk. *It's 1630... 1631. Each minute feels like an eternity.*

Various phone calls came into the duty hut as the evening trudged on. He recorded all the reports from the rovers just as his fellow shipmate did when *he* roved. *Oh, yeah.* Corey pulled out his phone, took it off of silent, and read several messages he received throughout the day. *My foster parents want to know if I'll be back home for Thanksgiving.* He stared at his reflection against the mirrored screen. *Home... has it ever been?* He continued onto the messages in the group chat Selene set up.

<u>Selene</u>

Corey this is Selene. I think someone is following me. Can I meet you on base?

<u>Thursday 1140</u>

<u>Selene</u>

I've got to find my

Thursday 1141
Joseph

Selene, can you send me that last text? I didn't get it all. Corey, are you still holed up on base?

Thursday 1809

Selene never responded to Joseph. Shit. Corey called Selene's number... *it went straight to voice mail.*

Corey called Joseph's cell phone number... *it went straight to voice mail too.*

Corey messaged the group.

Corey

Corey here. Still, on base, please check in. Selene? Joseph?

Thursday 2030

The duty phone rang. *Is it them?*

Corey picked it up. "Barracks 323. Petty Officer Parker speaking. How may I help you, sir or ma'am?"

"Hey man. It's Charles. I'm out here at the Linden Inc. Steak House near loop 340. Can you pick me up?"

Corey shook his head. *I guess not. How would they know this phone number anyway?* He tapped his black pen against his notebook on the duty desk. "Dude, what the fuck are you doing out there this late?"

"Look, I just *need* you to come to pick me up," Charles pleaded.

Charles sounds... off. Ticking seconds from the clock taunted Corey's mind. "I've got thirty minutes left until I have to rove again and it's getting late. You know I can't just use the duty van for shit like that."

The phone went silent.

"Some chick stood me up, alright. Just hurry up and come pick me up, this place is about to close," Charles said.

I thought he'd never admit to something like that. Corey sighed. "Fine. Alright. I got you. I'll leave right now so I'll have time to sign the keys back in. But you owe me, homie."

The line went silent again.

"Hurry and... I'm sorry." Charles hung up.

As Corey put the duty phone back on the receiver, he hesitated. *Maybe Charles was heartbroken for the first time and just too embarrassed to admit it.* He walked out of the barracks, got in the duty van, and drove off base toward the restaurant. *First Selene and Joseph, now Charles. Good thing I took my anti-anxiety pill today.* He stopped at a red light halfway to his destination. Heavy drops of rain pelted the front windshield of the white duty van. *Shit, this is the last thing I need. I didn't bring a poncho or anything to protect my skin.* It took most of his concentration to see the street signs and road markers as he squinted to enhance his field of vision. Corey used the fastest windshield wiper setting he could. *I need to find out what happened to Selene and Joseph.* He checked his phone for notifications and none were recent.

Shit! Corey swerved to avoid a poorly parked car. *Oh, crap.* He regained his bearing as he continued down the desolate highway. *I shouldn't be out in this weather.* He arrived at the Linden Inc. Steak House parking lot. The chattering of patrons of this popular restaurant was replaced by the sound of the rain. Large droplets smacked the top of the lamp posts that lined the now-vacant parking lot. He surveyed the area for his taller shipmate. *The inside lights are off.* Only the outdoor spotlights at each corner of the restaurant beamed down on their respective area. Radiant beams of light from the parking lot lampposts couldn't penetrate the dense volume of rain. *Where is he?* Corey swiveled his head as he attempted to peer beyond the watered veil. *If he stands out here for too long without an umbrella or raincoat he'll get blotches on his skin. Maybe that's why he seemed off when he called?*

Corey pulled out his phone in an attempt to speed dial his friend. *He better answer.*

A looming dark figure huddled underneath a jacket, knocked on the passenger's side door. *Shit.* Corey looked up and unlocked the doors.

Corey looked on as the door opened. "Damn it, Charles, you scared the shit out of —"

Abruptly, the driver's side door flung open. Corey froze. *Who just opened the door beside me?* Someone reached in, unlocked his seatbelt, and pulled him out.

Corey struggled against the stronger assailant. "Get the fuck off me —"

"Come with us Mr. Parker, please don't make this difficult."

How the fuck do they know my name? A man's large hand covered Corey's mouth with a wet cloth rag. The frigid water droplets splashed off of his face as he continued to struggle. Corey tried to scream but the firm pressure of the cloth against his mouth was inescapable. It muffled any sound he could muster.

He breathed in. *What is...?*

His legs became heavy.

His arms waivered. *Why me...?*

Corey found it harder and harder to resist his captors. The blink of his eyes transgressed the passage of time. His heart thumped louder as each singular moment expired. A car's door latch clacked through the damp night air. *I can't... make out what they're saying.*

He faded in and out of consciousness.

"Let's go... got what... came for."

IN MEDIAS RES

Seven Years ago.

I glared at the other thirteen hand-selected students in the auditorium. Each of them frantically wrote in their notebooks doing their best to catch up to the professor's lecture. I tapped my pencil against the notebook on my lap. *Nothing new... of course.*

The professor of Advanced Applied Physics scratched chalk on a blackboard to expand on the quantum states of entangled nuclei separated by a particle accelerator in near absolute zero degree environments.

So tedious. The clacking of chalk hitting the blackboard and the noise from my pencil fused to enrapture my mind in a melodic lullaby. *So tired.* I wiped my eyes to break the spell of boredom, which this lecture cast upon me.

A foreign girl with glasses and freckles leaned in from my right. "Another rough night studying?"

Studying? This? I read these findings and the associated two-hundred-page peer-reviewed conclusion two years ago. "Yeah. I just can't catch up on sleep with all these classes." I adjusted my posture.

She placed her hand on my shoulder and squeezed it, sensually. "If you need someone to help tutor you, I can make myself available. Just let me know." She winked.

I don't have time to make acquaintances. I nodded. "Thank you. I'll let you know if I need the help." *From someone who knows far less than me.*

She sat back as I continued to tap the pencil against the notebook. Yawning, the professor's monotone voice dulled the lecture and dazed my mind.

My eyes grew heavy as my head dipped.

I blinked. *Stay awake.*

As time marched forward, the darkness between my blinks lasted longer. *No... I can't...*

My eyes shut.

As the backdrop of my consciousness enveloped my dreams, a dark being emerged from the gray haze that filled the background of my mind. "Get me out...you must... find a way."

I pleaded into the void, "I'm trying. I need to get more information. I've researched every physics, metaphysical, astral, and biological subject at this college."

"You must... transfer... my body..." Slithering echoes of the entity drew closer.

I retracted. "What more can I do?" *I don't even know what I'm looking for.*

"Save me... you must find a way... I am... you're my only..." The source of the being changed direction.

It was much closer. *It's never been this close.*

I swung my arms back and screamed in all directions. "No, go away! Leave me alone!"

An ominous dark figure reached out from the void with a writhing tendril and wrapped it around my neck. *What the...?* It revealed the resemblance of a face. Its skin was infinite darkness with speckled celestial bodies as eyes. Within the celestial bodies, stars systems went supernova, collided with each other, and their red luminance portrayed anger and hatred.

I can't breathe. The figure's flailing mass tightened its grip on my throat. "I will *never* leave until you bring me back."

It seared its gaze onto my soul.

After a whimper and wheeze, my matte, gray, internal world shook and then crumbled away. Its vice-like grip released as it slithered off and receded into the darkness of the void.

My eyes opened to a blurred classroom existence.

"Hey, hey." The foreign girl shook my shoulder. "You better stay awake. Professor Higginbotham's final exam is one of the hardest in the whole advanced curriculum, or so I've heard."

I can't stay here and absorb this professor's prehistoric theories. I coughed and caressed my throat. *His consciousness has become more violent.* It was difficult to swallow. I got up from my seat and walked down the steps toward the exit.

The professor tilted his head. "Excuse me, sir. Please return to your seat."

I sighed then strolled toward the professor's chalkboard and erased the theoretical arithmetic equations.

"What do you think you're doing, young man?" he asked.

"You're all blind. You're not looking beyond this realm," I transcribed the answer to the proposed theoretical equations that I solved in my spare time. Knowledge from various studies and papers I learned by way of other advanced physics experts from around the world poured forth on the blackboard.

As the professor stood slack-jawed, he gasped at the simplified and practical answer that was written across the surface of the chalkboard.

"Please email me your final exam professor and I'll reply in my free time with the answers." I looked up at the promiscuously-dressed, blond, foreign student. "He might need you to tutor *him*, however, *I'll* have to pass, my dear."

Walking out of the auditorium, I tugged at my throat again. *Patience.*

I swallowed some saliva. *Have some patience. I'll find a way to get you back... and be rid of you forever... Father.*

CHAPTER TWELVE

THE PAST THAT CONTROLS THE FUTURE

Present-day.

The overhead halogen light made it hard for Joseph to open his eyes. He lifted his hand and covered his vision as he gathered his composure. *Ugh. Is it that light again?* He closed his eyes and massaged the temples of his head as he rolled out of a cushioned couch. He looked in front of him and saw a vending machine next to a brightly lit sconce. To his left and right, the gray brick walls were vacant and foreign. Joseph wiped his eyes as he sat upright to regain his senses. *Where am I?*

A girl's voice echoed behind him. "He's up, finally."

Joseph turned around. *You two!*

Selene and Corey rushed over to his side.

Wincing, Joseph wiped his eyes with his left hand. "Selene. Corey. What are you doing here? Where are we?"

Corey scratched his head. "This looks like some underground facility. The last thing I remember was being abducted... I think they were former military."

Great. Joseph sighed. *The last thing I need. More nameless faces.*

Selene sat next to Joseph with her legs crossed. "When I dropped Corey off I went back to my hotel and my mom was gone." She leaned toward him. "I saw a suspicious-looking man with a green polo shirt and khaki pants. So I used the side stairs to go outside the hotel. I tried to text but a black van pulled up and that's all I remember."

Corey looked toward Selene. "Yeah. I got your text."

Joseph stood up and massaged his temples. "Some feds came to my condo, but I shushed them away. The last thing I remember hearing was the sound of my dogs' whimper. I tried to fight... but I passed out." *It's still a haze.* "We'll just call for help. I have my phone right —"

He reached for his phone but found only empty pockets.

"No good, huh? My wallet, phone, and watch were gone when I woke up. It was a little while before you two," Corey said.

Fucking bastards. "Wait, you're in the military. Do you have anything to do with this?" Joseph loomed over Corey.

Corey stood up and walked around the couch to meet Joseph's gaze. "Look, sir, I don't know what kind of world you're living in, but the military doesn't just abduct civilians for no reason... much less one of their own."

They could have just ordered him to sit in with us. Joseph scoffed at Corey as he walked away. "Another cog in the machine."

Selene rose her fingertips to her lips. "This can't be a coincidence, right? It's gotta be about the dreams."

"How?" Corey asked. "I didn't tell anyone. I didn't even believe it when *you* told me."

Everyone wants dirt on me. Joseph crossed his arms. "Someone must have hacked into my computer. It would have tipped them off with all the research." *I should have known.*

Joseph looked down at Selene. *Poor girl. She's mumbling to herself.* "How are you holding up?"

Selene looked down at the floor, paused, then looked up at Joseph. "Oh, hmmm. I'm worried about my mom. I wonder if she's in a different room."

Corey leaned his hand against the neon-lit vending machine on the far wall of the room. "How do they expect us to get an Aspen soda without our wallets?"

Does he understand how fucked we are? Joseph paced around. "You seem to be taking this pretty lightly, kid. If you plan to convince me that these guys are gonna just let us walk out of here, I'd advise against it."

Corey looked back at Joseph. "Why? Have you tried to open the door?"

Joseph smirked then shook his head. *That's a dumb suggestion.*

Selene jumped up, turned around, and squatted in the seat. *What is she doing?*

Joseph placed his hands on his hips. "Don't be stupid. Why would they kidnap us, stick us in a windowless gray room, and leave the door unlocked?"

Corey stared intently at the door in the back corner of the room. Joseph uncrossed his arms and raced over to the door as Corey followed closely behind.

Joseph turned the knob but it would not turn. *I knew it.* "Damn. I'd hoped you were right, kid."

As Corey walked away, the door was flung open.

A tall man in an unmarked black uniform stood by the open door. Shortly thereafter, two armed men dashed into the room and surrounded them. "Good. You're all awake. Please, follow me to interrogation room five down the hall," the older man who stood by their only exit said.

So they are *from the government.* "You can't hold me in here without letting me call my lawyer. I know my rights," Joseph said.

Corey rose both of his hands above his head and backed away from the guards. "I want to speak to your commanding officer. We didn't do anything wrong."

Selene stood up on the couch. "Where's my mom?"

The man stood by the open door and looked at Selene. "Look, I get it. You're all scared. You're not in trouble. Special Agent Tucker is going to meet you in another room, sit down with you, and ask you a few questions. Then, you can be on your merry way."

Joseph crossed his arms. *Yeah, right.*

"Did you guys abduct her mom too?" Corey asked.

The man motioned toward Selene. "I have no clue what you're talking about, ma'am. Our instructions were to pick you up and bring you back here for questioning. That is all."

"And exactly, where is *here*? You bastards took my property without my permission. I know that's against the law," Joseph said.

He let out a sigh, clasped his hands as the wrinkles on his face tightened. "If you could please just follow me, answer the agents' questions, and we'll give your stuff back to you. Simple."

Joseph held his arms out. "Why should I trust you?"

Corey turned to Joseph and leaned in. "I don't think we have a choice."

Joseph clenched his fist. *There's always a choice.*

"What do you think, Selene?" Joseph turned back toward the couch.

Selene's gaze fixated on the man by the opened door. She jumped down from the couch, walked up to him slowly, and stood silently in front of him.

The armed guards raised their weapons and trained them on Selene. "Stand down!"

Joseph staggered back. *Shit, shit. What is she going to do?*

"Hey, now. We should all calm down." Corey extended his arms above his head.

I don't think she can read a room. "Selene, what are you doing?" Joseph asked.

Standing inches in front, Selene narrowed her eyes as she glared at the taller man's face. She stood; unwavering.

Joseph's eyes widened. *Whoa, this girl's got some balls.*

The tall, older man by the door stared right back at the bold teenaged girl.

Selene's face relaxed.

She turned her head and walked into the hallway.

Lowering their weapons, the guards backed off.

Corey exhaled as he looked at Joseph. "I don't think she understands how bat-shit crazy that situation could have been."

I'll be damned if I get shown up by a little girl. Joseph followed as the guards escorted them out of the room. Dimly lit, exposed electrical conduit ran overhead throughout the hallway. Several rooms with cloudy door windows lined the corridor. On the left side at the end of the passageway light extended down from an open door. He walked into the room with a table and four chairs. Three yellow chairs on one side and a black metal folding chair on the other.

Corey walked in past Selene toward the farthest chair. "I guess I'll sit here."

Selene sat in the middle.

Joseph stood for a minute and surveyed the room. *This is no way to treat someone like me.* Then sat down.

Corey glanced down at a metal bar that went across the bottom of their feet. Two guards came into the room with loose shackles in their hands. They knelt and cuffed their ankles to the bar below their feet.

What the fuck? Joseph stood up. "Hey, what is this? I thought we weren't under arrest!"

The tall man leaned in from the hallway. "This is just a precaution. We wouldn't want you to have an outburst and harm our agent, would we?"

One of the guards approached Joseph. "Sit down, sir."

Joseph stood there in defiance. *These assholes are going to hear from my lawyer.*

Another guard walked up to Joseph and moved his hand to the black pistol on his waist. "Please."

I guess we don't have a choice after all. Joseph sat down and crossed his arms.

Corey raised his hands by his head and offered no resistance. One guard attempted to cuff Selene's ankles. She jolted her legs toward her chest and wrapped her arms around her knees.

Joseph glared at the man by the door. "Come on. If a little girl can hurt your agent then they need to get better training."

As the guard looked up to the man at the door, the taller gray-haired man nodded then motioned his men to exit the room.

Joseph smirked. *About time they listened to me.*

Selene stuck her head between her knees. "Thanks."

Joseph leaned toward Selene but said it loud enough so everyone could hear. "No problem. Someone needs to show these assholes some manners."

Gritting his teeth, the man by the doorway said, "Special Agent Tucker will be with you shortly. Don't go anywhere." He closed the interrogation room door and locked it.

After a brief moment of silence, Selene sat back in her chair and stared off.

She's got to be scared. Joseph looked over to Corey. *Either way, I need to find out what's going on.* "Hey. Mr. Military. Do you recognize their uniforms? Who are these guys?"

Corey extended his feet until the shackles were taut. "I've never seen those uniforms before... and my name is Corey, not Mr. Military."

Whatever, kid. Joseph ducked his head far enough back to view underneath the table where they sat.

Tapping from the other side of the interrogation room door grew louder and faster as someone approached. The door slowly opened and in walked a dark-haired olive-skinned woman dressed in black. She had a slender and upright physique. *She must be in charge of these assholes.* She walked around on the opposite side of the table where they sat. Underneath her right arm was a folder full of documents. The edge of a few pictures extended beyond the folder's border. She had an identification tag on the left side of her black blouse with big letters on it that spelled out C.P.A.

"The C.P.A.? What are we in here for? Tax evasion." Joseph grinned.

The black-haired woman leaned in and stared directly into Joseph's eyes. *Her gaze reminds me of a certain manager slash agent.* "I assure you, Mr. Godwin, that the Center for Paranormal Activity doesn't give a shit about your taxes."

Joseph sneered. *Finally, someone who knows who I am.*

"You've been brought here to discuss a very important matter. It is not out of the realm of possibilities to say that your lives are at risk," she said.

Sitting upright, the agent glanced at the others. "But it's more than just *your* life. Think about your mother's life, Miss Selene Alicia Garcia. Think about *your* career, Petty Officer Parker, that is, if you still have one after this."

Corey sunk in his chair as he placed his fingers to the sides of his temples.

Joseph inhaled, exhaled slowly, and leaned forward. "So you know our names and our personal lives. What do you want from us? If our lives are at risk then explain why you brought us here? Where is *here* anyway? And —"

"My name is Special Agent Tucker. All of your questions will be answered, but first, let me tell you about our agency and why we had to bring you here in such a manner. Deal?" she asked.

Tilting his head, Joseph crossed his arms. *Do I even have a choice?* "I'm listening."

Agent Tucker placed her elbows on the table and she clasped her hands together. "As you may have gathered from the name, we deal with paranormal activity in this version of Earth."

Perspiration glistened off of Corey's forehead. "What do you mean by 'this version of Earth', ma'am?"

Agent Tucker leaned in. "Yes, this version. What you all experienced recently was a rare phenomenon known as a *quantum entangled dream-sharing event.*"

Joseph laughed, "Okay, that's funny. You can let us out now. This is ridiculous." He tugged at his wrist restraints but they would not give way. *I knew it. We need to leave.*

Agent Tucker's face offered no expression. Undaunted. Stoic. "Are you done?"

She's serious. Joseph sank into his seat. "Fine... continue."

"You see, normally most of our dreams are related to daytime events our subconscious experiences. We think about some stressful or exciting event from that day and, subconsciously, our dreams manifest that feeling and imagery. Occasionally, we dream about ourselves in different environments where we might look or feel like a different person altogether."

Selene raised her hand.

Joseph looked over. *Does she think this is a classroom?*

Selene lowered her arm back down to her waist. "Oh, like how we all dreamed about each other but we were different versions of ourselves?"

Agent Tucker narrowed her eyes and smiled. "How perceptive of you Miss Garcia." She refocused her gaze on Joseph. "Yes. What you three experienced is an even rarer phenomenon in which you all dream-shared the same alternate reality."

Joseph's eye widened. *This goes beyond what I read about.*

"How is that possible?" Corey asked.

Agent Tucker held out her hand. "Well... every night, millions of people across the globe do this regularly. We peer into alternate realities all the time."

Joseph looked at Corey and shook his head. *I call bullshit.*

Selene looked down at the fingertips on her lips.

Agent Tucker sighed. "I can tell by your expressions that you don't believe me. I will try to explain it the best way I can. You see, our brains operate at a certain frequency. This whole universe operates on a resonant frequency. However, when we sleep, our brains can subconsciously adjust our brain's resting resonant frequency. This allows our conscience to peer into alternate realities."

Joseph tilted his head. *How the hell?*

Agent Tucker continued. "For example, if I brought a radio in this room and tuned it to 99.5 FM you would only be able to listen to country music, but if I tuned it to 103.3 FM then you would only be able to hear classical music. Even though all the frequencies are in this room, invisible, bouncing around everywhere, the radio can only tune into one frequency at a time. Our brains perform the same function. We are the radio, *tuned* into this universe with every cell of our being. Rarely, though, our brains can change the resonant frequency that our conscience attunes to. This allows our subconscious to *receive*, much like a radio, on a slightly different frequency."

Holy shit. "That. That makes sense," Joseph said.

Receiving a file Agent Tucker slid to him, Joseph opened the folder. Several research documents and pictures spilled out in front of them. *Is she going to let us look at all of this?*

She sat back in her chair as they poured through the file. "In 1968 through 1973 the U.S. Government performed different experiments with willing participants and the effects of LSD and other hallucinogens on the brain. A brilliant scientist named Dr. Authur Bonovich continued that research. He detailed a discovery that came out of an experiment in this report. Dr. Bonovich hypothesized that people could enter an alternate reality via shared dreaming and their subconscious could cross the boundaries of this reality to another universe altogether. So convinced of his theory, he included himself among the willing participants. As you can see from the pictures and records, he was never able to conclude his research."

Names redacted. Locations redacted. "All the results of his experiments have been blacked out, of course. I can't make out a damn thing," Joseph said.

Agent Tucker stood up and paced about. "That's because details of these experiments are classified above top secret. What I know is that something happened during the experiment. Something... which left Dr. Bonovich in a comatose state. His body went to his next of kin. That's all I can tell you."

Joseph threw his arms up but was caught by the wrist restraints. *Fucking chains.* "Are you saying that we're somehow doing this on purpose? Special Agent, let me tell you, if you try to arrest us for perpetrating this 'dream-share' event, I'd advise against it."

"No, Mr. Godwin, our objective at the CPA is to keep this phenomenon from happening again," Agent Tucker said.

"If you're part of some secret government agency trying to help us then why did you snatch us up like some would-be assassins? Why did you stalk me at the noodle house? And —"

"Not sure about the noodle house, but my associates tried to warn you, Mr. Godwin. Unfortunately, another interested party knew of your existence. Some other entity was observing you. We had to take drastic measures before another *quantum entangled dream-sharing event* occurred. I hope you understand."

Joseph put his elbows on the table and rested his chin on his clasped hands. "And how are you going to do that exactly... by killing us?"

The room fell silent.

Joseph focused his attention on the agents' lips.

Agent Tucker gathered the documents and pictures, then pulled the file back toward her slowly. "Of course, we'll —"

A loud alarm rang out inside, as red flashing lights lit the hallway outside the blurred window of the interrogation room door.

Agent Tucker's eyes widened. "Wait right here." She held out her open hand. "I need to see what that's all about."

None of this is sitting right with me. Once the agent left the room, Joseph attempted to remove his ankle restraints. *Paranormal experiments by the government. They'll imprison us for the rest of our lives at best.* He looked over toward Corey and Selene. "Whatever is going on in this facility we need to get away from here. Now!"

CHAPTER THIRTEEN

THE AGENCY OF DUTY

L eaving the room, I lock the door behind me and look back at the two guards stationed by the door. "No one enters or exits that room except for me. Copy that?"

"Yes ma'am, Special Agent Tucker," one of the guard's replies.

I rush down the hallway and around the corner to the situation room. *I hope this is a false alarm.* "What's the status?"

The head security supervisor tilts his head back. "An external parameter alarm tripped, ma'am, however, I don't see an intruder or animal that may have caused the issue and the security guard roving topside is unreachable via radio."

This isn't normal. I scan the video monitors. *Nothing looks out of the ordinary, but the timing of this intrusion isn't a mere coincidence.* Continuing to look at the monitors, the southern gate camera goes dark. The camera at the eastern auxiliary shed displays white static. *Some entity knows of this facility and is here for these civilians, I'm sure of it.*

I tap the security supervisor on his shoulder. "I'll evacuate the civilians and get them to another facility. Alert all security personnel to prepare for a breach."

"Yes ma'am, roger that." The security supervisor radios the other security personnel in the facility.

I run back into the room and open the door. *I need to keep these civilians safe.* "It looks like someone is here for you." I kneel to unlock Joseph's ankle restraints.

"Who's here?" Joseph chimed in.

Selene assists Corey with his restraints. "Why us?"

I need to put their minds at ease so they trust me. "I don't know, but you have to follow me so I can take you to someplace safe."

"Hold up, why should we trust you, ma'am?" Corey asks.

I unlock their last restraints. "Look, we don't have time for twenty questions."

Joseph places his hand on my shoulder. "At least tell us what's going to happen to us if we go with you or —"

A distant gunshot echoes through the passageway outside of the interrogation room. *Shit, they're already inside.* "Go check that out!"

"Yes ma'am," both of the guards yell as they rush off.

"Look, you'll have to trust that the U.S. government wants to keep you safe." Their collective glares reveal an obvious distrust for the government. *They won't budge unless I give them some reason to trust me.*

"You three sharing an alternate dream reality isn't just rare, it's dangerous. If more people dream share into an alternate reality, then it's possible to create a tear between our realities or worse."

I stood. *We've gotta hurry.*

"What do you mean worse?" Joseph asks.

"Two frequencies can't exist in the same space without adverse effects. There are examples of this happening all over the world. Like the Bermuda triangle, places where people and large objects suddenly disappear. Anytime you hear stories of mysterious figures appearing and disappearing in homes. People have memories from lives they never lived. All these events and places are examples of when our universe bleeds into an alternate one. I know it's a lot to take in, but we don't have much time. Now that you know all this, will you please come with me?" I hold the door open. *Make. A. Decision.*

"I believe her. We should go." Selene walks forward. *Finally.*

"Not this time, Selene. Please, let me." Corey inserts himself in front of Selene.

I funnel the civilians behind me as I exit the room. *That's assuring.*

To the left, down the hallway from the direction of the control room, gunshots and flashes of light illuminate the hallway. *Shit.* Flushing the civilians around, I back away from the source of the commotion. *They're relying on me to get them out of here.* I hesitate. *I can't provide backup for my men. Remember your sworn duty, Angela.* I use my hand to signal to the three civilians to head right, against the nearest wall down the dimly lit corridor. Hypnotic sirens blare out as red lights above my head continue to strobe. *I may need to return fire.* I draw my Glock 9mm and keep my finger off the trigger. Directing the civilians further through the corridor, I move toward the garage. *I've kept my gun proficiency up at the local gun range, but I've never shot someone. If we can get to the garage, we can escape and head to another safe house.* Following the darkened path, we make our way toward a fully lit underground parking structure. I keep looking back and motion for the civilians to continue moving.

Stifled silence drowns out the humming of the sirens. *Are the guards coming?*

High-pitched gunshots pierce through the blare of the sirens and the pounding of my heartbeat; calamitous and nerving.

"Move quickly, keep your head down, and don't make any loud noises," I say to them asserting the need for caution.

Shit. I can't drive and engage my weapon at the same time. We make our way to the garage area and dash toward the nearest black armored vehicle. *I need to hand my weapon to one of them. How about Joseph? No... He'll ditch us at the first opportunity. Selene seems just as scared as anyone would be in this situation.* I survey the underground garage for potential hostiles. "Get in the back and keep your head down. I'll drive." *Corey has to be it, he's had training in the military and should be used to stressful environments.*

I put my weapon on safe and look over to Corey. "You sit in the front with me. Selene and Joseph, please get in the back with your heads down low."

As we get in the black, armored SUV, one of the heavy doors shut. A loud thud echoes throughout the garage. *Shit!* I get the keys from the center console.

"Corey, you've been trained in using a firearm, right? I need you to watch the entrance and shoot if you see anyone that doesn't look like me or the guards, got that?"

I hand him the firearm. *It's life or death.*

"You can count on me. I'll let you know if I see anyone, ma'am." Corey holds the weapon out of the passenger side window and aims it toward the corridor we came from.

I smiled. *Thank god he seems... reliable.* Heavy footsteps close in on us from the passageway.

Corey turns to me. "Ma'am, people with narrow lights are by the garage entrance. Is that a good or a bad thing? I can't tell."

"Call me Agent Tucker, and we don't carry high-beam lights on our personnel so that's bad. We need to leave now." I turn the key. *Fuck seat belts.* Then stomp on the gas pedal.

Joseph and Selene duck in the backseat as we make our way out of the garage. In the rearview mirror, two tall muscular males in full tactical gear armed with automatic weapons stood at the ready.

"Get down!" I brace them for the gunshots coming from the rear of the SUV, but the armed men do not fire. They simply stand and reach for their radios as we drive off. *They must be professionals; knowing that the bullets fired at that range will not penetrate the exterior hull of this vehicle.* We exit the garage and pull out onto a dirt road that leads off the base. *No guards, no lights.* I scan the surrounding compound grounds as we leave toward a grass clearing. *Nothing about this seems right.*

"Hold on. We need to get you all to safety first, then we can figure out what to do next." Looking into my rear-view mirror I hold my breath... *No one is following us. ...* then exhale.

"Who are they? What do they want from us? How did they know we were here?" Joseph asks.

Man, he needs to ease up on the questions. I keep my eyes jumping from mirror to mirror. "I don't know, Mr. Godwin."

Selene cowers in the corner of the backseat and covers her ears.

I've got to calm them down. "Okay, look, remember when I said the fact that all three of you dreaming of the same reality wasn't just rare that it was also dangerous?" I glance ahead at the nothingness before me. *No one's following us. Good.* My heart rate steadies. *Their immediate need for answers would just create more questions. However, I need them to understand the gravity of the situation.*

I turn my head but continue to look forward keeping my eyes on the road. "Just think, if all three of you could theoretically view into another reality, anyone could use that as a window to learn things not meant for this universe. On top of that, others in said reality could use that same window to peer and learn things that may destabilize this existing universe. The U.S. government can't let the public discover this, but apparently, someone wants to use this opportunity to —"

A blinding light penetrates the vehicle's windshield. *Shit, I've gotta slow down.* Slamming my foot against the brakes, the vehicle comes to a stop. A loud thumping emanates from above the SUV. *It's a helicopter. How the hell? They must have flown at high altitudes to mask the noise and then descended when the timing was right. Damn it, being in an armored vehicle offers us protection but also insulates us from the sound.*

Screeching from a loudspeaker broke the hum of the propeller in the otherwise silent and still night. "Agent Tucker, please release your hostages. We cannot allow the U.S. government to have access to these individuals. We would like to resolve this peacefully; however, we are prepared to use force if necessary," A calming, yet assertive and masculine voice says.

They know who I am and they know why these civilians are with me. It doesn't look like I have a choice, but... if I see a safe opportunity to escape, I'll have to take it. "Corey, hand me the gun." I reach out and take my gun from him.

A tap on the driver-side window on my right startles me. *It is a tall man in full tactical gear like the man I saw in the parking garage.* An AA-12 Atchison Assault Shotgun taps the window again. *Those have been illegal since congress deemed them inhumane for military use. They must have gotten behind my field of vision during my temporary blindness. Damn.* I put my hands up and place the firearm on the dash to show my compliance. *I can't risk their safety.*

Glancing in the rear-view mirror at Joseph and Selene, I turn sideways toward Corey. "Hey, these people don't seem to want you all dead. Or me for that matter."

Selene pokes her head between the two front seats. "How do you know that?"

"I'd be dead right now, and they would have taken you by force. I'm sorry, but... I can't risk your lives with some type of daring escape. It'll be okay." *I hope.* "Just do what they say."

I try to sound confident but the truth is, that I've never been this *scared in my life.* A heavily armed man shows up on the passenger side of the vehicle. Several other armed men open up the doors and instruct all of the civilians to exit the SUV and get in the helicopter up ahead. One of the men opens my door.

"Lay on the ground with your hands behind your head!" he states in a loud commanding voice.

Getting out of the SUV, I raise my arms in compliance. *Am I going to die?* His hard carbon fiber AA-12 presses on the back of my skull. *Where did I go wrong?* I lay face down on the dirt road. *Should I have sheltered in place inside of the interrogation room?* My heart beats out of my chest. *I did what I was supposed to do, right? Right. I have...* Roadway dust particles burst up my nostrils as I breathe. *No regrets.*

"Don't fucking get up if you know what's good for you," deep raspy voice commands.

Will these be the last words I ever hear? I shut my eyes. *Each moment feels like an eternity.* The pressure of the weapon releases from the back of my skull. I stay perfectly still. My breathing is eerily calm while my heartbeat is going a mile a minute. The hum of the helicopter propeller fades in the distance.

The stillness of the night consumes every sound around me once again.

I look around and raise my head. *Am I alive? Are they gone?* I get back into the SUV and sit.

My hands shake as I grasp the rearview mirror. *What the hell just happened, Angela?*

I need to head back to base to assess the situation. My people may be injured or worse. Before driving back toward headquarters, I survey the area. *Was it just a nightmare?* I slam my fist into the steering wheel. *I am truly sorry Joseph, Selene, and Corey. I hope you guys are safe. My superiors are going to have my ass.* While I speed back to the compound, the wheels kick up dirt and gravel behind the SUV. *Who would have the resources to pull off this type of job?*

I must find the answer or we may all be in grave danger.

CHAPTER FOURTEEN

FALLING DOWN THE RABBIT HOLE

Roaring helicopter propellers amplified the tension in the air of the cabin where Corey sat. His thick sturdy build swayed side to side as far as his restraints would let him. As the helicopter hit mild turbulence, his heart jumped. Thumping from his heartbeat echoed louder and louder as the helicopter ascended into the clear night sky. Corey's chest moved up and down, even under two layers of clothing. His hands trembled uncontrollably, and his vision blurred. The back of his neck beaded sweat. *I'm so hot that I want to rip off my shirt and run my face under cold water.* He looked to ground himself at this moment, but the trembling traveled into his arms and legs. *Shit, I need to stop this... without my medicine.* His heart pounded faster... harder.

He took deep breaths to calm himself, but his breaths were sharp and shallow.

His vision fell into darkness. *I can't seem to focus.* He grasped at his chest and held onto the fabric of his shirt. *Is this what dying feels like? I'm high above a forest surrounded by strangers. No solid ground. Alone. I don't know what I'm doing.* Corey closed his eyes as hard as he could. *My life is over. I'm going to get kicked out of the Navy with a dishonorable discharge. Then, where will I go?*

He sank into his seat.

The maddening thoughts of impending doom cradled his soul into the abyss of despair. *I don't know how much time passed before I was able to sit up and steady myself—it could have been thirty seconds or an hour.*

Corey opened his eyes, slowly inhaled, and forcefully exhaled. Two of the armed men sat on either side of Selene. With eyes closed shut, she retreated into her seat firmly pressing the hearing protection against her ears. *I wish I stabilized the rocking as fiercely as she drowned out the sound. I hope she's okay.* Corey stared at the large automatic rifle held by one of the burly men dressed in black tactical gear. *That doesn't look standard issued.*

He pointed at his AA-12. "Don't worry about this, sir. This is for your protection! Just relax and enjoy the ride!"

That's what they all say until you get out of line. Corey wiped his face with his sleeve. "Who are you guys and where are you taking us!?"

"Who are we? We just saved your asses! We're headed to headquarters, and I'll let the doc explain everything else. We just do his heavy lifting!" He grinned.

They don't look like they're in any military uniform I've seen. Corey sneered. *No military outfit would just raid a government compound. Wait, does he mean* doc, *like a* Navy Corpsman?

Joseph leaned in. "I guess we're going to another compound and these guys are our escorts!"

Corey looked into Joseph's eyes. *How are you not freaking out right now?*

Multiple lights in the distance caught Corey's attention. As they approached the lights, they brightened to reveal a multi-level fenced-in mansion. The large red-brick mansion sat atop a hill surrounded by sparse woods. *I bet it's big enough for an extended family to live in.* As the helicopter descended onto the helipad, Corey noticed several armed guards patrolling the perimeter grounds. *Looks like they don't want intruders. What are they protecting in there?* Cameras, security lighting, and two rows of barbed wire atop tall fences covering the exterior of the well-kept property. A grand home was secluded amid thick evergreens and beyond those trees lay rough mountainous terrain. *Pretty fancy for a fortress.* As the helicopter landed and the engine wound down, a group of men approached the helipad before the propellers stilled.

"Please come with us, sir. You're guests here. Don't worry, no one will harm you while you're staying with us." One of the men attempted to help Corey out of the helicopter.

Corey waved their gesture off and jumped onto the concrete helipad. "No thanks, I've got it."

Corey glanced back at the others. Joseph was helped off on the opposite side. Selene stared intently at the man's open hand. *She's prolly scared out of her mind after all that.* He walked over and stood in front of the armed guard. "Let me try."

He turned to Selene. "Hey, are you okay?"

"Oh it's you," Selene said as she gathered herself. "Yeah, just give me a second." She closed her eyes, released the grip from around herself, exhaled, and then removed the hearing protection hardware from around her ears. She opened her eyes and nodded. "Okay, I think I'm good now. It's just another adventure, right?"

"Sure..." *If you say so.* Corey helped her down from her seat onto the concrete below.

They were driven toward the front entrance of the mansion in a golf cart-sized transport on a cobblestone driveway that led to tall white columns which lined the entryway. Extravagant arched windows adorned the front of the mansion on either side of a filigreed red door. *This place looks like a house on the cover of a Christmas magazine.* As the red front door opened, a brown-haired light-skinned man of average height stepped out from a well-lit foyer. *He's not like the armed men who were in the helicopter or like the ones patrolling the perimeter grounds.* He was slender and pale but stood straight and proper. An uneasy shimmering gaze from his hazel blue eyes pierced through a pair of thin-rimmed glasses. His attire conveyed a sense of fashion, matching the mansions stately exterior; elegant, yet simple.

"Hello, Petty Officer Parker, and Miss Garcia. Of course, every aspiring theater buff knows you, Mr. Godwin."

Corey glared up at Joseph. *Do They?*

"I hope your rescue wasn't too brazen. I didn't have time to contact you before the U.S. government detained you." He extended his light-skinned hand to greet Corey.

Corey furrowed his brow and crossed his arms. *How does he know our names?*

He retracted his hand from Corey's vicinity. "Ahem. My name is Dr. Kreiner, but please feel free to call me Henry. You must have had quite an ordeal, please come in, you're quite safe here, I can assure you."

Reaching back, Dr. Kreiner held the front door open. Joseph gazed at the surrounding statues and expertly designed landscapes. Selene raised her right-hand fingers to her small chapped lips, looked down lost in thought, but did not budge. The guards did not try to force them into the house.

Corey leaned back. "So you're the *doc*, I presume?"

"Is that what my men call me? You can call me whatever you prefer." Dr. Kreiner smiled. "It's been a long night and you must be famished. We have world-renowned chefs that will make you anything you want. And the truth is that you three are some of the most important people on the planet right now."

Joseph's head perked up as he turned his attention toward Dr. Kreiner. "World-class chefs. Say no more. I'm starving, and this mansion is exquisite Doctor."

Joseph placed a hand on Corey's shoulder. "You can stay out here if you'd like but I'd advise against it," he said, strolling toward the entrance.

Of course, you'd go into a gaudy mansion without question. Corey shook his head. *Why does he think we're important? Because we shared a dream. Gimmie a break.* "Who are you guys and what is this place?"

"We are interested in saving the world; nay, this reality, and we need your assist —" As Selene approached, Dr. Kreiner looked on.

Corey narrowed his eyes. *What does he mean by* this reality? *Is this what Agent Tucker mentioned?*

Selene stared at the doctor and circled him like a lioness scouting her prey. She looked him up and down as if she was trying to find a blemish in his being.

Corey tilted his head. *What is she doing?*

Dr. Kreiner continued on but intermittently recoiled as if bothered by Selene's movements "Uh, we need your assistance and we couldn't wait for our incompetent government to lock you away forever, so we rescued you while we had the opportunity." He turned his head around toward Selene. "Um... can I help you with something, Miss Garcia?"

"You haven't slept much, have you? Plus, you're nervous. Also, I need to get a hold of my mom to make sure she knows I'm okay," Selene said as she returned to Corey's side.

What's her deal? Corey shook his head.

Henry's pale cheeks turned a pinkish hue. "I've been up a few days... planning your rescue and anticipating your arrival. I hope that you'll at least hear me out. It's very important to me and all of mankind that you listen to what I have to say, so... yes, I'm a little nervous," Henry composed himself. "Ahem, as far as a phone call, I can arrange for that."

Corey took a step back as he stared at Selene. *She was right.*

Selene looked at Corey then toward Joseph who waited by the luxurious red door. "Good enough for me. I'm hungry, too."

"What? Wait you two." *Am I the only sane one here?* Corey grimaced. *I'm beyond exhausted at this point. That anxiety attack took it out of me.* He put his hand on his forehead and sighed. "Look, I don't know what you or your goons are up to, but... if you wanted to harm us back there... you would've already done so. I'll roger up... for now."

Walking past Dr. Kreiner, Corey stepped through the threshold into the illustrious mansion. The doctor followed Corey into the beautifully decorated foyer and closed the red door behind him. Swirling black and pearl marble tiles reflected the light off the crystalline chandelier mounted high up on the vaulted ceiling. Beyond the entryway, a massive center room led to two aged wooden staircases running up either side. Bubbling water cascaded from the top rungs of a porcelain fountain between the staircases. High above the staircase on the back wall of the second-floor pathway was a large portrait of an older man sitting in a chair. *Must be from some famous painter I've never heard of.*

Walking up the left side of the staircase to the second floor, Dr. Kreiner escorted them down a wood-floored hallway. "Please, follow me to your quarters where you can rest."

I'm exhausted, but I don't know if I can sleep with everything that's happened. While remaining vigilant, Corey shuffled around the corner through the wall-papered corridor.

"You can order what you want from the room. Our chefs are available around the clock, so do not hesitate to give them a ring. I'm sure you have a plethora of questions, however, please try to rest as it is quite late. We'll gather back up in the morning down the stairwell in the cafeteria," Dr. Kreiner said.

Corey surveyed the deep, yet well-lit, hallway. *No guards around.* Dark stained wooden doors and filigreed arches paved the walls forty feet long. At the end of the hallway lay lush green plants in golden brown vases. *I haven't seen a guard inside the mansion, yet.*

Joseph ran his hand against the intricate woodworking of the sconces that lined the passageway.

Dr. Kreiner pointed to a door on the right. "You'll each have a room to yourselves. Corey, you are in the suite closest to me. Selene, you are —"

"Thank you, but no thanks." Selene stepped out from behind Corey and moved toward Joseph. She tugged at Joseph's sweater and looked up. "Can we all just share a room for tonight?"

She must not fully trust them either. Corey smiled. *Smart girl.*

Joseph looked down at Selene then motioned to Corey. "Sure. I don't have a problem with it. How about you, Mr. Military?"

Corey shook his head. *I'm just cautious. You should be, too.* "Yeah, fine... I'm down."

Dr. Kreiner pushed the bridge of his glasses up the ridge of his nose. "Of course. I'll have the staff bring fresh linens and another mattress to this room."

Walking past the doctor, Corey turned the brass doorknob and held the door open for Joseph and Selene. "Thank you."

Joseph and Selene walked inside he stood at the doors' entrance. Corey looked on as Dr. Kreiner walked off, around the corner, and out of view. *Finally.* Corey walked inside, turned around, and locked the door. He stood there, held his ear up to the door, and then surveyed the area. *No footsteps. No guards. Good.*

Joseph laid in the king-sized bed as he propped his feet on a pile of pillows. He clasped his hands behind his head. "Corey, relax. Look at this place; does this look like a prison? It's better than a waiting room, or worse, an interrogation room where you're drilled by some secret government agent."

He has a point. Corey scoffed. *Still.*

Multiple living spaces were connected within the luxurious suite. In the bathroom, light reflected off the golden faucets that contrasted against the porcelain sinks in an expertly crafted wooden triple vanity. Pure white marble floors made way for a cast iron golden clawfoot bathtub that could fit an entire family. As Selene stood in awe, Corey glanced at his rugged reflection in the large wall-mounted mirror. Various scented grooming products lined the seafoam-colored shelves.

Corey walked out of the bathroom. "So who needs to use the head first?"

"Head?" Selene asked.

"Sorry, it's a habit. Bathroom," Corey said.

Joseph leaped up. "Oh man, I've needed to piss ever since we left the helicopter, do you all mind?"

Corey shook his head as he walked over to the window and pulled the curtain aside. Armed men patrolled the parameter and spotlights mounted on guard parapets illuminated the dark woods that surrounded the mansion. *Shit, I don't think they'll let us just walk out of here.*

Joseph walked back into the main bedroom area and kicked off his brown loafers. "That's one hell of a bathroom. Almost as fancy as some of the hotels in Dubai. All clear, if anyone else wants to use it."

"I'd like to shower, but..." Selene rummaged through one of the handcrafted white wooden dressers.

Joseph poked his head over her left shoulder. "That's nice of the good doctor, clothes are available and they're all white. I can't speak for his taste, but at least we'll know that they're clean."

With a handful of white clothes, Selene maneuvered around Corey and stood at the bathroom French doors. "I need a shower. Please stand guard to make sure there's no malarkey happening around here."

Corey whispered to Joseph. "What's a malarkey?"

Joseph shrugged as water from Selene's shower tap-danced in the background.

Corey paced back and forth by the large second-story window. "How can you be so relaxed? Selene, I get it, she's just a kid, but don't *you* realize the shit we're in? I've prolly been rung up on charges of desertion by now. Do you know what that entails? My career, everything I've built. Gone." His heart raced. "Worse than that, federal Imprisonment and not a cushioned waiting room like with Special Agent Tucker. Literal breaking big rocks into little rocks. Bread and water only.

Real-life shit." As he hovered near the bed Corey leered into Joseph's brown eyes.

Joseph stood up. His fair-skinned complexion turned red against the greying blondish brown hairs of his beard. He towered a full head length over Corey. "Okay, Mr. Military. What are you, twenty-three or twenty-four? You're both kids so enough with the tough talk like you're in charge. You're clueless about how the world works. What's all the hoopla going to get you? Now they know that you're quick to anger. Belligerent!"

Corey furrowed his brow. *He doesn't know me.*

Joseph rose his left index finger below Corey's chin. "Pick your battles, kid. Look around. Do you think they'll just let us walk out of here?"

What? He noticed too. Corey's eyes widened.

"Of course, I realize the shit that we're in. I'm just smart enough to understand that you can't let people see you panic. Perception is reality."

I didn't think... Corey inched back.

"What about the girl? She's so freaked out that she mumbles to herself."

Corey broke his gaze from Joseph's eyes. *She does?*

"Do you think all of your bravado and questioning changes the fact that we need to find a way home?" Joseph asked.

As he backed away, Corey's shoulders sank.

Joseph retracted his finger and sat back on the bed. "Besides, they wouldn't harm someone like me without raising a few eyebrows, so stick close by and keep —"

A knock echoed from the other side of the dark wooden door.

From the bathroom, the water from the showerhead splashing against the bottom of the bathtub went silent.

Corey squared up toward the door. *I hope someone comes in here looking for a fight. Fucking bring it.*

Joseph stood, walked to the door, and turned to Corey. "Keep your cool."

Corey nodded as Joseph opened the heavy wooden door.

As the door creaked open, a figure stood within a darkened shadow on the far side of the hallway wall. Two circular lights emanated from the darkness like the vulturous eyes of a demon lurking in the shadows, waiting to devour their souls.

CHAPTER FIFTEEN

THE DOCTOR OF TIME AND THE TWINS

Selene walked out of the bathroom in the upscale suite inside of Dr. Kreiner's mansion. *Different soaps, oils, and scented lotions; I've never had that many options growing up.* She placed her folded dirty clothes on the love seat in between Corey, who was aimed to pounce at any unwanted guest, and Joseph, who stood tall and resolute against the open door.

She glanced at the dark figure in the hall. *Someone with shiny glasses, no tray of goodies, and looks like that doctor guy.* "I thought you were someone with food, Doctor K." Selene dried her dark brown hair with a white towel.

Dr. Kreiner stepped out of the darkness into the light of the room, adjusted his glasses up the bridge of his nose, and then looked at Selene. "Doctor K... that's a new one."

He's got puffy eyes. Selene looked on as she dried her hair.

He handed Corey a set of bedsheets. "Here you go, Mr. Parker."

Corey accepted the linens.

Joseph coughed.

Selene tilted her head. *That sounded disingenuous, but he* is *getting old... like mom.*

Corey gritted his teeth. "Oh...Um...Thanks." He set the sheets down on the love chair in the corner of the bedroom. "Dr. Kreiner... um, Henry. You're a legit doctor, right?"

Dr. Kreiner nodded. "I hold degrees in astrophysics, biology, chemistry, and psychology. I can show you each of my graduate thesis's if you're interested."

Corey shook his head. "No need."

Selene gasped. *I am!*

"I don't suppose you could get a hold of any Amitriptyline?" Corey asked. "It's for my —"

"A common prescription recommendation for anxiety." Dr. Kreiner nodded. "My men told me you had a hard time on the helicopter, during your rescue, Mr. Parker. I'm sorry about that."

Selene stood in the middle of the bedroom. *Does Corey have anxiety? He's usually so steady. I wonder if my brother Alex had anxiety and we couldn't afford the doctor visits or medicine. Is that why he left us? I need to find out what happened to mom.*

Selene walked up to Dr. Kreiner. "I need to get back to Waco and find my mother. She's probably at the hotel terrified, or worse."

Dr. Kreiner clasped his hands, walked to the dresser, and turned to face the three of them. "This is why I wanted you in separate rooms. I retrieved sensitive, personal information about your mother, Miss Garcia. Are you sure you want Mr. Godwin and Mr. Parker present?"

Selene's eyes widened. *His demeanor and tone convey... bad news. Oh no.* "What is it? I don't care if they hear. I just want to talk to my mother."

Dr. Kreiner motioned to Joseph. "Please close the door, Mr. Godwin."

Joseph obliged.

Selene sat at the edge of the bed in front of Dr. Kreiner. *I don't like this.*

"Selene, your mother was admitted to the downtown Waco General hospital the day the government abducted you," Dr. Kreiner said.

Selene clenched the sheets at the edge of the bed. *Oh no. Mom.*

Corey placed his hand on her shoulder. "I'm sorry, Selene."

Joseph crossed his arms. "That's terrible news... but... how did you know about it? A patient's name and personal information are kept confidential until they've notified their next of kin."

Selene looked back. *Joseph is... right.*

Dr. Kreiner tilted his head and smiled. "Miss Garcia has a brother. Additionally, I'm a renowned entity in the medical community and have many connections. Someone of your stature should know how well-informed you can be once you've established a network, isn't that right, Mr. Godwin?"

His smile looks like mine when I try to smile in the mirror. Selene stood, held herself, and stared into Dr. Kreiner's eyes. "What's her status? Is she okay? Is she conscious? Stable?"

Dr. Kreiner shook his head. "She's stable but unresponsive. That's the latest information I've received. I'm going to work tirelessly throughout the night to get a better update, Miss Garcia."

She fidgeted with her fingers at her side. *He's not telling me everything.*

Dashing past Dr. Kreiner toward the window, Corey opened the golden-laced drapes. "Why not let her go then? I'm sure you could take Selene straight to the hospital in your military-grade helo. Isn't that right, Henry?"

Selene looked out the window. *Corey is... also right.*

"Unfortunately, I've also been informed that your friends at the CPA are standing by at the hospital." Dr. Kreiner leaned in toward Selene. "I'll find a way to get you in contact with your mother as soon as she recovers, but it's an enormous risk to let you get abducted again."

Joseph stood next to Selene. "He's got a point, my dear. We know how *they* treat guests. Remember the interrogation room and ankle restraints?"

Selene raised her fingertips to her lips. *At least I know she's safe. Dr. K wasn't lying about that... but he wasn't telling the whole truth. Even if I make a scene here, where would I run to?* Selene paced back and forth. *She's safe. I can handle a night here.* She stared into Corey's confident yet soft eyes. She tilted her head adjacent to Joseph's overbearing yet protective posture. *I... will trust them.*

She nodded. "I can't go back to Waco until I know my mom is going to be safe. If Agent Tucker and her team grab us again, there's no guarantee that they'll let us go."

Corey sighed. "She's prolly right."

She turned to Dr. Kreiner. "Please let me stay here until you find more details about my mother."

Dr. Kreiner nodded. "That's the least I can do, Miss Garcia. Stay hcre as long as you need."

Selene exhaled. *I'm continuing the same adventure, I guess.* "Also, do you have a set of headphones I can borrow? Noise-canceling preferably, and..." Her stomach grumbled. "Food, please."

"Of course, I'll see about the headphones. And I'll have the chefs make you some sandwiches expeditiously and have my staff bring up a tray with bottles of water. Afterward, however, please try to get some rest." Dr. Kreiner exited the room.

Selene waved. "You as well, Dr. K." *He needs it more than I do.*

As Joseph nudged Corey's side, he flinched. "Oh... yes... Thank you, Henry," Corey said.

She raised her eyebrow. *Why isn't Corey fighting back?*

Corey closed the door behind Dr. Kreiner, then locked it. "I guess we're captives for another night."

Selene pulled back the comforter and bedsheets of the second queen-sized bed. "I don't think we have a choice." *I hope my mother is resting peacefully.* She nestled herself underneath the sheets and blankets as Corey and Joseph took their turns utilizing the shower. *Do we have a real choice if we're all supposed to follow God's plan?*

A knock came from beyond the aged wooden door.

"It's one of Dr. Kreiner's assistants. I have your food," he said from the hallway.

Selene jolted out of the bed, sprinted across the room, and reached for the handle. *Praise be to God.*

THE NEXT DAY DURING the latter part of the morning, Corey sneaked out past the threshold of the room inside Dr. Kreiner's mansion, slash prison. He looked down the corridor. *Any roving watch guards?* He grabbed at the soft tufts of down that made up his white garbs and shook his head. *Man, good thing Charles isn't here. He'd rip on me so hard for wearing this.* Corey tip-toed down the gaudy mansion hallway.

Joseph and Selene followed.

I hope my friend made it back to base safely. He inched toward the staircase toward the main entrance from their rescue, slash capture. Restained wooden floorboards creaked as he walked down the corner of the hallway. *Shit!*

Selene and Joseph mimicked Corey's every move.

Corey stood still. *That's right, just follow my lead.*

One of the brass handles clanked from a door down the corridor, slash cell block. *The guards found us, oh shit.* They focused their attention on whoever would appear. *I'm sorry guys.*

From the mysterious doorway, a fair-skinned woman with fiery red hair walked out into the middle of the hallway. She wore loose-fitting white garments similar to their own.

Corey's eyes widened. *Who the hell is that, another prisoner?*

Her head turned toward the room as she kept her gaze on Corey. "Marko, come out here."

Who is she talking to? Corey looked beyond the pale girl.

"I think the Doc invited some more guests," she said with an unfamiliar foreign accent.

Corey stared at the fairy-figured woman. *Is she related to Puck?* He shook his head. *Why was puck the first thing I thought of?*

A slender, small, light-skinned man emerged from behind her. He wore white shorts and a buttoned-down white short-sleeved shirt. His nose and mouth were hidden behind in a book.

Corey squinted. *I can't make out the title.*

He looked up, closed it, and then glared at them through his silver glasses.

They both have the same eyes. Corey took a step back.

The woman's hazel-colored eyes narrowed, and her cheeks rose as she smiled. "Hello, don't be frightened. My name is Saara." Saara gushed. "Finally, I'll be able to talk to other people besides my lame-ass brother and the Doc."

Brother and Sister? Corey stepped toward her with his arms open. *Henry must have kidnapped them from their family, that bastard.* "Were you captured by these guys too? We're going to find a way out of here if you want to join us?"

Saara raised an eyebrow as she put her small hands on her curvy hips. "What? No one captured us. We came here on our own after being contacted by the Doc. Weren't you guys invited here in the same way?"

Joseph crossed his arms. "The US government illegally abducted us and the good doctor saved us, fed us, and then gave us an exquisite suite to stay the night."

"Imprisoned us you mean." Corey peeked his head around the corner of the hallway. *No guards coming up the stairs either. Strange.* He held out his hand toward Saara. "My name is Corey."

Saara stared at Corey's hand.

"I think he wants you to shake his hand, Sis." Marko hugged the book close to his chest.

"I know, I just don't think everyone should have to touch hands to greet each other." Saara folded her arms.

Ouch, maybe she is *related to Puck.* Corey retracted his hand and turned to Selene. "This is —"

Selene stepped past Joseph, beside Corey, and waved. "Selene. It's nice to meet you, Saara. I also don't like hands... when they're used for greeting people. Hello, Marko. My brother's name is Alex."

Marko sneered. "Hmph."

Corey pointed his thumb toward Joseph. "The surprisingly fit-looking old man here is Joseph."

Joseph closed his eyes and shook his head. "Alright, Mr. Pudgy, who are you to judge my experience and dietary standards?"

Corey rolled his eyes. "And as Joseph mentioned, we got here late last night. This whole situation is shady as hell."

Marko stepped beside Saara. "Where are you all from?"

"We're from all over the United States. What kind of accents are those?" Joseph asked. "Both of you sound... foreign."

Corey smiled. *Glad you asked about it first, I didn't want to seem rude.*

"Oh, loujan kiitos." Marko pointed at Joseph. "You looked Russian at first glance. We're both Finnish and were personally invited here to help Dr. Kreiner with his research."

"What research?" Corey said.

Selene rose her fingertips to her lips. "Alternate reality research I'd bet. A quantum entangled dream-sharing event." She looked up at Corey. "That's what Agent Tucker called it."

Marko gripped a book by his side. His arm covered most of the title.

Corey squinted, again. *Da— W— och... is all I can read.*

Saara leaped in front of Selene and clasped the sides of her shoulders. "I knew it! You guys can do it too," Saara said.

Selene stood there, stiff with her eyes wide open.

I'm pretty sure Saara scared Selene right out of her skin. Corey chuckled. *Poor girl.*

Saara slapped Corey's arm. "I thought we were the only ones that shared our dreams or whatever-entangled-quantum-thingy she said."

Ow. Corey held the side of his arm. *So, they're not being held against their will?*

Marko shrugged his shoulders. "No shit, sis. Why else would Dr. Kreiner spend valuable time, resources, and effort to bring them in?"

"Ugh, whatever, bookworm." Saara furrowed her brow then pushed past Joseph. "Can we continue this chat after breakfast? I'm suuuper hungry. If you want to have some of the best food you've ever eaten then follow me. Friends."

Friends? Corey looked at Selene and Joseph. "What the hell, I am super hungry, too."

Is this an elaborate trap? Corey followed Saara down the staircase through the door to the main story of the stately manor. On the other side of the large mahogany door was a cafeteria-like facility with six freshly cleaned white tables. *Where is everyone else?*

Three chefs stood behind a large rectangular opening with a counter.

Saara walked up to the window. "Good morning, Chef Ramiro, let's see... can you make me an omelet with steak, shredded pork, chicken, mushrooms, peppers, and tomato."

The chef nodded and walked to the back as Saara grabbed a tray off of the stack in front of the metallic window, then she walked down the counter toward the drinking fountain.

Marko reached for a tray then turned to Corey. "Just order what you want for breakfast and one of the chefs will make it and send it to the end of the line for you to pick up. It's no use trying to stump them. I've tried. They can make any food item you can come up with."

Marko turned to the second chef. "I'll just have my usual, thank you."

The chef turned around and prepared Marko's meal.

Marko waved his book in the air as he walked away. "Go ahead, give it a go."

Corey grabbed a tray, laid it upon the counter, and turned to a female chef. "I'll take some pork chops, two eggs over easy, some sausage links, and a side of grits." *I hope that's not too much.*

The chef nodded. "Of course, sir. Is that all?"

"Yes, that'll be all." *Do prisons have food like this?* "Thank you, ma'am." Corey walked down toward the drinking fountain. *High-class fancy executive prisons do.*

Joseph stepped up to the window. "Yes, Chef, do you have any fresh fruits, yogurt, and granola?"

The chef smiled. "Yes sir, we get fresh produce delivered every few days."

Joseph nodded. "I'll have your finest of each if you please."

Of course, he'd order the most pretentious items. Corey shook his head.

Selene ordered a simple dish, grabbed her drink, and then walked to the white, marbled table where the others congregated.

Saara shoveled food into her mouth without care. She smiled at Corey as bits of egg dangled off of her chin.

Her lack of self-consciousness is endearing. His dark-skinned cheeks blushed as he looked down to eat. He scooped a spoonful of grits into his mouth and smiled back at her.

Selene coughed. "So, you mentioned that you were invited here. Where is here? What does Dr. K want to do to us?"

Thanks, Selene. We were having a moment. Corey smirked. *She really can't read a room.*

Saara continued to eat, then hit her brother on the arm.

"Ow." Marko winced. "Since my sister can't stop stuffing her mouth, I'll have to explain."

Joseph put his drink down on the table. "I'm glad someone around here can."

Marko placed his book on the white tabletop. "We were brought here because my sister and I shared dreams multiple times throughout our lives. We thought that this was normal for twins, however, Dr. Kreiner told us that our dreams were unique. It was because we have the same relative dream but at different times. While I can't say for sure, I'd wager that you were brought here due to similar reasons, no?"

Corey put down his fork. "That's just great. You're saying that some mad scientist wants to dissect our brains. All because of a stupid dream."

Selene leaned in. "It wasn't a stupid dream... well, maybe it was, but remember what Agent Tucker told us?" She swallowed the last of her food. "She said that it was dangerous."

Corey struck his empty drink atop the table.

Everyone stopped eating and turned their attention toward him. "She said... that the very fabric of our universe was at stake."

The cafeteria door flew open.

Corey looked on. *Who the hell —*

"Not only our universe, Mr. Parker." Dr. Kreiner stood at the opened doorway. "A reality beyond ours hangs in the balance. Our fates... no... all fates, will be in *your* hands after today. What will you choose, life... or death?"

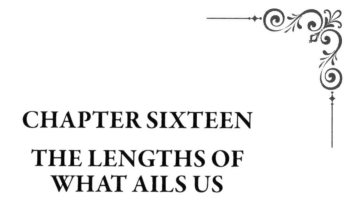

CHAPTER SIXTEEN

THE LENGTHS OF WHAT AILS US

Selene clutched one of the mansion's cloth napkins close to her chest. *God, please watch over mom.* "Did you hear anything else about my mom, Dr. K?"

Dr. Kreiner poured himself a cup of coffee at the drinking fountain, then pulled a chair to the end of the white table and sat. "They're running a test on her blood to figure out what happened. I'm hoping to get you in contact with her as soon as she wakes. Otherwise, she's still at rest in stable condition." He blew the steam off of his coffee.

How many cups did he have before that one? "Oh." *I should be there, but I'm stuck here.* Selene pushed her tray of unfinished food away. "Thank you."

Saara chugged her glass of chocolate milk. "Hey, Doc, what do we have on the schedule for today?"

Dr. Kreiner sipped his coffee. "After you all finish, I'd like to bring our new guests to the laboratory and show them around."

Corey put his fork down. "There's a laboratory here? I should have known, with the security around, this wasn't a normal mansion."

Joseph placed his utensils on his tray of half-eaten fruit and yogurt. "Well then, my good doctor, there's no time to waste."

Selene nodded. *Corey is right, we need to find a way out of here.*

Dr. Kreiner glanced across with the table, then stood. "Very well. Please leave your plates on the table, my staff will clean up behind us. Now, please follow me."

Saara jumped up and dashed through the cafeteria door.

She's got a lot of energy. Selene followed the group behind Dr. Kreiner past the central foyer, around the corner into a room with an elevator, where Saara stood.

"Way to ruin the secret elevator reveal, sis." Marko opened his book and continued to read as they walked.

Saara put her hands on her hips. "Damn... I hate it when you're right." She shrugged her shoulders. "I just love the elevator rides."

Selene poked her head around Joseph's frame. *Secret elevator? That's so cool.*

Dr. Kreiner shuffled into the elevator and reached into his white, lab coat pocket. He pulled out a flat, clear, plastic card with a computer chip molded into the middle of it. "Firstly, I see that you've met Saara and Marko. These guests have been here for a few months."

Selene ventured into the elevator after Marko. *He's got silver eyes, like a wolf.*

Corey inspected the room before wandering into the large white elevator.

Dr. Kreiner inserted the clear, micro-chipped card into the side panel internal to the elevator. "Now that you three are here, I can proceed with my *important* work. Some would say, the most important work of our lifetime."

Marko peeked up from behind his book. "Aren't you being a little dramatic, doctor?"

"Not at all, Marko." Dr. Kreiner pushed the L2 button on the metallic panel.

Selene stared at the panel. *If the mansion is on the L3 level and the laboratory is on the L2 level, then what's on the L1 level?*

"I don't know what the U.S. government said to you three. Undoubtedly, they mentioned that they captured you because of the quantum entangled dream-sharing event you all experienced, correct?" Dr. Kreiner asked.

As the roomy elevator descended below, Selene nodded. "That's right, Dr. K." *I knew it... and that's the same name Agent Tucker used.*

Dr. Kreiner turned his head. "Well, these two have also shared a similar event. Of course, their dream-share event is less rare as the brains of fraternal twins have a closer harmonic link. You see, all beings in this universe operate on a certain frequency which is regulated by our brains and —"

I know this one. Selene threw her hand in the air. "Like a radio tuned into the frequency of this universe, right?"

Dr. Kreiner used his finger to push his glasses up the bridge of his nose. "That is correct Miss Garcia. I see the government did explain a few things before we arrived. Unlike radio, however, we do not get to choose the frequency we are attuned to. From birth, every human brain operates on a subset of that frequency. While I may operate at 8.000034 hertz you may operate at 8.000055 hertz. This is so that our consciences do not interfere with each other's."

After an abrupt stop, the large metallic elevator doors opened.

Selene stepped out ahead of the group. Glass rooms lined the freshly waxed, white-tiled hallway. *It's so quiet.* Several medical personnel dressed in white lab coats, blue latex gloves, and safety goggles scurried about. Some of them wrote notes in aluminum notebooks. She inhaled. *It smells so clean, like alcohol and... industrial steel. This is what a laboratory is supposed to be like.* She pressed her face against the nearest glass room to their left. *The beakers and test tubes are sorted by volume. Of course, they are!* Selene smiled.

Joseph ran his finger across the windows of the first room to their right. "My good doctor, how did I get entangled in a dream with the others? Shouldn't that be impossible if my brain was hardwired to separate my conscience from theirs?"

I didn't think of that. Selene turned her head. *Good one, Joseph.*

"Please follow me." Dr. Kreiner walked into one of the glass rooms down the hall. The doors slid apart like that of a grocery store entrance. Inside were three oversized monitors on the wall. Each of them had videos of various people laying on bed-like objects. One of his assistants sat in front of a keyboard. He put down his pen and metallic notebook as Dr. Kreiner entered the room. "Dr. Keith, please pull up trial case study number forty-four."

"Yes, sir, right away." Dr. Kreiner's assistant faced the monitor and speedily typed on the keyboard.

Once he pressed enter, a video played on the center monitor.

Saara clapped her hands. "Oh, I know this one. This is one of *our* successful experiments, right Doc?"

Selene covered her ears with her hands. *Too loud.*

"Are you okay, Selene?" Corey asked.

Selene released her hands down to her side and nodded. "I'm fine, please continue Dr. K."

"Yes, well, when we sleep our brains can alter our operating frequency, as it were. Specifically, during our deepest periods of sleep, it alters the delta brain wave pattern as you can see here on their vitals readout." Dr. Kreiner pointed to the brain wave pattern on the device inside of the video monitor.

Selene leaned in toward the monitor. *They look so peaceful. Dr. K can't be as evil as Corey said, can he?*

"Our conscience can jump to a universe that operates on that frequency. This happens more than you realize. Have you ever been in a dream where you see your younger or older self in a different setting surrounded by different circumstances?" Dr. Kreiner asked.

Corey crossed his arms. "I had a dream where I was back home in Charleston, South Carolina with my real mom and dad... It was as if I never joined the Navy. It wasn't an exciting dream, though. I just thought it was weird."

Guess, I never asked about his past. Selene glanced at Corey. *I miss mom... and dad.*

Dr. Kreiner pointed his finger in the air at no one in particular. "That, Mr. Parker, was your conscience peering into an alternate universe. This phenomenon is not as rare, as you can see. However, the rarest phenomenon is what *you three* encountered. For multiple individuals to share the same frequency at the same time is extraordinary."

Was that part of God's plan? Selene bit her lip. *Maybe we just need to have faith and put in the work ourselves, right mom?*

Marko's face rose from behind his book. "It's not uncommon for twins though, correct, doctor?"

"That is correct, Marko. Fraternal twins come from two different eggs, however genetically they share the same brain development early on. Two people can dream-share when they synchronize to the same operating frequency. As seen, at the three-hour and twenty-two-minute mark. Dr. Keith, if you please." Dr. Kreiner placed his hand on his assistants' shoulder.

"Of course, doctor. One moment, please." His assistant hit a key on the keyboard to fast forward the video to the precise timestamp.

Selene observed the vital monitors on the video. Gradually, the delta brain wave pattern mimicked one another. *They're in sync.*

"How do you get them into a deep sleep at the same time? I can hardly remain asleep when my baby girls romp at the foot of my bed. I doubt that I get enough good sleep to venture into some crazy alternate reality, like Mister Bookworm and Miss Cheerleader."

Selene's eyes widened. *Do you sleep with babies at your feet? What the heck, Joseph?*

"Oh... that's where the drugs come in handy." Saara grinned.

Corey looked at Joseph.

Selene rose her fingertips to her lips. *Like with* her... *in the needles... of my nightmares?* "What drugs?"

Dr. Kreiner nodded. "Yes, please follow me." He walked out of the room, down the hall, and strolled into another glass room.

A woman in a light-blue scrub, yellow gloves, and safety glasses mixed a brown-tinted chemical into a cylinder and measured its contents. She wrote in her metallic notebook as the group entered the room.

"Dr. Nguyen, can you explain to our guests, what that substance is?" Dr. Kreiner asked.

Smiling, Dr. Nguyen turned toward the group. "Of course, Dr. Kreiner. The substance is called Dimethyltryptamine. To be more specific, a modified version of it. Dimethyltryptamine at its core is a chemical substance that occurs in many plants and animals. It's both a derivative and a structural analog of tryptamine. It was used as a psychedelic drug for various cultures, mostly used for ritualistic spiritual journeys. Thanks to Dr. Kreiner's contribution, we manipulated its compounds to induce a stable deep sleep while we kept the psychedelic side effects to a minimum."

Marko talked into his pages. "We just call it DMT since Dimethyltryptamine is a mouthful, to say the least."

I thought this was about dreams, not drugs... I can't... not like her. Selene shut her eyes and raised her hand. *I have to tell them.*

An armed guard burst into the room, ran to Dr. Kreiner, and whispered into his ear.

Selene opened her eyes and lowered her hand. *What's going on?*

"I see." Dr. Kreiner tightened his lips and nodded.

The armed man left the laboratory.

Dr. Kreiner turned to the group. "It's Selene's mother. She's regained consciousness and has requested to speak to Selene."

Mom! Selene's heart fluttered.

"My lovely Saara, can you escort Mr. Parker and Mr. Godwin up-stairs to their rooms?" Dr. Kreiner leaned toward Corey and Joseph. "Please go with them, will you? I'd like for Miss Garcia to have a little privacy with her mother."

Joseph herded Corey to follow Saara out of the laboratory into the elevator. "Of course, my good doctor. We'll await further word. Besides, I think we need to digest what was learned this afternoon."

Selene paced back and forth in the room as the group exited the floor. *I need to get out of here. Mom needs me by her side. She doesn't have anyone else and —*

"Do you remember an incurable disease in an alternate reality you journeyed to?" Dr. Kreiner asked as he approached Selene.

Selene stopped and turned. *Incurable disease...* "No, sir, but in that alternate reality, people lived on the streets." *Just like* she *does.*

Dr. Kreiner pushed his glasses up the ridge of his nose. "That doesn't happen in this world. A layer in the upper stratosphere was de-stroyed decades ago due to pollutants. It was too late to prevent the horrid rain that, has since, limited our ability to venture outside for long periods."

Selene closed her eyes and massaged her temples with her finger-tips. "The details are fuzzy, but I don't recall incurable diseases in my nightmares... or dreams."

Dr. Kriener pulled out a large phone from his lab coat pocket and presented it to Selene. "Before you talk to your mother, I need to tell you the results of her blood work."

Selene took the phone and held it against her chest. *Oh, no. His face and tone...* "Tell me, please."

"Your mother has the same disease that's ravaging Europe's popula-tion. It's a virus we've never seen. She's one of the few new cases found in the United States. She's been quarantined at the hospital. I'll give you some space, please take your time," Dr. Kreiner stepped out of the glass room to the other side of the door.

Selene's eyes watered. *No.* She wiped her eyes and called her mother. *I need to be strong.*

"Mija, oh thank God." Her mother's voice shook.

God? Selene sniffled. *The plan is all messed up.* "How are you doing, Ama? Are you hurt? Are you in pain?"

"Calm down, Mija. I'm fine. Are you safe?" her mother asked.

She's lying. Selene gritted her teeth. "You don't have to say that anymore. I'm not a little kid... and yes, I am safe. The doctor here told me... what's wrong with you."

"They're giving me antibiotics, vitamins, and are going to let me walk around a bit. The doctors and nurses are friendly. I wish I could see you... You're going to be a great scientist, I mean, biologist someday," her mother said.

Selene smiled. *Biochemist, but close enough.* Her eyes widened. *Oh no, how can we afford this?* "Ama, don't worry about the hospital bill, I'll work extra shifts. I'll work the weekends and —"

"Mija, you always get wound up on things like that. I've already asked about it. Someone paid for my ER visit and long-term care, too. See, there are still generous people in the world. It's all a part of God's plan. The scientists are smart, they'll figure it out, and I'll be back on my feet in no time. Just as long as you're safe, Mija... that's all that matters," she said.

Who would pay for a stranger's medical bills? Selene paced back and forth as she looked at the phone. *It couldn't be...* She glanced at Dr. Kreiner as he stood by outside of the glass room. "Ama, as soon as I hear anything, I'll give you a call. Hopefully, I can see you soon."

The phone went silent.

"Ama, are you still there?" Selene's heart raced. *Oh, no.* "Mom!?"

"Cuidate, Mija. Promise me that you'll never change. I love you very, *very* much," she said.

"I promise..." Selene's eyes watered. *Why did she say it* that *way?*

Her mother hung up.

Selene gently tapped the glass with the phone to get Dr. Keriner's attention.

Dr. Kreiner walked in and held out his hand.

Selene placed the phone in his hand. *I need to know.* "Dr. K...did *you* pay for my mother's hospital bills?"

Dr. Kreiner nodded. "Yes, of course, Miss —"

Selene wrapped her arms around Dr. Kreiner's body as tears ran down her light-brown cheeks. "Thank you, sir."

Dr. Kreiner stumbled back as Selene squeezed. "Ahem. Well, then."

"Sorry." Selene wiped the tears from her eyes. "I need to leave. Please, just let me go."

"I see." Dr. Kreiner crossed his arms, then stepped out into the hallway with the door open. "You're free to do as you please, Miss Garcia."

He's going to let me leave? Selene composed herself then waltzed past Dr. Kriener out into the hallway and headed toward the elevator.

"However... I thought you wanted to help me save your mother's life." Dr. Kreiner's words echoed throughout the hallway.

Selene stood still. Resolute. *What does he mean?* She turned around. "I thought you said that the disease was incurable?"

Dr. Kriener pushed his glasses up the bridge of his nose. "In *this* reality, it is..."

LATER THAT EVENING, Joseph poked his head out of his room. *Any guards out here?* No one walked by. He softly closed the door behind him and wandered toward the lower floor of the mansion. *It's eerily quiet.* He strolled by the porcelain fountain in the middle of the foyer, ran his hand through the water, and looked around. *No guards here either. Interesting.* His fingertips fondled the tempered steelwork of the banister railings. *This place is too clean. Too well kept. Like no one lives here.* He looked up at the crystals that dangled from the high vaulted ceiling chandelier. *How could someone so young accrue these resources? Honest men of science are paid far less than me.*

Dr. Kreiner approached Joseph from the right side of the mansion. "Mr. Godwin. Are the accommodations up to the standards of some-one of your status?"

Joseph was startled. *Shit.* He smiled. "It's excellent, Dr. Kreiner. Hopefully, I can help you in any way possible. Although, I wish this place had a convenient store, to tell you the truth," he chuckled.

"Are the chefs not able to fulfill your needs?" Dr. Kreiner asks.

Joseph shook his head. "On the contrary, my good doctor, the food here is excellent. It's better than some of the best hotels I've stayed at. No, it's embarrassing to admit, however, I like to have a cigarette with my meals. Our self-serving government illegally confiscated my belong-ings, so, I'm out."

Dr. Kreiner nodded. "I see." He walked toward the entrance, opened the red door, and looked back. "Follow me, Mr. Godwin."

What are you up to, my good doctor? Joseph followed the doctor outside into the still clouded night. Puddles of water spotted the cob-blestone driveway. Dr. Kreiner waved his hand at one of the armed men that patrolled close by. The guard rushed over to him then he whis-pered in the armed man's ear. The armed man nodded then ran off. Dr. Kreiner pulled a thick and unwieldy phone from his front pocket. *It's not a slim, top-of-the-line, stylish cell phone that a wealthy person would have.*

Dr. Kreiner handed the phone to Joseph. "This is a satellite phone. Please call your manager, I'm sure she's worried."

Is he for real? Joseph grasped the thick, silver, satellite phone and opened it. "Thank you, Dr. Kreiner."

"I'll give you some privacy," Dr. Kreiner said and then walked down the driveway and stared at the night sky.

Joseph stared at the numbers on the keypad. *Should I call the au-thorities?* He looked around. *I wouldn't know where to send them even if*

I did. He clenched his fist. *Julia has to be freaking out, considering I never explained why never meet back with the San Francisco client.* He sighed. *I'll get an earful, but I need to tell her to look after Roxy and Velma. My girls are probably worried sick.* He called Julia.

"Hello, Julia Petrovski speaking. May I ask who's calling me this late in the evening?" Julia asked.

Joseph grinned. "It's your biggest client."

"...I hate you. Do you know that?" Julia asked.

Joseph's smile faded from his rugged cheekbones. "Yeah... about that —"

"Why didn't you tell me that you were working on a side project?" Julia asked.

Joseph's eyebrow raised. *What?* "Umm..."

"Joseph, I'm your manager, but... I thought we were on better terms than that," Julia said.

What is she going on about? "Listen, Julia, my dear. I don't know what you've heard, but —"

"Don't play dumb with me. Your million-dollar side project," Julia said.

Joseph pulled the phone away from his furrowed brow and held it at arm's length. "Million-dollar what?"

"I'm just glad you finally included me you son-of-a-bitch," Julia laughed. "I thought you were leaving me for another agent, then you go and make a deal without me, but include me in the retainer. Ugh, I could kiss you if I wasn't married."

Joseph massaged his forehead with his left hand. "I must have hit my head, my dear, what are you going on about?" *Also, you're married?*

"Oh shit, that's right. Your new client said that this project was hush-hush, but would make you the most famous man in all of history. A little dramatic for my taste, but the eccentric clientele has always been your forte," Julia said.

New client... Joseph glared at the doctor standing off to the side. *I see.* "Yes, well, ahem. You know I couldn't leave you out of this. Not after all we've been through." *I'll have to play along. If he knows about Julia, then maybe there's more to him, and this place, than I thought.*

Ferrel dogs howled from the distant mountain range as the sunset behind the burnt-sienna-colored, rocky peaks. *My baby girls!* "Julia, my dear, I don't know how long I'll be working on this one, so please watch after my girls."

"Yeah, yeah. I know the drill. I'll stop by your condo and pick them up to stay with us in the meantime." Joseph smiled. *Thank goodness.*

Joseph cupped the receiver with his hand. "Listen, just in case you don't hear from me in a week or two, call —"

The armed man from earlier rushed over to Joseph and handed him an open pack of cigarettes then walked toward Dr. Kreiner. *So, that's what they were whispering about earlier.* Joseph nodded, grabbed the pack, and mouthed the words *Thank you.*

"Are you alright?" Julia asked.

Joseph put the pack of cigarettes in his right pocket. "Never mind... just make sure my girls are taken care of, my dear."

"Don't worry about that. This is your chance, Joseph. I want you to focus on making this your greatest work ever. Who knows when something this big will come around again. Be remembered... forever."

She's right, but... Joseph nodded. "Right. Goodbye, Julia, my dear." He closed the satellite phone, then walked toward Dr. Kreiner. *Let's find out what this is all about.*

"Do I have *you* to thank for my manager's sizable retainer, good doctor?" Joseph asked.

As Dr. Kreiner turned and held out his hand, Joseph returned the phone to him. "Of course. You should be compensated for your time and effort. You saw what I'm trying to do here. You're vital to its success."

Yeah, and it's worrisome. Joseph crossed his arms as his gaze pierced through Dr. Kreiner's glass lenses. "And... what if I refuse? Will you let me walk out of here of my own volition?"

Dr. Kreiner took a lighter from his pocket and lit it in front of Joseph. "You're free to do as you wish. I'll have to find someone else to make history with."

Joseph grabbed a loose cigarette from the pack he was handed, put it in his mouth, and leaned into the flame. He inhaled, meandered beside Dr. Kreiner, and blew smoke into the crisp night air. "Answer me this, my good doctor, I get that peeking into another reality is astounding, but we're hardly the first to experience it. I don't understand what role we're to play in this."

"I'll show you all tomorrow. Then, if you're still unsatisfied, I'll escort you anywhere you'd like to go, deal?" Dr. Kreiner handed the lighter to Joseph.

Is he referring to the experiment with Selene and Marko? Joseph sneered as he put the lighter in his pocket. *You place your faith in such bit actors, doctor, but sure.* He nodded. "Deal."

A searchlight atop a nearby parapet illuminated their general position. The light enveloped the entire grassy patch where they both stood.

He shielded his eyes and looked away. *That light, again? Or...* "Can you tell them to not do that?"

"I apologize, but I'm afraid it's only standard practice. I have them sweep the perimeter every two minutes." Dr. Kreiner leaned toward Joseph. "Are you sensitive to light, Mr. Godwin?"

Every two minutes. Interesting. Joseph blinked. "Not usually... maybe I'm getting more sensitive to it in my old age." *He saw it too. I thought I was going senile.*

Dr. Kreiner walked past Joseph back toward the red door of the mansion. "Give me tomorrow and I'll show you the answer... the answer to everything in this universe... and beyond."

Joseph followed. "I'm inclined to help in any way I can, my good doctor. After all, you paid for my professional expertise." *The others, however... can exit the stage sooner rather than later.*

CHAPTER SEVENTEEN

GATHERING THE EDGES

The next afternoon, Joseph followed Corey, Saara, and Dr. Kreiner into a waiting room on the second subfloor of the laboratory below the fortified mansion. One wall was replaced with a glass window. Joseph slipped his hands into his pockets as he stared through the thick glass. Selene and Marko lay on two separate beds in the next room. Selene wore a white robe and laid perfectly still with a black cap-like device clasped around the top of her head. A black pair of headphones surrounded her ears. *She seems... peaceful.* Marko clutched his book, at his side, on the cushioned metallic bed. He had a similar black device on his head. *What are they wearing? They look ridiculous.* Strands of cables ran off the head-strapped devices through the headrest of the beds. *The good doctor seems more like a mad scientist.* Medical personnel in bright white lab coats scurried around the inside. Two scientists conversed with each other as they wrote notes and ensured that all the equipment functioned properly. *I can't hear a word.* He smiled.

Overhead, a black and white sign read: Sleep Synchronization Test Facility #3.

Corey walked to the far side of the wall and placed his palm against the window. "I hope you know what you're doing, Selene."

Joseph turned his head. *Same for you, kid.*

Saara stood at the window beside Corey. "How long does it usually take, Doc? I'm usually the guinea pig laying there, not the wide-eyed little kid watching from outside of the cage."

Joseph walked over to the cushioned seats of a burgundy-colored couch and sat. He rested his head against his clasped hands. *It's like they're anticipating some shocking revelation to burst forth from the room. No patience.*

"Well, either of them may fall asleep shortly, however, who knows how long it may take for them to sync their delta brain waves." Dr. Kreiner penned notes in his aluminum notebook then glanced at the silver watch on his right wrist. "In the eleven experiments we tried with you and Marko, it took an average of one hundred and thirty-three minutes for both of you to sync up. Even so, you were only able to produce the intended results three times."

Joseph raised an eyebrow. *So precise.*

Corey turned around. "That's all?"

Joseph smiled. *Smooth one, kid.*

Dr. Kreiner rose his head from the notebook. "Yes, Mr. Parker, but the chances are like lightning striking in the same place. It is quite miraculous we were able to reproduce the results at all."

Does he think having me here will raise the statistics? Joseph placed his left ankle on top of his right knee and sat back.

Dr. Kreiner shook his head. "If only... I was able to gather more data. Observation and documentation can only get us so far. We need to find a cure for Miss Garcia's mother's condition."

Joseph looked around the room. *It's a pretty big gamble, but I need to get out of his scrutinizing gaze.* He turned to Dr. Kreiner. *Like that unknown girl at the convention center and her screenplay, there's only one way to get your big shot in show-business.* "Why don't you join them, my good doctor?"

Corey crossed his arms. "Like he'd become the guinea pig to his twisted experiment. That's what he wanted us for, remember?"

Joseph glanced up to Dr. Kreiner. *Good, kid. Just like that.*

Saara smacked Corey on his arm. "That guinea pig reference is my thing."

That's right, Mr. Stiff. Joseph chuckled as Corey grasped his arm. *I like her.*

Dr. Kreiner pushed his glasses up the bridge of his nose. "So, Mr. Godwin, what you're proposing is that the combined energy and frequency in the proximity of their total consciousness quantum entangle the harmonic frequency of *my* delta brain waves into *their* alternate reality. Even if I've never ventured into their alternate reality previously?"

I have no clue what he said. Joseph sneered. "Precisely, my good doctor. I'm surprised a man of your caliber never thought of it."

Dr. Kreiner crossed his arms and held his chin as he stared into space.

Saara looked at Corey and Joseph. "Doc, you're not considering going in there with them, are you? Who's gonna keep an eye on the mansion?"

The fifty or so armed men patrolling the grounds, but point made. Joseph stood up. "Well, my good doctor, what will it be?" *Show me your commitment to making history.*

Dr. Kreiner paced back and forth at the back of the room behind the couch. "Please make yourselves comfortable. I'll have the staff bring down water, coffee, and snacks," he said dashing out of the waiting room.

Corey unfolded his arms and rose an eyebrow at Joseph. "This makes things... interesting."

Saara and Corey rushed to the observation window.

Joseph followed. *Is he going to join them?*

Dr. Kreiner entered Sleep Synchronization Test Facility #3, took off his white lab coat, and rolled up his sleeve. One of the other doctors handed him one of the black helmets as he laid down in a sleeping apparatus. He conversed with an assistant as she administered a brown substance intravenously. *That's the DMT he showed us before.* All three had plastic bags hung by their bedside. The brown substance dripped and mixed with the clear liquid in their bags. *All the actors are on the set.*

Joseph walked toward the biometric monitor screens and tapped on the glass with his left index finger. "Hey, Saara, how safe is this? They're pumping you up with drugs and watching you from afar. Doesn't this seem weird to Marko and yourself?"

Saara turned toward Joseph and tilted her head. "Hmm, I never thought about it that deeply. I just figured that this was a good cause and I think deep down Marko and I figured we owed the Doc for the kindness he'd shown us. If that means some doctor and his assistants watch me sleep, as long as I'm not naked, it's not that creepy."

People watch me perform far sketchier scenes for money. Joseph nodded. "I guess you're right, my dear."

An assistant walked in with a tray full of finger foods, pastries, and a thermos of coffee. A second assistant walked in with plastic cups, plates, and utensils from the cafeteria. They set them down on the corner of the room on the end table next to the burgundy-colored, cushioned couch.

They ate various foodstuffs and conversed with the staff as they waited to see if Selene, Marko, and Dr. Kreiner pulled off an improbable anomaly.

Joseph walked to the window as the staff exited the room. "Their brain waves read between twelve and thirty-five hertz, according to Dr. Kreiner's assistant, that means they're not in a heavy dream state yet, but close." *It's close enough.*

Corey jumped up from the couch. "I can't take it anymore. What the fuck are we doing? What does Dr. Nutjob think we are, mice for his experiments?" He turned to Saara as she choked down a cream cheese pastry. "His hired goons abducted us from a US Government facility.

That act alone breaks countless laws! We have a system and structure for a reason. Stability."

Perfect, kid. Joseph rushed over and clenched fistfuls of Corey's white shirt. "Look, Mr. Military. How many times have I told you? Calm the fuck down!"

Corey's nostrils flared, his lips tightened, and his eyes narrowed as he gripped Joseph's wrists. "For the last fucking time, old man, I don't take orders from you!"

Saara's eyes widened as she retreated for the couch. "What the hell? Damn macho-ass, crazy Americans."

Joseph sneered at Saara. "You stay out of this, little miss cheerleader."

"Leave her out of this, fucking drama queen." Corey puffed his chest out and cocked his fist back.

Joseph shoved his face inches in front of Corey's. "I fucking dare you."

Saara cowered behind the couch.

Corey surveyed the room as his face returned to normal. "I think we're close enough that the listening devices installed in here, like the ones in our rooms, won't pick us up," he whispered.

Joseph gritted his teeth and leaned in. *Good job kid, now...* "Here's what I found out about the perimeter guards and how we're going to escape."

The real act begins... tonight.

CHAPTER EIGHTEEN

DOWNLOADING... IN PROGRESS

An overcast sky drizzles rain droplets on my face as I lean against a painted, brick building in a trash-laden alleyway. *Shit, Selene, when the fuck did you get here?*

Oh no, I have to go inside.

What was that? I reach my left arm out and let the drops of rain wash across the scar tissue by my kick-ass chimera tattoo. *It's just a little rain.* Fire dwindles from a spray-painted barrel off to my right as the stench of garbage hits my nostrils. *I cover my nose, then look around. Where the fuck am I?* Shielding my eyes from the sun as dawn approaches, I gather the goods in my backpack and get up. The coldness of the early morning atmosphere chills my bones. *I need to leave.* Further down the alleyway, I stumble toward the source of the horrid stench. A blue, repainted, industrial-sized dumpster towers over my sightline. *Medical waste.* I grasp my head. *How wasted was I last night?*

Ama would never let you come home like that.

My eyes jolt open as I turn. *Who the fuck said that?* At the far end of the alleyway a green, neon-color, garbage truck drives by. *No one is between me and the street. Ugh, I must have had a* real good *time.* I reach in my backpack to check what's left of the drugs and party favors from last night. An opaque bracelet slides down my light-skinned, slender, bruised, right arm and settles on my wrist. It reads:

Patient: Garcia, Selene
DOB: 12/06/2001
Sex: F
Dr. Oslow #244624
Texas Health Presbyterian Hospital
Allergies: None

What the fuck, was I in a hospital yesterday? Every time I go into a hospital, they try to restrain me and force me into a sobriety box. Looking to the bottom of my empty backpack drops of rain dangle from my long, unkempt, black hair and drip onto the asphalt beside my dirty white shoes. *Shit, where's my stuff?*

Why can't I move on my own?

I shake my head. *These thoughts... It must be a side effect of something I tried last night.* I close the main compartment of my backpack and sling it across my right shoulder. *They must have confiscated it at the hospital.* Back and forth, I pace in the alleyway between the medical waste dumpster and rust-ridden barrel of burning debris. *I can't believe the hospital jacked my shit... but, I don't think they'll let me stroll in without good cause.*

Use the bracelet as an excuse to go and see what floor Dr. Oslow works on. I need to find a cure...

Great idea... but, I need to get my shit back. It must be in some confiscation bag or something. Walking around the corner, morning traffic continues along the busy downtown street; a car horn wails beside me.

Too loud.

I cover my ears. *What am I doing?* I lower my hands down from the side of my head. A vibration stirs from my backpack. I stop to open the small front pocket of my black, worn backpack. Looking down at the screen of my cell phone, I see the date along with twelve new messages from Alex, mom, and dad. *I hope I wasn't so fucked up last night that I called them.*

Dad... is alive?! I need to talk to him.

No! When did I start arguing with myself? I bet the hospital called them. *Well too bad, I'll just leave as soon as I get my shit back.* I put my cell phone away after deleting all the messages. *I don't have time for family drama right now.* As I walk up the hospital entrance, I glance at my reflection from the glass window beside the doors.

You don't look like a visitor, you look like a zombie.

Ain't that the truth, but I don't give a shit how people see me. Why am I?...never mind. Covering the bracelet with my black hoodie sleeve, I walk up to the receptionist. *Maybe, this is the beginning of a mental breakdown or some shit.*

"Yes ma'am, Dr. Oslow told me that he needed to see me for a follow-up medical examination."

A frumpy middle-aged lady looks at me, raises her eyebrow, and then faces her computer. "Name, please?"

Shit. If I use my real name then I'll have to dip out quick before they check into it further.

Ama said that you shouldn't lie.

"Shh, shut up," I whisper.

The woman leans in. "I'm sorry, what was that, young lady?"

Damn it. My hand shoots up in the air. "Selene Garcia, ma'am."

With a glare of judgment, the same glare I always get, she continues to type. *Come on, I can't live without my fix.* I retract my hand and arm and analyze them in front of my face. *Why did I raise my hand? I'm not in a schoolroom.*

The lady finishes typing. "Ah, yes. Go ahead, Mrs. Garcia." She motions her head to the side. "The elevators are behind me down the hall. Dr. Oslow is on the fifth floor."

Oh my fucking god, it worked! I fabricate a half-believable smile. "Thank you, ma'am."

That was a good smile.

It was? Are you some sort of demon that lives inside me, now? I walk toward the elevator and push the button for the third floor. *'Cause,* that *would be fucking cool.* Down the hallway, I purposefully stride. *Just march straight ahead so no one feels the need to come asking me what I'm doing on this floor.*

A group of blue, scrub-wearing nurses approaches ahead. *Oh, shit.* I dip into the nearest restroom and listen at the door. *The nurse's station is always occupied so that'll be hard to get by. Well... Demon, do you have any solutions?*

I listen for anything.

Silence. Of, fucking, course. As several footsteps and accompanying medical jargon pass the restroom, I glance above my head.

It reads: Men's Restroom.

I shrug my shoulders. *I could walk into a patient's room and tell them that I'm here to visit so I can seem less suspicious. Then I can play the* caring granddaughter *card.*

So, you are *smart. Why are you living on the street?*

"Shh, shut the fuck up," I whisper. *Why can't I turn you off?*

As I open the door, I poke my head out of the men's restroom. *No one is coming.* I dart toward the nurse's station. Walking down the hallway, a security person talks into his radio. *They're actively looking for someone. Fucking old bitch. She must have set me up.*

Bolting into the closest room with a patient, I search around their bed to find some type of identification without waking them up. *It's a man and he's the only one in the room and he didn't react to me hiding behind the curtain, so...* There is a silver metal folder at the foot of his bed. I look back at his face and vitals to make sure he doesn't wake up while I invade his personal information. *He looks... peaceful and... familiar.*

That's wrong. You're not allowed to know the patient's personal information if you're not the next of kin.

Okay, now I know you're not a demon. You're a lame imp or maybe a lower-class angel. I flip open the metal folder and start rummaging through the paperwork. *Now let's see what your name is so I can pretend to be your loving granddaughter.*

Age: 34. *Okay... Maybe I can pretend to be your daughter instead.*

Name: Mäkinen, Marko. *That's a weird name and it says here he's co-matose.*

Marko... he's here? But where's —

Well, that means I don't have to worry about waking him up. I chuckle. *So, I can ignore you, imp, and continue my train of thought.* I close the aluminum medical folder and head to the nurse's station to play the caring daughter role. *Now to get what I came for. My fucking stash in Dr. Oslow's office.* Exiting the room, I walk up to the head nurse who's sitting behind a round wooden desk.

I form the cutest, dimple-filled, smile that I can. "Excuse me, ma'am, my father is the man in a coma in that room." I point in the general direction behind me. "Can you tell me where Dr. Oslow's office is? I'd like to talk to him about my father."

I need to ask her about recent diseases that —

I bite down on my lip. *I'm ignoring you.*

She raises her head from her computer screen. "That man's only living next of kin is a thousand miles away and is a white Scandinavian male. What is your name, young lady?"

Fuck. I step back. "Oh, my name? Uh... it's S-s-Sandra Makinain."

She stood up in her blue scrubs. "Are you lost, miss?"

Shit. I stumble back. "No thank you, ma'am, I'm fine."

She turns to the nurse next to her. "Mary, call security. I think we found Miss Garcia."

Goddamn it. I turn and run down the hallway toward the elevator.

Don't run away, please, I need to ask them about the cure.

Shut the fuck up. I press the down button several times but the elevator doesn't open fast enough. *Why won't you go away?* With restraints in their hands, several men run toward me. *If you are a demon, at least, help me!*

"Stop!" A security officer appears from around the corner.

I run around the end of the hallway toward the stairs and reach for the doorknob. *Fuck me, it's locked!* One of the men comes from behind and squeezes his arms around my body.

"Get the fuck off of me! Rape! Get the fuck away!" I flail as violently as I can.

He throws me, face down, to the cold sterile floor. "No, I don't want to go!" *Save me. Someone!*

A needle penetrates my right ass cheek.

Get off of her! She doesn't need your help!

Then help me! Kill them or something! Writhing under the weight of their bodies, I arch my shoulders as a knee pressed against my back. One of them cinches leatherbound restraints around my wrists. "No, fuck! You don't have my permission. No! *Please* don't take me to —"

My vision gradually fades to black.

I can't see through her eyes anymore.... No!

Mom... Mom...

I need to save her... No!

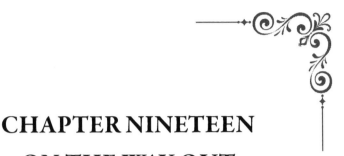

CHAPTER NINETEEN
ON THE WAY OUT

Corey slapped his palms against the viewing window. *What's going on?*

Selene's heart rate skyrocketed as she opened her eyes wide. Flailing her arms and gasping for air, glistening sweat dripped from her forehead from underneath the black helmet-like device.

I knew it, this is too dangerous. "It's Selene, she's awake. Follow me." Corey rushed out of the waiting room and opened the laboratory door. *Just wait, Selene.*

Joseph and Saara followed.

She needs me. Corey dashed to Selene's side and helped her sit up. Moisture from her dark brown hair covered his hands as he removed the headphones and monitoring device from her head.

Joseph stood at the head of her bed. "Are you okay, my dear?"

"I... was being chased." Selene placed her hand against her temple. "You know, one of *those* kinds of dreams."

Opening his eyes, Marko sat up and stabilized himself against the back of the bed as the cables dangled from his head. "I'm a little foggy still."

"Marko, did you see anything? Did you see Selene or the Doc?" Saara asked.

Straight to the point. Corey rubbed his shoulder. *...just like her jabs.*

Marko looked away as an assistant pulled out the clear tube from his arm. "Thanks for asking, sis. I'm doing fine."

"What —" Selene winced as another lab assistant removed the needle from her left arm. "What doctor?"

Dr. Kreiner lay on the other side of Marko. His delta brain waves were steady as he slept.

Joseph hovered above Dr. Kreiner then looked at Corey. "I wonder if he's in a separate dream world."

We need to get away while we have the chance. Corey stabilized Selene as she stood up. "Maybe, he's prolly better off as a guinea pig."

Saara perked up and narrowed her eyes toward Corey.

Corey flinched. *I know, sorry it was the first thing I thought of.*

Selene used Corey's shoulder to counterbalance herself. "He's going to turn himself into a guinea pig?" She listed toward Corey's chest as the cables from the head device resisted their efforts. "I'm confused."

I've got you. Corey stabilized her as she tried to stand.

"Welcome back, my dear. I see that the drugs didn't change your personality." Joseph walked toward the health monitoring devices. "Selene, did you find what you were looking for? Did you find a cure for your mother in the other universe?"

Selene shook her head. "No, but... it worked. Dr. K was right."

The room fell silent.

Corey's eyes widened. *No way.*

Marko brushed away his sister. "She's right." He turned to Selene. "You looked different. You were much less... *refined* than you are now. I called out to you but you didn't hear me, just like the pretty girls dressed in blue."

Corey turned toward Marko. "Pretty girls?"

"Yea, sometimes when we've dream-shared one of us would see pretty girls dressed in blue." Saara handed Marko his book.

Selene turned to Marko and peered into his eyes. "Mäkinen! Marko and Saara, is that y'alls last name?"

Marko nodded. "Yes, it is. So it *was* you that I saw. Why couldn't you hear me?"

Selene shrugged her shoulders. "You were in a hospital. I think you were... in a coma. It's still hazy, but I think you were next to a nurse's station. They were all —"

"Dressed in blue, right?" Color faded from Saara's rose-tinted cheeks.

Selene nodded. "I didn't see anyone else in the room. I don't get it? How did you see the same thing as Marko?"

Staring slightly in front of her, Saara furrowed her brow. "I don't know."

A third lab assistant entered the room. "Please, ladies and gentlemen, let us come in and aid Mister Marko and Miss Selene. After they regain their footing they can join you all in the cafeteria."

Corey handed Selene off to an incoming assistant. *They're relying on me to be the voice of reason.* "Yeah. We'll wait outside until you're both ready." *To get them out of here.*

"I agree." Joseph leered into Corey's eyes.

It's about that time. Corey marched back and forth with his arms crossed. *Come on, we need to hurry this up.*

Selene and Marko walked out of the glass room as Dr. Kreiner woke.

Joseph glanced down at his watch as he walked to the elevator. "Ladies and gentlemen, let's discuss what transpired."

Saara ran into the elevator ahead of everyone. "I'm starving!"

Marko clutched his book to his chest. "As always, you show the utmost concern for your older brother, sis. Should we wait for the good doctor?"

Selene rose her fingertips to her lips.

Selene must be trying to make sense of this whole thing. Poor girl. I need to get her out of here. Corey shuffled next to Marko. "Older? I thought you were twins."

Marko turned and selected the L3 button on the elevator panel. "We're twins, but I was born first, therefore *I am* the oldest."

"Don't forget the nerdiest too." Saara bounced on the heels of her feet as the elevator ascended.

Corey chuckled. *Nice one.*

Selene raised her hand without touching anyone. "So let me get this straight, both of you have a dream where you're a guy in a coma. But only one of you can see the pretty girls in blue, I mean, the nurses?"

Saara stopped bouncing.

Marko adjusted the frame of his glasses. "Where was my sister? Was anyone else in the room?"

Selene put down her hand. "Only your name was on the hospital medical paperwork." She shook her head. "No one else was in the room. And... there was something about the next of kin... but, it's still fuzzy."

Marko nodded. "I see. Thank you for confirming something that we've been trying to find an answer for, Miss Garcia."

Joseph leaned in. "It's so unbelievable, yet I don't think you'd lie. We've experienced a similar scenario. I'm sorry you weren't able to find a cure."

Selene's lips tightened. "I'm homeless, or... *she's* homeless. I used to hate dreams with her, but now I feel sorry for that version of me. Now that I know... she's real."

The elevator fell silent as the doors opened to the room with a large, brown, leather chair, fireplace, and wooden mantle. No one said a word on the way to the cafeteria.

Everyone looks so depressed. Corey followed Saara as she shuffled through the cafeteria door. *Even Saara stopped being so bubbly.* "Don't worry everyone. Joseph and I —"

Joseph nudged past Corey toward the white tables. "If this alternate reality is not a bad dream, then what we've seen, done, and who we've been is... real?"

Saara turned a white chair around, sat down, and then rested her soft, rose-tinted cheeks on her arms. "So, I'm some guy laying in a bed? That's lame as hell. I wish I was a fighter pilot or rock star."

Dr. Kreiner opened the cafeteria door, was helped by an assistant, and walked in. "Unfortunately, that's not how it works, Saara."

Selene turned to Dr. Kreiner. "Are you okay?"

Dr. Kreiner nodded. "Yes, Miss Garcia. I'm fine. But more importantly, my assistant told me the experiment was a success."

Selene sat at the white marble table. "It was. I was the same age, but Marko was an older gentleman in a coma. How is that possible, Dr. K?"

I never thought about that. Corey folded his arms and leaned against the cafeteria wall. *Let see if you can explain this.* "In our dreamshare, quantum, whatever event, I was an old man, and old man Joseph was a young short-haired stoner guy."

Marko and Saara looked up at Joseph with collective eyebrows raised.

Joseph's cheeks turned a reddish hue that lit up against his light-skinned stubble face. "Listen, I was as shocked as you. I'm trying to make sense of this whole thing, just like everyone else."

"Yes, well..." Dr. Kreiner grunted as he struggled to sit in one of the white chairs. "Mr. Godwin, were you, perhaps, a planned pregnancy or an accidental birth?"

Saara raised her head. "For shit's sake, Doc."

Joseph waved his hand. "It's okay, Saara. I was an accidental child. My parents had me while they struggled to balance family and a so-called *career*. Please, continue, my good doctor. I don't want you to leave out a single detail."

Saara gritted her teeth and nodded. "He's right. I'll shut up. Please go on."

Kr. Kreiner raised his index finger. "*If* Joseph's mother and father decided to use a contraceptive, then Joseph may have been born later in that universes timeline, versus this universes timeline where he was an accident. As such, there could be a discrepancy in age but the flow of time would remain the same. Our choices have a ripple effect that can alter the shape of reality upon our universe. Some of them have a bigger effect on your timeline, and some, have such an effect on the timeline that they alter human history."

Marko stumbled forward and braced himself against the table with his arm.

Perfect timing. Corey unfolded his arms. "Marko, are you going to be alright?"

Marko nodded. "Just give me a minute."

Corey walked up to Dr. Kreiner and leaned by his ear. "Henry, maybe we all need some fresh air. Is there a chance we could venture outside?" He stared into Dr. Kreiner's dark brown eyes. "I'm worried about you and the others."

Corey's heart rate increased. *Say yes...*

Dr. Kreiner sat back in his seat and leered back.

Corey's palms moistened. *Come on...*

Dr. Kreiner glanced out toward the group. "Perhaps you're right, Mr. Parker. I think we need to take in some fresh mountain air." He utilized Corey's larger frame to rise from his seat. "What say you, Marko and Miss Garcia?"

They nodded.

Corey handed Dr. Kreiner off to Joseph as they walked out to the foyer. *I'm counting on you.*

Joseph offered his arm to Dr. Kreiner. "Please allow me to help until the effects of the drugs wear off."

The group made their way through the foyer past the porcelain sculptures. Saara opened the red front door then narrowed her eyes toward Corey.

Corey made his way to Selene, glancing at Saara. *I know, I know. We're on our own from now on.*

AS THE GROUP VENTURED out to the cobblestone driveway, Corey escorted Selene toward the perimeter gate. *It's still open from the fresh produce delivery earlier, just like we thought.*

A searchlight from the parapet sentry aimed toward the wooded area in front of Corey. *Come on...*

Narrow beams illuminated the area ahead of the group at the edge of the woods. *Wait for it...*

After two minutes the light shifted toward the far side of the compound. *Now!*

Corey grabbed Selene's wrist and ran through the open steel perimeter gate.

Joseph restrained Dr.Kreiner to the ground. "Go, now... run away. Don't worry about me, just go!"

Marko stepped forward. "Selene! Where are you taking her?"

Saara intercepted Marko and extended her arms outward. "This is their choice, brother. *You* stay out of it."

Dr. Kreiner writhed underneath Joseph's larger frame. "Did you have to worry about the rain in your dreams, in that other reality?"

What is he getting at? Corey pulled Selene as fast as he could toward the surrounding woods. *We only have two minutes until we're noticed.*

Dr. Kreiner reached out with his hand as Joseph held him down. "You never worried about the acidity of the rain in that reality because they found a solution to it! Think about the lives we could save... Selene's mother! You're abandoning this universe, Mr. Parker!"

Consolidating clouds of darkness smothered the remaining moonlight. A siren rang out over the bullhorns that surrounded the looming gray parapets at the corners of the compound.

Corey gritted his teeth. *What's his point?*

Selene looked back. "What about Joseph? It's wrong to leave him behind."

If we can make it to the woods then we can make it to civilization. A radiant beam of light cast its elongated shadows against the grassy exterior. He ran faster.

No one pursued.

Not one gun fired.

Corey turned his head. *Good, we need the head start.* His heart pounded. "This was his plan, he's been playing the part and was willing to stay behind so we could escape. I... misjudged him."

We made it. Corey trampled over dead, frail branches and pine cones at the edge of the woods. A light from behind exposed a shadow ahead. *What the —*

The earth underneath his feet vanished. *Shit.*

Corey tumbled down a small ravine. Small branches, dirt, and leaves flew around them as he rolled. *Oh, crap, we're going to get caught.*

Selene fell alongside him.

Corey looked up the hill as they hit the shallow bottom. *No one's following us... for now.*

Selene jumped up from the floor and backed away from Corey.

Corey walked away from the mansion toward the chirping of cicadas and rustling branches. "Come on, Selene, we've gotta go."

She raised her fingertips to her lips. "I don't remember worrying about rain. I have vivid memories of sleeping in dark alleys, doing horrible things... but not rain that hurts, massive tsunamis, or sickness like the one that's spreading through Europe right now. It's the same sickness that mom has."

A flash of light blinked in the distance beyond the top of the ravine.

They're on to us. Corey stumbled forward and leaned his hand against a large tree. "We need to go."

Cracking electrons ripped through the sky. *Shit. We won't make it for long without protection for our skin. We need to find shelter along the way.*

Thunder rumbled across the countryside and vibrated his chest.

Selene slammed her hands against her ears. "I can't."

We don't have time for this. Corey raised his arms. "What can we do about your mom, dream-share? That's nuts."

Selene leaned against the roots of a large tree. "You *are* like my big brother, after all."

What's that supposed to mean? Corey stared at her small frame silhouetted amongst the small branches and fallen leaves against the growing darkness.

"He runs away from his family when things get difficult, too." She sniffled.

I'd never abandon my family, like... they *did.* Corey walked over to her, knelt, and put his hand on hers. "I know that you're scared but we need to get back to civilization."

Selene gazed into his eyes. "I'm not sure if I can trust Dr. K. He's hiding something from us. But... I can't trust you, either. I'm... different than you or the others. I know I am, yet..." She wrapped her arms around herself and hummed. "You're scared, just the same."

Barking dogs and men yelling echoed from the direction of the mansion.

What is she saying? Corey released her hand and stood up. *Of course, I'm scared.* "Either way, we need to go."

Selene shook her head, faced the mansion, and then wiped the debris of shattered leaves from her white sweatpants. "God be with you, Corey. I'm sure there's a plan for me, but I can't say the same for the rest of the universe. I *need* to find the truth for myself. I *need* to try... even if I have to do it alone, for mom."

She scaled the ravine and wandered back toward the bright lights.

"Selene!" Corey looked up from the shadows.

Corey paced back and forth. *What is she doing?* Looking back at the darkness of the woods, he punched a nearby tree as hard as he could. "Fuck!" The intense sting from his knuckles exacerbated his rage. *Of course, I'm scared.* Multiple flashes of light danced close to the woods. *What am I doing?* A putrid wind ran its fingers through the curled hairs on Corey's head. *God's plan... we should worry about Henry's plan, first.*

Corey trudged up the ravine and met with several guards. *I'm trapped here.* They escorted him back to the mansion as he meandered back through the gate toward the cobblestone entrance. *No one will come.* As he approached the red door, no one said a word. *Abandoned... again.*

Saara stared at him.

Joseph helped Dr. Kreiner on his feet. "Yes, well, my good doctor. I thought the kids deserved to make their own way. I hope you understand."

Marko comforted Selene as she walked into the mansion.

Corey's feet dragged and his shoulders slouched as the guards left him at the foyer. *I'm fucking useless.*

Dr. Kreiner dusted himself off. "Yes, well, you're surprisingly menacing, Mr. Godwin."

Joseph lowered his head. "Sorry."

I failed you... old man. Corey shuffled up the staircase in silence.

He walked into his suite slash prison cell.

The heavy dark wooden door closed shut behind him.

SITTING IN THE CUSHIONED loveseat of his bedroom, Corey stared out the window late into the midnight hour. *What am I going to do, now?*

A knock came from the door which broke him out of his thoughts. *It's prolly a guard, checking on me.*

As Corey opened the door, Dr. Kriner stood at the far side of the hallway. "Mr. Parker, can I have a word with you?"

He's going to lock us down indefinitely, I'm positive. "Sure," Corey said.

As they ventured down the staircase into the main area, Dr. Kreiner leaned against the porcelain fountain. *Did Joseph put too much weight on him?* "Are you okay?" Corey asked.

Dr. Kreiner nodded. "I'm fine, Mr. Parker. These experiments take a toll on the mind. Additionally, my body isn't in perfect health, I'm afraid." Gathering himself, he walked into the side room left of the main entrance. "Please follow me."

I don't have a choice... anymore. Corey followed the doctor into the secret elevator room. A thick wooden desk anchored the middle of the room in front of a freshly lit fireplace. Radio's and relics from the early twentieth century lined the top of the red brick mantle. *Nothing in here looks like it's been made in the past twenty years.*

Dr. Kreiner sat in a brown, leather, throne-like chair on the other side of the wooden desk. "My father sat in this chair... for *many* late nights... trying to solve the most complex problems of his time," he chuckled as he ran his fingers across the age-worn upholstery.

That's the first time I've heard him laugh. Corey maneuvered in front of the fireplace mantle. "Are you laughing because we're stuck here as your little guinea pigs or because of something else?"

Dr. Kreiner composed himself. "I'm sorry, I just found some personal irony... humorous." He cleared his throat. "I brought you here because this room contains a landline to the outside." He pointed to the phone sitting at the edge of the hefty mahogany desk.

Corey turned his attention to the dated, red rotary phone. *Does that old-ass thing still work?* His eyes toggled between Dr. Kreiner and the phone. That's *my chance to call for help, but...* "Why would you tell me that? Is this some sort of test of loyalty or some psycho head-shrink bullshit?"

Dr. Kreiner leaned forward. "My father worked for the government thus *this* phone is a classified line to some of the most influential people in your chain of command, Mr. Parker."

An armed man walked in and stood by the entrance. "Sir, he's waiting on the other line."

Dr. Kreiner nodded, and then the armed man walked out of the room.

Corey massaged his throbbing knuckles. *Why did he bring me here?* "Who —"

As the old red phone rang and rattled against itself at the edge of the desk, Dr. Kreiner remained stoic. "I believe it's for you, Mr. Parker. Please, answer it."

The phone rattled and rang again. *No one knows that I'm here... so who...* Corey inched toward the phone and picked it up.

"Hello, Petty Officer Second Class Parker," a familiar voice said.

Corey's eyes lit up. *I know that voice.* "Is that you...? Captain Crawford?"

Captain Crawford laughed, "What's the matter sailor did you forget the sound of your skipper's voice? I'm not issuing orders from the 1 M.C. but I assure you, Petty Officer, it's me."

No fucking way... how? "Sorry, sir. I'm just shocked to hear your voice."

Mumbled military conversations echoed in the background. "You're telling me. I was equally shocked when the Commodore briefed me that one of my sailors was pulled from TAD orders in Waco, Texas for his expertise in matters of national security."

Corey's eyes widened. *National security. What's he talking about?* "Sir, I don't —"

"Now, after I bragged to the Commodore that my sailor was one in a million, he questioned why you hadn't made Chief yet," he said.

Corey raised an eyebrow. *I wish I was a Chief... but...* "I'm not up for Chief, yet... I'm only a second class, sir."

"Well, I can't have a representative of my ship be a mere Second Class, no disrespect, but I think we need to fast track you a little. The Commodore agreed, so, as of this moment, you're a Petty Officer First

Class. And, when the time comes, later this year, you'll be at the head of the line for Chief. How does *that* sound?" he asked.

What!? I can't believe it. I can't wait to tell Charles, he'll be so mad... Oh, shit! "Sir, that's fantastic news and I'd be honored, but Charles... I mean, Petty Officer Carter was with me on the night we..." *Damn, should I tell him? ...No. Not now.* "Did he make it back to base, sir? Or back to the ship?"

The phone went silent.

Corey turned to Dr. Kreiner. *Did he have anything to do with this?*

Dr. Kreiner sank into the brown leather chair and stared at the ceiling.

"Yes, of course. Petty Officer Carter was accounted for on the muster sheet today," Captain Crawford said.

Corey leaned against the desk and exhaled. "Oh, thank god, sir. You don't know worried I was about —"

"Yes, well, I'm sure you're being pulled in all directions due to your newfound responsibilities, Petty Officer *First Class* Parker. We're all proud of you here and look forward to hearing about your continued success. Remember, I'm counting on you to represent my ship, and the US Navy, with honor, courage, and perseverance," Captain Crawford said.

Corey's smiled. *This is so much to take in.* "Roger that and thank you, sir."

Captain Crawford hung up.

Corey placed the red phone receiver back on the aged base. *They're all counting on me... what am I doing?* "I've been so wrong, Henry..."

Dr. Kreiner stood up and walked around the desk toward Corey. "I think we've both been dishonest with each other. It's late, I'd like to meet you all back in this room, tomorrow. I've explained bits and pieces but it's time for you all to understand what's truly at stake."

So, something was *off about this whole thing.* "What's at stake?" Corey asked.

Dr. Kreiner put his hand on Corey's shoulder "Right now everyone has a different agenda. We'll meet back here tomorrow morning. Until then, I need you to step up and be a leader. Can you do that for me?"

Corey tightened his lip. *Why me?* "Even after what Joseph and I did?"

Dr. Kreiner escorted Corey to the door. "You did that out of fear. I would have done the same thing. It's my fault. I thought you wouldn't understand so I kept information from you. Your superiors have faith in you and..." He nodded. "I should too."

My foster parents... Charles... Chief. Corey gritted his teeth. *They've always trusted me to do the right thing.*

Dr. Kreiner held the door open. "Tomorrow is a start for a new reality. Your decisions mark your path to a different future. Fortune or failure, it's up to what you do from now onward."

He's right. It's up to me. Corey nodded. "I'll give it my best." *For everyone.*

CHAPTER TWENTY
THE APPROACHING DAWN

After breakfast, Selene followed the others into the room with the elevator. Kindling wood crackled in the fireplace, while a hint of pine rose from the warm glow. On the top of the desk in the middle of the room lay five clear cards with microchips embedded in their centers. *Isn't he worried that someone will take them?* Selene poked her head out from behind Joseph as they gathered around the large wooden desk.

"Do you think the Doc made those for us?" Saara asked.

Marko adjusted his glasses. "It would seem like a logical conclusion, sis. Although, the timing *is* odd."

Selene glanced at Marko's empty hands. *Where's his book?*

Dr. Kreiner walked in. "Ah, I'm glad you're all here. Please, each of you take an access card and follow me."

"You're seriously going to give us the ability to move about freely, my good doctor?" Joseph asked.

Corey grabbed an access card then tapped Joseph on the shoulder. "Of course, old man, we're not prisoners here, remember?"

He seems to be in a better mood after what happened yesterday. I guess we all needed to rest. Selene reached down, picked one up, and then stepped aside. *With this, I can ask Dr. N about how she chemically modified the Dimethyltryptamine.* She raised the clear access card to her lips.

Maybe they'll let me review the compounds needed to create a cure for mom.

Dr. Kreiner walked to the bookshelf and pulled a book halfway out. The bookshelf slid into the wall to reveal an elevator. "This way, please. I want to make sure we're clear about what's at stake."

Selene followed Dr. Kreiner and the others into the elevator. *Marko was right. That was cool.* She smiled. *Like the old horror movies, mom would let me watch with her. She said it was because I'd get scared.*

Once they all huddled in the spacious metal elevator, Dr. Kreiner used his access card then selected the L1 button. "Your access cards will give you the ability to go down to the L2 level, the main level on L3, and outside if you wish. Unfortunately, you're restricted from going down to the L1 level."

Selene tilted her head. *But... we're going down to level one right now.*

Corey chuckled. "Why? What's down there? Are you making weapons of mass destruction? Or creating alien-human hybrids? Or —"

Dr. Kreiner turned to Corey and narrowed his eyes. "I'm going to show you." He rose his index finger. "This one time. So that you understand the weight of your decisions and so you can see that I have nothing to hide from you. Maybe... you'll trust me."

He's serious. Selene clutched the access card to her chest. *No matter what happens.* She shook her head. *I have to save mom... even if it means I'm interfering with God's plan.*

The elevator came to a stop.

The metal doors opened.

A limestone cavernous underground hallway lay ahead of Selene and the others. *It smells like... earth, but not like South Texas soil.* She shivered. *How far down did we go?*

Dr. Kreiner walked out into the corridor. Pipes and electrical cabling lined the walls. "Yesterday's experiment gave me the data that I needed to make a new hypothesis. I knew that your conscience resonated with the very cells of your being, your DNA. However, Saara and Marko's experience challenged the core of my research. There was no way to verify that what Saara saw was the same as Marko's or that it was a figment of her subconscious. Now... I believe that Saara and Marko occupy the same body."

The light down here is dull... unlike the bright white laboratories above. Selene raised her hand to her lips and looked at Dr. Kreiner. "Are you saying that the Marko lying in a coma, from the other universe, has Saara's DNA too?"

Dr. Kreiner pushed his glasses up the bridge of his nose. "That is exactly what I've implied. In very rare cases during the embryonic stage of birth, one of the fraternal twins can absorb the other. The outcome from this is that the child born will have two sets of DNA."

Saara hit Marko on the arm. "Eww. You jerk face."

Marko grabbed his shoulder and turned away from Saara. "Ow! You act like I had something to do with that in a different universe. It's nature, deal with it, sis."

Saara scratched her head. "Wait, so Doc, does that mean that I'm dead in that other place?"

"Technically, no, since you're DNA still exists. This is different from being dead," Dr. Kreiner said.

"How do you know such things?" Joseph asked.

"With tests, of course." Dr. Kreiner walked to the first door and stood with his hand open to his side.

Along the wall that led to the room were half windows where the bottom half was obstructed with reinforced steel. Selene peeked into the room. In the center of the room, three people lay on metal surgical tables with the top of their heads facing each other. *Are they dreamsharing, too?*

Dr. Kreiner scanned his access card on the outside door panel and entered the room. "The precious data needed to form my hypotheses stem from these rooms. My recent theory states that the resonant delta waves, which your conscience rides on, will try to find the closest harmonic frequency available in this universe... or the next."

Selene stood at the entrance. *One man was short with lighter skin and tattoos along his left arm. One older woman had blond hair and a tan. The last one was a tall African-American guy but wasn't much older than me.* She reached for her head. *They all wore devices on their heads, but they are different than the ones that Marko and I wore. These look... like prototypes. Wires dangled and components were exposed. We had electrodes... these look like... probes. Inserted right into their br —*

"Miss Garcia, are you alright?" Dr. Kreiner stood in front of Selene.

Selene looked at Dr. Kreiner's face as the group glared. *Oh, I must have... never mind.* "Sorry. Please continue, Dr. K. Who are these people?"

"Volunteers." Dr. Kreiner picked up their medical documentation folder that was set on the steel table at the far wall. "These test— people are seeing if they can dream-share with different languages. What happens in the unified reality? Do they keep the same language barrier? Interesting research to say the least."

"How long have they been under, Doc?" Saara wandered around the bodies.

Dr. Kreiner thumbed through the documentation. "Approximately... one hundred and thirty-two hours, thirteen minutes and..." He looked down at his black watch. "Eighteen seconds."

"Henry." Corey hovered over the African-American man. "And in that time, how long have they been dream-sharing?"

Dr. Kreiner sighed. "Unfortunately, Mr. Parker. I'm still waiting on lightning to strike."

Selene glanced up at the conduit that ran across the ceiling. *There's no way that lightning will reach down here.*

The steady beeps from their monitoring devices broke the stillness.

"Can anyone tell me what happens if you're in the middle of viewing an alternate reality, via the dream state, and you're about to die?" Dr. Kreiner asked.

I've been scared to death a few times seeing how she *lives.* Selene raised her hand. "I wake up."

Corey nodded. "Yeah, I've dreamed of falling off a building or I wake up a split second before I crash into something. I've hit my head on my rack a few times because I sat up too fast."

"Precisely, Miss Garcia and Mr. Parker, your consciousness collapses back to this reality. It returns to the physical brain that housed the original frequency entwining the universal quantum wave." Dr. Kreiner placed his hand on the end of the metallic table where one of the bodies slept. "Now, what do you think would happen if the opposite occurs? If *you* die here while your conscience is viewing an alternate reality."

Selene shrugged her shoulders. *I don't know this one.*

"This way please." Dr. Kreiner walked out of the room and down the hall.

Several armed men marched by in a single file line. At the end of the hall two heavily armed men guarded a large wide steel door. *Are we going to head in there?*

Dr. Kreiner scanned his access card again and walked into another room. Obstructed by canvas pull-down shades, all the windows were covered.

Against the far wall were massively oversized metallic drawers. *I've seen those before... on a science field trip.* Selene tightened her lip. *Why would he need* this *down here?*

Dr. Kreiner walked over to the nearest drawer, unlocked the handle, and pulled it out. A blue cloth was draped over a body-shaped mass.

Joseph backed away. "What exactly are you doing down here?"

"I told you that I'd show you everything." Dr. Kreiner turned. "When you die while you're peering into an alternate universe... your conscience is lost... It has no physical body to return to so it merges with a similar harmonic frequency among the quantum wave. In other words —"

Selene pushed her way past Dr. Kreiner to the cloth-covered body and removed the edge of it to expose whatever horrors were hidden beneath. *This is real-life human trials, Joseph.*

An elderly Native American woman's wrinkled brown face lay smiling on the metal slab drawer. *She seems... at peace.* "It merges with our alternate self. Isn't that right, Dr. K?"

"What? No way," Corey said.

Dr. Kreiner narrowed his eyes. "Astute as ever, Miss Garcia. Yes, this is how we explain people with *old souls.* Or if they have an innate skill for something that they never tried before; a *natural* if you will. That person has incorporated memories or abilities from an alternate version of themselves. Unbeknownst or *otherwise.*"

Selene covered the elderly woman's face back with the blue cloth. *I won't let this happen to mom.* She gritted her teeth.

Dr. Kreiner slid the drawer back in and locked the handle. He walked out of the morgue and further down the dimly lit corridor remaining far away from the heavily guarded area. He scanned his card, again, on the panel outside a dulled black door.

Four male fully clothed volunteers slept on separate flat metal beds, as Selene peered through the window. Instead of dream cap devices, tubes dangled from their arms which led to liquid-filled bags that hung by the wall. Pink-hued sustenance ran through some of the tubes and a light-brown fluid ran through others. *Is that for nutrients? How long have they been there?*

At the edge of each occupied metallic slab was a plastic sign that read:

Dimethyltryptamine Test Sample 7

A scientist dressed in blue scrubs, gloves, and a white mask handled vials of light-brown liquid in the corner of the room. Selene poked her head out from behind Dr. Kreiner. *It's Dr. N!*

Corey walked in ahead of everyone. "I don't see health monitoring equipment. What did *these* folks volunteer for, Henry?"

Dr. Nguyen turned in her seat, hopped off, and placed the vial of liquid in a plastic bin next to her notebook. "Oh, Doctor Kreiner. I didn't know you were bringing... guests down here."

Joseph walked around to the furthest volunteer and poked her side with his finger. The volunteer physically reacted to his prod. "Yes, well, at least *these* are alive. What dastardly thing are you using *them* for, my dear doctor?"

He's agitated. His breathing is accelerated. Selene tilted her head. *Has Joseph never performed a science experiment before?*

"Dr. Nguyen, if you please." Dr. Kreiner extended his hand toward the sleeping individuals.

Dr. Nguyen's olive-toned arm reached back for the vial and presented it to Joseph. "As you've seen, the Dimeth — I mean, DMT, is effective enough to provide the sedation and lucidity to help increase your chances to dream-share." She brought the measured vial back in front of her bright, brown eyes. "Unfortunately, there are still some residual side effects."

Is she trying to see the molecules with her eyes? Selene nodded. "She's right. When I woke up, it was like I was still asleep. I was unable to regain control of my limbs for a while."

"And I was exhausted, even though we slept for several hours," Marko said.

Dr. Nguyen clutched the vial in her small hand. "Well, what *you* had was an extract from test sample six. Once these volunteers wake up, I'll hopefully have test sample seven ready for you all."

"Ready for *us*?" Joseph asked.

"Thank you, Dr. Nguyen, we'll get out of your way." Dr. Kreiner motioned to the group. "Last stop, follow me." He walked out into the corridor and stood in front of a room just before the guarded tall double door.

Selene squeezed her lips together. *I guess we're not allowed in there.*

He stepped through the opening on the left. There were no windows. Instead, several monitors were covering every wall of the room. Against the center wall, a singular large screen was powered off.

What does he view on that one? Selene wandered into the room and looked at the bottom of the remaining video screens. *They're from different geographical coordinates across the world.*

In the middle sat a long wooden conference table. Two remote controls rested at the edge of the table. The various videos displayed the inside homes or warehouses, wooded areas, deserts, and arctic environments.

Dr. Kreiner closed the door behind him, picked up a remote control, and walked to the front of the room with the large blank monitor at his back. "Please observe this video." He pointed to the top right monitor in the farthest corner of the room.

The video displayed a wooded area from an unknown latitude and longitude.

Small trees and some branches off of the larger trees moved with the wind. Selene squinted. "Dr. K, I don't see —"

"Please, keep observing." Dr. Kreiner turned to the video and looked on.

A grayish blurred image faded into view. As the picture cleared the ethereal silhouette of several people walked across the middle of the woods. The ghastly image transformed back into the woods again.

They looked like... ghosts. Selene's eyes widened. *Mom said ghosts weren't real. God sent our souls to heaven or hell.*

Another video showed a person laying on a gray couch inside of an upscale metropolitan office, talking to a female therapist.

Joseph scoffed as he pointed to the therapy session. "Now, I know that's illegal, my good doctor."

Dr. Kreiner pointed the slender black remote toward the monitor. "Please listen, Mr. Godwin." Their voices became louder as the volume increased.

"When did human rights activist, Nelson Mandela, die?" the slender well-dressed therapist asked.

"He died on a bed in his villa around two thousand and thirteen," the man said.

She wrote in her notebook. "No, Mr. Slater. Nelson Mandela perished in a prison, as he awaited trial, in the 1980s."

"What?" the man asked.

Joseph turned to Corey. "I remember that day. I was in grade school and we had to write a paper on his legacy. The teacher rolled in an old television so we could witness the funeral and everything. What is that guy talking about?"

Jotting a few sentences in her notebook, the therapist continued, "It's alright, Mr. Slater, let's move on. In nineteen thirty-two American aviator, Charles Lindbergh's twenty-month-old son was kidnapped. Whatever happened to the child? Please take your time as this was a long time ago."

"I remember this one. The child had been killed not long after he was abducted, I think it was a blow to the head. Tragic. I can still see the headline documenting the event's anniversary from a magazine I read not too long ago," he said.

She leaned in. "I'm sorry Mr. Slater. It remains one of the longest cold cases in American history. Unfortunately, for the Lindbergh family, the child was never seen again."

The man sat up. "That's impossible. I remember it clear as day, goddamn it!"

Dr. Kreiner paused the video. "This is what happens when our universe and an alternate universe bleed into each other. Alternate memories mix with our own. It's happening more frequently, I'm afraid, with very bleak consequences." He pointed at the screen on the back wall behind everyone.

The group turned around in unison.

It's a video from the sky... looking down at the ocean somewhere. Selene squeezed the access card in her pocket. *I don't like this.*

An aerial view from *something* flew through dark, ominous clouds. As the camera shook in the prevailing winds, sporadic blue and purple lightning flew across the screen.

"Where the hell is that thing headed, Doc?" Saara asked.

Joseph crossed his arms. "The Bermuda Triangle, I'd wager."

"Not quite, Mr. Godwin. This is drone footage from the Indian Ocean south of the equator," Dr. Kreiner said.

Soaring above the deep blue water, small white caps crashed against the oncoming towering waves. A purple-hued ring of lightning created a small crack against the dark clouds. The drone video screen shook violently before a cloudy black image appeared.

Selene moved behind Joseph. *Even during the biggest country storms, I've never seen lightning that went sideways and stayed for that long.*

Bursting light flashed across the screen before mysterious purple lightning opened a portal.

Flying toward the reddish-purple glow, the drone disappeared into the portal and straight through to the other side.

Smash!

As it crashed against a large, rocky, black structure, the cracked video screen tumbled to the bottom of whatever it hit. Glowing red rock seeped down toward the camera, enveloping it. The video cut to static.

The room fell silent. *What was that?*

Dr. Kreiner pointed with his remote and paused the video. "It hit a volcano. In the middle of the Indian Ocean where nothing should exist. An active volcano from another reality. More of these anomalies are happening. More people are peering into another universe, like you five, but I don't think it'll stop there. The human brain can't attune to two frequencies at the same time. One universe will have to give."

Selene stared at the static-filled monitor. *He wouldn't reveal this unless he needed our help.* She stepped forward. "What do you need from us?"

"You five are special. You've got an unexplainable pull to that other reality. I'd love to study the Godwin phenomenon further but we don't have the luxury of time," Dr. Kreiner said.

Selene looked up at Joseph. *When did he —*

"My good doctor, you can't be serious? I don't think I heard you right." Joseph's cheeks turned bright red against his light skin.

Dr. Kreiner nodded. "It was your idea, after all, Mr. Godwin. Your name will be attached to the greatest phenomenon of the modern world since Tesla's theory of relativity."

Joseph ran his fingers through the greying brown hair and walked toward the corner of the room.

Selene glanced at Joseph. *He's speechless.*

Dr. Kreiner shook his head. "I need time to find answers. There is a possibility that if I can understand the harmonic resonance of the other universe then I could devise a way to avoid this calamity."

But... Selene raised her hand.

Dr. Kreiner glanced at Selene. "And of course, in the process, discover the cure for your mother. The longer I can remain in that universe the more knowledge I can accumulate."

"Is the other *you* a scientist, too, Henry?" Corey asked.

I never thought about that. Selene put her hand down to her side.

Dr. Kreiner pushed his glasses up the bridge of his nose. "I don't know. Unfortunately, I couldn't make contact with my *other* self. But I'm certain with all five of you I'll be able to make a stronger connection."

Selene narrowed her eyes. *He's not telling us everything.* "Are you being completely honest with us, Dr. K?"

"You're too perceptive for your age, Miss Selene." Dr. Kreiner sighed. "Yes. I left out *one* key piece. I'll need you to remain in a sleep stasis for at least... one hundred and sixty-eight hours."

Marko shook his head. "Insanity. That's one full week, doctor."

Corey threw his hands up. "You know, why not go for a month or hell, a year, Henry?"

Dr. Kreiner's face turned somber.

The color went from his cheeks. Selene shivered. *This isn't good.*

Dr. Kreiner placed the remote control down on the conference room table. "That's because, Mr. Parker, we don't have a year. According to the data from the surveillance videos, the frequency of clashes between universes, and the rate of sub-atomic decay instabilities, we only have *three months* before the collisions become irreversible."

Oh, no. Mom. Selene raised her fingertips to her lips. *I won't be scared.* She tightened her lips. *Even if I have to live with... her.* She clenched her hand into a fist. *She's lost... and angry. I won't let her universe become my reality.*

Joseph emerged from the corner of the room. "If it's so damn important, then why the hell didn't you abduct us, like our good-for-nothing government, and strap us down?! You've got the muscle for it, doctor."

Selene stepped back and scrunched her right shoulder to her right ear. *Joseph's got a point, but why is he so angry?*

Dr. Kreiner shook his head. "Please, calm down. It doesn't work like that, Mr. Godwin. I've theorized that your pull to the other reality is based on a need. Not a fear. Something provokes, appeals, guides you to that timeline. Forcing you isn't an option, otherwise..." He walked out of the room.

Something... guides me? Selene followed the others into the damp corridor toward the large elevator. *I don't know if God's plan involves another universe, but...*

Dr. Kreiner stopped at the end of the cavernous entryway and turned around. "I need for you five to make a choice. I'll give you tonight to decide. It's sudden, but we don't have time to waste. I'll be in Sleep Synchronization Test Facility Four at nine AM exactly, awaiting your decision."

Is this just another adventure? Selene tightened her lips.

Dr. Kreiner gazed into Selene's eyes. "Will you let our universe, and the things that you hold dear, crash and burn like the drone in the video, or will you help me cross over and save our reality?"

Selene nodded. *I don't know if I can do it alone but... I'll find a way, mom.*

CHAPTER TWENTY-ONE

ONLY THE STRONGEST WILL

L ater that evening, after they all dispersed to their rooms, Corey walked into the luxurious bathroom and set his clear access card on the counter of the gaudy vanity. *No longer prisoners, unless we choose to be.* The stillness of the night unsettled his heart. *They're relying on me.* Scrutinizing his reflection in the mirror of the bathroom, Corey focussed on his deep, dark-brown eyes. *My Captain, the Chief, Charles, Selene... the twins... and even... the old man.* As he ran his palms underneath the running water, he washed his face hoping the cold refreshing splash would rejuvenate his spirit. *My country... this whole damn universe. I can't abandon them...* Corey dried the moisture off his face with a white cotton hand towel. *So, why do I feel... off?* He shook his head. *What's wrong with me?*

His breaths became shallow.

Sweat beaded on his forehead.

His heart rate continued to rise.

Shit... It's coming. Corey clenched his eyes shut. *Stop.* He inhaled. He slowed his chest to decompress. *Why can't I control this, after all this time?* His heartbeat reverberated in his temples as he exhaled.

The pills Henry gave me! Corey's eyes shot open as he rushed to the mahogany nightstand by the bed. He pulled the bottle of Amitriptyline from the wooden drawer. *But... can I trust him?* As he hesitated, the pills rattled inside the bottle from his unstable grip. *If everyone else can, then...* He opened the container, ran back to the restroom, and swallowed two pills with a handful of tap water. He closed his eyes as he splashed water on his face. Corey tried to use the chilled spigot of liquid as a barrier to shield the external calamity from his mind. *It's not working.* He furrowed his brow. *I can't rely on pills, I need to calm myself. Think...*

A sweet gentle woman's voice called out to him. *Whose voice is that?*

Images of children playing, laughter, and emotions like love, pride, and joy invaded his thoughts like a bayonet piercing through his childhood trauma. *Are these...*

His heart calmed.

The interval between his breaths slowed.

A tear ran down Corey's sturdy bronze-tinted cheeks. *What was that?* He sniffled. *They're memories? But, whose —*

A knock came from the wooden door of his chilled, luxurious suite.

As Corey opened his eyes, the images and voices faded away. "Who is it? If it's you, Henry, I thought you said that we had all night to think about it." Dashing toward the door he wiped the tears with the back of his hand.

"I need to talk to you. May I come in, please?" A soft female voice asked.

That sounds like... He opened the door.

With her hands behind her back, Saara stood at the threshold and, through her hazel-colored eyes, looked up at Corey. The smell of lavender wafted into the room. Her vibrant red hair lay on her shoulders in contrast to the bright, white, long-sleeve top she wore. "Am I interrupting anything?"

Why didn't she just burst in? Something's gotta be on her mind. Corey scratched his head. "No, please come in."

She waltzed in and sat at the edge of his bed. "I've never been down to the bottom level. The Doc must trust us a lot... or the situation is that... fucked. It's a lot to take in ya know?"

Tell me about it. Corey closed the door then sat at the other end of the bed. "Really? I assumed you knew more than us since you and Marko had been stuck here for longer."

Saara laid back on the bed with her hands behind her head. "My brother... is the main reason I'm still here."

She's cute when she's not hyper-aggressive. Corey pulled a pillow from the headboard and laid across the bed parallel to Saara. "What would make you think that?"

She turned to Corey. "He's got a photographic memory and I don't have anything special about me... besides being half a comatose guy." She sighed. "I just want to be useful to the Doc."

That is *cool, but...* "Saara, I think you're being too hard on yourself. I think this whole situation is too much for anyone to take in. Besides, you're special to me." Corey jolted his head over to Saara. "I mean you're special to all of us. We're in this together, right?" *Smooth one, idiot.* He half-smiled. *Charles prolly would've clowned on me hard for that one.*

She scooted her fairy-like figure closer to Corey. "I know why you did what you did. I thought you were a coward, running away like a scared little kid. But... Selene, right?"

His heart rate increased. *Another panic attack?* Corey exhaled. *No.* "Yeah... I thought I was doing the right thing by her. I should have talked it out with you and your brother. Joseph and I found listening devices in our rooms and —"

Saara laughed, "Yeah, dummy. What if we were sleeping and shouted out something of importance or plotted to kill the Doc? If you were that rich and let strangers walk around your mansion freely, wouldn't you want all the surveillance you could?"

She's got a point. Corey glanced up toward the ceiling. "I guess... you're right."

Saara slid toward him, again. "Ya know, Corey, I'm kind of scared about tomorrow. Us... saving this universe. Maybe... I'll be able to dance in the rain. My mom told me that's what they used to do, before... when it wasn't snowing outside, of course."

"And find the cure for Selene's mother." *Maybe this is the place where I belong.* Corey turned his head to find Saara's face was inches away. *With her...*

As Saara smiled, her dimples sank into her supple fair-skinned cheeks. "You *really* are a good man."

Hints of lavender from her being intoxicated his senses.

Placing her hand on top of his, she whispered, "We're in this together, right?"

"Yeah..." Corey's heart fluttered. "I won't let anything happen... to you."

He squeezed her hand as he leaned in.

Saara's hazel eyes narrowed as her mouth drew closer to his.

His palms moistened. *I can't believe it.*

The warm softness of her lips brushed against his full, brown —

An expanse of blinding light shot across the room.

Corey closed his eyes and turned away from her face. *What the hell? It's that light again.* He winced. *Shit. I blew it.* He blinked to regain his sight. *She's going to think I'm disgusted with her or something. Damn.*

"Fuck. Sorry, it's not you... I had something in my eye," Saara freed her hand from Corey's and wiped her eyes.

No way. Corey sat up. "Saara, did you see that bright-ass light, too?"

Saara sat up alongside him. "What? I thought only me and my brother could see it." She shook her head. "We only saw it every few years but then it's started to happen more often..." Staring at the corner of the room, her smile evaporated. "...recently."

Where did it come from? Corey shook his head. "Thank god, I thought I was going crazy. If you and Marko can see it, then maybe the others can —"

Saara stood up. "Sorry, Corey, I didn't mean to come in here and get all mushy." Her cheeks turned a reddish hue. "I just wanted to tell you that I planned on going through with it. I hope you're going to be there too."

She darted to the door and opened it.

Corey stood up. *Crap... did I say something wrong?* "Okay, Saara... you can count on me. Maybe, afterward, do you think we can... continue our conversation?"

Saara looked back.

Is she going to smack me, again? Corey flinched.

She nudged his thick brown shoulder with her small pale fist and gazed into his deep dark eyes. "I'd like that."

She closed the door behind her as she exited his suite.

Corey slouched down on the bed with a blank expression on his face. *What. The hell. Just happened?*

JOSEPH OPENED HIS EYES and looked over to the silver and gold filigreed clock on the wall of his suite. *Midnight... great.* He turned over in the luxurious king-sized bed and stared at the ceiling. *Is that what I'll be remembered for in the final three months of existence? Known in the scientific community... isn't the same as being world-renowned.* He kicked the thousand-thread-count sheets off to the side of his feet. *What did I* think *would happen?* Footsteps pattered and wooden floorboards creaked outside of his door. *I'm not the only one who's still contemplating, I see.* Sitting up, he flicked on the light from an etched porcelain lamp atop the nightstand by his bed. He surveyed each corner of the room. *No matter what I do or say, he's going to record it.* He glanced at the access card on the dresser, beside the pack of cigarettes, above his discarded white clothes. *Let's find out who's full of shit, doctor.*

Joseph exited his room, scuttled down the stairway, and opened the red door in the main foyer of the extravagant mansion. No one approached. The distant parapet searchlights kept their gaze on the edge of the woods. He pulled out a cigarette, lit it, and then wandered toward the closed perimeter fence. The searchlight scanned the fence entrance after two minutes. *Like clockwork.* He blew smoke into the cloudless moonlit sky during the small hours of the night. The cobblestone path that led to the access panel of the front gate reflected the moonlight like the stage lights on opening night. *People* always *have their agendas.* He pulled the access card from his pocket and swiped it.

Joseph's eyes widened as the blank bulb on the access panel turned green. A locking mechanism clanked as the steel gate hinged open. He flicked the singed cigarette butt down at the cobblestones beside his feet, tightened his lips, and shoved the gate outward. Rubbing metal screeched out into the barren driveway ahead that extended beyond the darkness of the night.

No bullhorns sounded.

Joseph stood and stared out into the hills and mountainous backdrop. *Come on.*

The searchlight panned over to Joseph. He smiled. *I knew it.* He shielded his eyes from the light. *It's not as bright as the first time.*

The searchlight turned away.

No alarms rang out.

Only the stagnant night air remained.

Joseph clenched his fist as he scoffed. *Why should I risk being here for one-second longer?*

As he took a step forward, one of the armed guards ran toward Joseph. "Mr. Godwin, Mr. Godwin. Wait!"

Joseph stepped back and lifted his chin. *I knew he was full of shit.*

The armed man stopped in front of Joseph. His breaths were heavy and labored. His large black-coated, guard dog ran up to Joseph.

Smiling, Joseph knelt. *You're too playful to be guarding a place like this.* The dog's tail wagged as he scratched behind the dog's ears.

"Mr. Godwin, before you leave, I wanted to say that most of the guys around here don't know who you are," the armed man exhaled.

Joseph glared back.

"I know, right? That's crazy." The armed man nodded. "But *I'm* a huge fan. I've seen you perform at least seven times. My wife and I made it our goal to see you, right around our anniversary, every year."

Joseph turned his attention toward the big-eyed, long-snouted canine. *Don't worry Roxie and Velma. Daddy's coming home real soon.*

He looked down at the dog's smile and sagging jowls as Joseph rubbed his belly. "Oh, wow. He's usually not friendly around strangers, you must have a real gift, Mr. Godwin."

Joseph patted the dog on the side. *Good boy, I hope your loyalties are rightly founded.* He stood and faced the shorter armed man. "I suppose you're here to return me to my quarters."

He shook his head. "No sir. We've been instructed to let the doctor's guests roam as they please."

Joseph sneered. *Well played, my good doctor.* He looked to the moonlit path that led outward toward the countryside then glanced back at the upstairs windows of the mansion. *Corey will launch himself headfirst, there's no doubt. Selene's inquisitive persistence will land her in danger for sure.*

Corralling the large black guard dog to his side, the armed man mimicked Julia's voice. "Don't you want to be great? Don't you want to be remembered? People who say no to opportunities will never be remembered. Isn't that what you told me?"

What the fuck? Joseph stumbled back. *Julia!* "What?"

"I said, where are you heading out to, sir?" asked the armed man, in a raspy deep voice.

Joseph shook his head regaining his thoughts. *That's right...*

He stroked the stubble on his chiseled jawline. *I'll be damned if those kids etch their names in history as the saviors of our universe without me.* With his chin raised, he looked down at the armed man. "I'm not heading anywhere. I was simply checking your ability to keep someone like *me* safe in this place. If you let any harm come to me and my associates, I'd advise against it."

The guard's eyes widened. "Uh, yes. Yes sir."

As Joseph stormed off up the cobblestone driveway toward the red door of the mansion, gnashing his perfectly white teeth. *I'll show everyone who THE FUCK I am.*

Any cost.

Any sacrifice.

Even if every one of them has an agenda.

Vowing to himself, Joseph raised his clenched fist skyward toward the full moon. *If there's an opportunity to cement my name in the history books...* "I'll take it!"

As long as the lights shine down upon me, I'll out-perform them all.

WALKING OUT OF THE suite's lavish bathroom during the early morning hours, Selene dried her dark brown hair and threw the wet white cotton towel on the bed. *Will someone do our laundry for us while we're under or should I ask to use their washer and dryer beforehand?* She dawned white sweatpants and a satin short-sleeved shirt before putting her long brown hair into a ponytail. *I hope we're not too gross after a week.* She shivered. *It doesn't matter how gross I get.* Putting on her socks and shoes at the edge of the bed, Selene glanced at the clock on her wall that displayed time in roman numerals. *Eight. Plenty of time to grab some food before I go under.* Her stomach grumbled. *Last time, I was starving afterward.* She caressed the soft light brown skin of the inside of her elbow. *I'm pretty sure I'll be fed through those tubes like the ones*

hooked up to those volunteers on level one. She stood up and grabbed the black headphones off of her nightstand. *It's all part of God's plan.*

As she opened the heavy wooden door, Selene stepped on something underneath her black and tan running shoes. *It's... a note.* She poked her head out into the hallway. *Who put this here?* No voices echoed through the corridor and the wooden floorboards remained silent. *Where is everyone?* She picked it up and it read:

Selene,

I don't know who else I can trust. My sister is acting strange since the doctor talked to her in private. Things do not add up. Find me and my sister in the other universe. You're the only person who knows which hospital we're staying at. Don't let anything happen to the other *us.*

— Marko

Selene tucked the note in her pocket. *I'll ask him about it at breakfast.* She trotted downstairs through the foyer and waltzed into the cafeteria. Only the chefs remained at the ready by the kitchen window. *Maybe I'm early.* She stood at the counter and ordered her food. The cafeteria remained vacant. Clattering pots, oatmeal boiling, and the smell of fresh fruits were Selene's only company. She grabbed her food and drink, walked to a desolate white marble table, then set a pair of black, noise-canceling headphones on the seat beside her.

Selene glanced up at the clock on the wall above the door. *It's already eight twenty-two in the morning. I should hear Saara's loud voice by now.* Her eyes watered as her chin trembled. *...and where's Marko?* A tear cascaded down her light brown cheek into her bowl of sogging oatmeal. *What was I expecting? There isn't anything in it for Joseph. Corey doesn't want to be here any longer than he has to.* She swallowed a spoonful of warm mush. *My brother left. My dad is gone.* She furrowed her brow and wiped her eyes with the bottom section of her white satin top. *It's alright.* She sniffled. *I'll save mom...*

Selene placed the black headphones across the back of her neck after she left the half-eaten bowl and empty glass on the table. As she trudged into the mansion foyer from the cafeteria, the sun crested over the mountains out the window beside the red door. *There's no turning back now.* She meandered into the room with the fireplace, large chair, and elevator-hiding bookcase. Once in the open and exposed elevator, she used her access card to go down to laboratory level two of the mansion. *Who used the elevator already?*

As the large metallic elevator doors opened, bright white lights illuminated the vibrant laboratory floor. Selene inhaled. *Clean and sterile air.* Lingering through the quiet corridor, she peeked into the other rooms. *Their vials and test tubes are still meticulously organized.* Her heart calmed. She took a right at the end of the hallway up to the door labeled Sleep Synchronization Test Facility #4. Swiping her access card on the reader outside the laboratory room, the card reader bulb turned green and the double-paned door opened.

As Selene walked in, Dr. Kreiner hovered over two large metallic cylinders. *Is that Marko and Saara?* Glass covers encased their bodies and their vitals displayed on the electronic readouts attached to the side of the apparatus. *Why did they start without us?*

Dr. Kreiner looked up, retreated to the desk at the far wall, and wrote in an aluminum cased notebook. "I see you're here bright and early. Have you made your decision, Miss Garcia?"

Beyond the glass windows of Saara's metal cylinder, maroon-colored satin bedding lined the interior. Selene reached out and ran her fingers across the cold metal frame. Displayed on a screen outside above the red hair of her sleeping head, Saara's brain wave patterns oscillated. Several gray and white cabled protruded her state-of-the-art monitoring cap. Wires and tubes converged into a large cable bundle that exited the back of the cylinder. *It's fancier than the ones that Marko and I wore.*

Selene approached Dr. Kreiner who continued to jot notes in his aluminum cased notebook. "I wanted to speak with Marko before we started, Dr. K., is he too far under?" she asked.

Dr. Kreiner glared back at their tubes then down at his notebook. "The twins... *made* their decision."

They did? Selene loomed over Marko's apparatus. *He seems peaceful and his vitals are stable so I don't think anything happened to him. Should I ask Dr. K if he knows anything?* She reached into her right pocket and clutched the note from Marko. "Did you notice something strange about —"

"I thought I would be the first one here. You know, to lead the charge, but I should have known you'd be itching to get this started, Selene." Corey burst into the laboratory room.

Selene looked back at Corey. *I can't believe he's going through with it after he attempted to escape.*

"It's about time *someone* from the government got off their ass for the good of the world." Joseph strolled in shortly after Corey.

Gazing into Joseph's eyes, Selene nodded. *The definition of conceited needs to be reevaluated.*

"Mr. Godwin, Mr. Parker, and Miss Selene." Dr. Kreiner closed his notebook and set it down on the metal desk at the far wall of the laboratory. "Welcome, have you made your decisions?"

Joseph crossed his arms. "What's the deal with Saara and Marko? Why are they going before us, my good doctor?"

Corey walked over to Saara's chamber and placed his hand on her headrest. "You know Saara, she prolly busted in here and demanded to get a head start," He chuckled. "And then hit Marko on the shoulder so that he'd accompany her."

Joseph uncrossed his arms and headed toward one of the open metallic cylinders. "Yeah... that sounds like the shenanigans they'd pull."

Selene released her grip on Marko's note and raised her fingertips to her soft pink lips. *That's a plausible scenario. I don't think the doctor would harm Marko, so maybe he was paranoid. Either way, I'll just have to find them in the other universe and convince* her *to check in on them.*

She bit down on her bottom lip. *Easier said than done. She hates the authorities... but... I'll have to go there for mom, eventually. Maybe I can convince the others to* —

"How about it, Selene? We're in this together, right?" Corey reached his hand out to Selene.

Selene looked up to everyone's stares. *I must have...* She looked down. *Corey's hand...* She genuinely smiled. *It's about more than a greeting.* She reached out and firmly pressed her smaller hand against his. *It's about a connection... right, mom?* "I'm in, of course."

Joseph rolled up his white sleeves. "You're all wasting your time. I'll force the other me to find the cure for her mother's disease. Just make sure you get my name right for the press conference, my good doctor." Smiling, he looked into Selene's big brown eyes. "No one will remember the person who quit halfway, but we'll *all* remember the person who succeeds."

His eyes are warmer than his words. I wonder if dad will be the same way in the other universe. Selene sniffled. "It's just another adventure." *One, where I'm not alone.*

Dr. Kreiner pushed his glasses up the bridge of his nose. "Excellent. I'll contact Dr. Nguyen and her assistants so we can get started. For now, if you could lay down on the modified extended sleep hibernation chamber," he said walking over to an intercom near the entrance.

As Selene laid down, small blue lights illuminated throughout the cylinder as it activated. She pulled the updated white and gray brain wave monitoring device over her head.

Dr. Nguyen and three lab assistants dressed in light blue scrubs surrounded Joseph and Corey's sleeping apparatus. They placed the brain wave monitoring caps on their heads and administered the Dimethyltryptamine intravenously.

Selene removed her shoes and scooted them to the side of her feet in the corner of the red satin-padded cylinder interior. *This is their first time, I almost forgot.* "Are y'all okay? It's not so scary."

"Don't worry about us, my dear. Corey shouldn't be able to fuck up the act of sleeping. I assume the government trained him to that level, at least," Joseph's voice echoed throughout the room.

"Fuck you, are you sure that you won't die from old age once we get started? I'd hate for you to get an award posthumously," Corey said.

The room went silent.

Joseph and Corey laughed.

Selene placed the state-of-the-art brain wave monitoring cap on her head. *They sure don't talk like pals but... they're laughing like they are. Is that how Alex and dad would've acted?* Air blew across the small, dark, brown hairs on the small of Selene's neck. She winced. *Too loud.* "Alright, then. I'm going to put my headphones on. Good luck and... thank you." She placed her headphones over her small ears. *Silence.* She took a deep breath and exhaled slowly. Her heart calmed as the lab assistants hovered over her. She stared at the ceiling extending her arm as they hooked her up to the needles and tubes. *I have to show* her *how lucky she is to have a family.*

Selene's vision glazed over as she blinked.

Her heart rate slowed.

Dr. Kreiner walked over to Selene and flashed a small penlight into her eyes. "Alright, she's the last one to go under. Remember to keep them in stasis until..."

Selene blinked. *What was that?* Her breaths slowed.

An assistant pulled the glass cover over Selene's body and locked it in place. She tried to reach out but only her fingers moved. *God... are you the one guiding me to the other side?* Selene's eyes fluttered between this world and the dream world. *I love you, Mom. I'll see you soon.*

As Selene's eyes shut in *this* universe, she hoped to open them once again... someday.

EPILOGUE

Two hundred and fifty-seven minutes into the future.

Trees and road markers pass in front of my view. Wet autumn leaves line the side of the highway. As I take my head off the glass, my attention turns to the driver. "Where are we going?"

We're going to see father.

Who said that? "Attica Correctional Facility in upstate New York, mister," the driver responds.

I wipe the debris from my eyes. *I must have imagined that.* "How long will it take to get there?"

Looking into the rearview mirror, the driver says, "It'll be another twenty minutes or so. Are you okay, mister? You fell asleep for a while there. Maybe you're still a little tired?"

I'm fine.

Exactly. "I'm fine, thanks." As I pull my phone out of my pocket to look at the time, I notice the background is of an older picture of a big house. . *I look so young in this one.* A man and a woman are posing. *My wife... ex-wife is holding our son. It's been so long. I miss those days.*

Love is just a construct we build with other humans. It's a chemical imbalance in our brains that —

You're wrong. Love is... Who is this? I shake my head.

222

I usually visit father on December thirty-first. I glance down. *My phone says it's November fourteenth. Why did I feel the need to go see him now?*

December has thirty days, imbecile. I need to tell father that everything is in place.

"What, no it doesn't. What do you mean *everything is in place?*"

As the car stops at a red light, the driver turns his head over his shoulder. "Excuse me, sir. Are you talking to me?"

Oops. I shake my head. "No, sorry." I raise my phone to his line of sight. "Just an email I got on my phone, thanks."

He turns back toward the road.

He's always unresponsive. Why do I ... you... think he would talk to me? I listen for a response. Nothing. *Am I going crazy?* My heart rate increases. *Is insanity hereditary?*

It's infuriating how incompetent you are.

Now I'm insulting... myself? When the luxury sedan arrives in front of the medium-security prison, I pull my wallet out and open it. *No cash. I'll have to see if one of my credit cards still has a credit on it. I'm late paying my rent, but I'll just need a little time.* I walk around to the driver's side window and hand the driver one of three credit cards from my otherwise desolate wallet.

Pathetic. The fact that you remain alive, is baffling yet... necessary.

Don't you think I know that? I just need to catch a break, life is unfair. They're not hiring jobs at my skill level and... what do you mean necessary? Who are —

"Sir, this card was declined," he says handing me my credit card back.

Damn. I slide him another credit card. It's also declined. *The third time is a charm... hopefully.*

"This one went through fine. Thank you, sir." A judgmental glare beams through the driver's window as he pulls away.

Up the cracked concrete steps of the Attica Correctional Facility and through the entrance, a whiff of stagnant air permeates my nostrils. *It smells like despair in here. Why am I here?*

To see father. It's your primary objective.

Do you think I'm a robot? Are you some type of sci-fi AI sent from the future to enslave humanity, but can only talk to me? Am I the chosen one? I look around as I meander up to the front desk. *Why aren't you answering me?*

An overweight, elderly, pale woman glares at my meager figure. "Yes, can I help you?"

Pay attention.

I shake my head. "Yes sorry, I'm here to see my father."

Heavy sighs come from the woman, visibly obstinant that she's been interrupted to perform her reason for existing. "What is your relationship to the patient?"

"I'm his only son, Dr. Henry Kriener..." *Why did I say that?* "I meant Bonovich, Henry Bonovich. Not doctor. My father is Arthur Bonovich. He... was a doctor."

His genius is wasted on this timeline.

She looks at me through the top of her bifocals. "Ah, the son of the famous Doctor Universe. He's been around since I was an intern. I don't know why you came to visit. He's medicated to hell and back. He kept trying to commit suicide, telling everyone that he was trying to go back to his reality. It's sad."

Your feeble mind couldn't comprehend a fraction of his brilliance, fucking Philistine.

What's your deal? I cough. *My head.* "Yes, well. I'd like to see him nonetheless. Holiday's and all."

She focuses her attention back on her computer. "Please sign in and have a seat, I'll have the wards prepare a room. According to his documentation, no sharp objects, or electronic devices are allowed. So you'll need to turn in your phone and car keys *if* you own a car, that is."

Reaching in my pockets, I pull out my phone and feel a small object in my left front pocket. *What the hell is —*

Leave it.

I hesitate, pull my empty hand from my pocket, hand my phone to the bitter elderly receptionist, and stumble toward a cloth-torn, faded, red chair.

I brace myself as I sit while the throbbing inside my temples gets worse. *What's happening?* Fading in and out, my vision blurs jostling my waking consciousness. *It's like I'm falling into a never-ending hole.* I grasp for the light ahead but consuming darkness envelopes my sight. *I'm falling further... falling... fall...*

I look down at my hands and my waistline. *This isn't my real body. This is... his.* I lift my hands in front of my face and analyze them. *Finally, it seems like the combination of all five of them allowed me to transfer my consciousness into this pathetic existence.* I glance down at my feet and perform checks on my motor skills. *Excellent. My hypothesis was correct.*

"Sir, are you alright?" the receptionist asks.

More than fine. I nod.

Motioning her lumpy, sagging arm, she says, "Good, they're ready to see you in the back. Good luck."

I stand and march toward the back. "Thank you, Miss Philistine."

A large muscular man wheels my father into a room with padded white walls. At the center stands one table and a single, bolted-down chair. Maneuvering him on the opposing side of the table, the strong-looking ward locks the wheelchair brakes. Dr. Bonovich leans to one side of the wheelchair, his gaze fixates on some undefined distance to his right. His overgrown gray and white beard contains mushed cream-colored debris. One arm is on the armrest and the other is curling toward his stomach.

His ward hovers next to both of them.

Dr. Bonovich mumbles, "Get. Third. Away. Recall it all! Or. Therm."

I see. The ward looks down as I sit in the chair. I look up and form the convincing smile of a simpleton. "Can you give us a little privacy? Maybe if I mention some personal family stuff I can jog his memory."

He rolls his eyes. "Ugh, fine. I'll be in the corner on my phone. Tell me when you're done."

"Of course, my good man. Right away." I nod as he retreats.

I lean in and turn to the side. *When is the last time they bathed him?* "Father. It's me."

His eyes remain in an absolute glaze. *Of course, I wouldn't answer this yokel either.*

Let's see if he's still sharp. I lean further in. "The third law of thermodynamics is that the entropy of a system approaches a constant value as its temperature approaches absolute zero."

For a brief moment, he glances into my eyes and blinks. *Yes, come on.*

I grin. "The test subjects are in position. The bridge was stable enough for me to travel here. Your research and notes helped tremendously." *And your money helped me amass a small fortune.*

His eyes scan the room without moving his head.

Good. I turn my ear as close as I can to his lips.

He stretches his fingers and whispers, "Ugh, I've been wanting to do that for some time now. Tell me, Henry. How... did you convince them to converge on the frequency of this universe?"

I attempt to push my nonexistent glasses up the bridge of my nose. *Hmm, I don't wear glasses in this universe, interesting.* "Convince?" I scoff. "No, father. You taught me that manipulation is far more effective than coercion. Study, observe, and then dissect your target's weaknesses. To use something as basic as love, fear, duty, and responsibility. Or feeding their ego and sensibility with material luxuries and lofty promises. You taught me to be the smartest person in the room, but to allow others to think you're the fool." I smirk. "I've gotten quite proficient at it, to be honest."

His ward looks on from the corner of the room.

He's paying too much attention to our whispers. I produce an exaggerated face. "Hey dad, the kids are doing great. Little Johnny is getting so big. Do you remember my little one?"

Dr. Bonovich mumbles incoherently.

In the past, I felt sorry for you. Now I feel only admiration. I can't fathom the fortitude to play the part like this for all these years. You're truly a man of science and perseverance. "That's right dad, the one with the red toy truck you bought him for Christmas... seven years ago." As I shake my head and smile, I motion to his ward. "He's getting better, I'm pretty sure."

Rolling his eyes, his ward returns to playing on his phone. *Good, simpleton.*

I bend down to his left ear. "With all five of them, the bridge should be stable enough for you to go back. I've told my attendants to let three remain in stasis... for now. As for the other two... I've figured out how to bring the blueprints with me."

My father raises his eyebrow. "I'm listening."

It's a solution that even you *didn't think about.* A smile emerges from my face. "Someone with a special mind." The smile fades. "Unfortunately, it came alongside a silly, simple-minded girl. At least she was useful, one last time."

Dr. Bonovich tilts his head to his shoulder to shield his mouth movements from the camera in the adjacent corner. "This is only the beginning, Henry. I only wish your mother were here to witness what we're about to do."

Mother... I grit my teeth. "She exists here, but..."

"I know, my son. As our energies balance themselves within the universal quantum wave, humanity's narrow perception tries to rationalize its existence on this plane with feeble constructs. Death. Life. Good. Evil. Greed. Altruism. They waste their lives struggling to find the meaning to those words without confirming the binding truth. You and I are different, never forget this. Now, did you prepare for my arrival?" Dr. Bonovich narrows his eyes.

Still expecting failure, I see. "Of course, father. Also..." I reach in my left pocket and covertly slide him a small white capsule. "This will get you back to our universe." *And out of my nightmares.*

I grasp his hand. "Yes, Dad! We'll all go to the old farm when you come back from your vacation!"

Dr. Bonovich mumbles incoherently.

Now to move on to the next phase. I stand up and dramatically wave my hand. "Goodbye father, I'll see you soon!" *Hopefully not too soon.* "I'm off to go visit your other son." I shake my head.

Walking out of the facility, past the dregs of humanity, I open my ancient flip cell phone. *Looking back is the reflection of a lazy, thirty-year-old, out-of-work degenerate, living in a shitty one-bedroom apartment.* I clutch my fist. *It's not the image of a prestigious dignified man of science.* My right hand relaxes. *No matter. Now that I have control of this existence, I'll be fine.* Opening my banking app, I input the access codes and review my bank account balance. *I retain his memories too. How interesting.* I sigh. *One thousand and fifty-eight dollars total... pathetic.*

Walking across the desolate parking lot to the grassy embankment beside a lone tributary, the bitter lake-effect temperature bites through my department store clothing. My unkempt brown hair gives way against the stiff upstate New York breeze. My eyes toggle beneath my eyelids, as memories pour into my conscious like a large file downloading into a dated hard drive. Quadradic equations, string theories, and statistical probabilities flood the deepest recesses of my mind. *Normal people would feel burdened with such intricacies. To me... it's comforting. They're the only friends I've ever known.* Grinning, I sit on a weathered wooden bench stationed along the lakeside. *Welcome home.*

With my eyes open, I call a car to take me to the airport. *I'll be seeing you soon, Marko. As for Corey, Selene, and Joseph.* I reach out to the canopied heavens above. *That's what I promised you three, isn't it?* Gray, overcast sky casts a shroud over my vicinity. *After all, I am a man of my word.* I nod. *One universe will have a secure future.* I look forward and laugh. *Unfortunately, I never said that* you *were going to be a part of that reality.*

You'll be trapped in this *shit-hole of a universe.*

To you, my reality is just a dream. To me... this one is simply a means to an end.

About the Author

Max grew up dreaming impossible dreams of an alternate life other than the one he had in a small town outside of San Antonio, Texas. Shortly after high school, he joined the Marine Corps where he traveled to Foreign Lands. Throughout his budding Marine Corps career, he studied military radar technology and decided to leave the Marine Corps after a memorable eight years to work in the civilian Radar Technical Community at Saab Defense Inc. in Syracuse, NY. During the following eight years, he met his beautiful and intelligent wife, Shirley. Eventually, Max and his growing family wanted to move away from the snow so he accepted a position working as a Government civilian for the US Navy specifying in emerging naval radar technology. Currently, Max resides with his wife, two handsome boys, and a small white Llasa Apso named Tesla in Virginia Beach, Va.

Read more at https://www.maximilianlopez.com.

Made in the USA
Columbia, SC
25 January 2023

30aae708-d115-47b7-8ff2-b26d9e83105aR01